The Buffalo Runners

G·K
Hall
&Co.

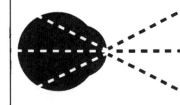

The
Buffalo Runners

Fred Grove

G.K. Hall & Co. • Thorndike, Maine

Published in 1998 by arrangement with
Golden West Literary Agency.

G.K. Hall Large Print Western Series.

The text of this Large Print edition is unabridged.
Other aspects of the book may vary from the original edition.

Set in 16 pt. Plantin by Al Chase.

Printed in the United States on permanent paper.

Library of Congress Cataloging in Publication Data

Grove, Fred.
    The buffalo runners / Fred Grove.
       p.   cm.
    ISBN 0-7838-0336-2 (lg. print : hc : alk. paper)
    1. Large type books.   I. Title.
  PS3557.R7B84 1998
   813'.54—dc21   98-29036

To Bill, my son and good friend

CHAPTER 1

At times Keith Hayden heard the guttural booms of heavy rifles on the purring wind, like spring thunder rumbling off there in the buffalo country to the west. Nothing changed across the rolling distance, a brown sea of swaying prairie always before his eyes, until he rode upon a swell of land and saw Fort Elliot's quadrangle of rambling frame and adobe buildings, flat and stark and dull in the cool December sunlight. And nearby the raw beginnings of a settlement rooting for life not far from a wooded creek.

He felt no marked relief at the sight of habitation again, and supposed that was because he had acquired a certain self-confidence while guiding himself westward from Fort Reno, Indian Territory, to this remote Army post in the eastern Texas Panhandle. Perhaps luck rode with him, too; several times he had observed parties of Indians, hazy horseback figures which vanished like dim whirlwinds.

Thus, he was now alert to watching about him, and avoiding broken stretches which invited ambush, and hiding the cone of his small fire in the hollows of the red hills and, while sleeping, holding the geldings picket rope, his senses lightly at rest.

Leading the pack horse, he turned toward the creek and passed numerous black mounds of buffalo hides stacked like hay. Below the fort, tents bloomed and wagons were parked up and down the creek. After the lulling solitude behind him, the clatter rising from the village sounded harsh and intrusive, and the few rough buildings were as blemishes spreading over the slope. He rode to the first saloon, tied up, and entered.

He saw several indifferent soldiers. Some smoky-looking, bearded men he took for buffalo hunters. A paunchy individual in a rumpled brown suit; Keith thought of a whisky drummer. And a gaunt Englishman wearing weeper whiskers and a deerstalker cap standing at the far end of the bar, aloof from the others while he toyed with a glass of whisky.

Keith ordered whisky. After the first fiery taste, he set down his drink and came to an understanding of the Englishman's full glass. He tossed down the drink, then, and listened to the desultory talk. The drummer complained of the hard trip from Dodge City. The soldiers grumbled. The hunters said little of anything. The Englishman said not a word.

Soon restless, though Keith wondered what he could expect to find in a frontier village which was scarcely more than a camp, he went outside. It was the same discontent that had urged him through the lands of the so-called civilized tribes in eastern Indian Territory. Movement was the only remedy he had for it. He turned next door into a low picket building which served as the main store.

"What's on west of here?" he asked the proprietor, and received a curious look in return.

"Nothin' much for a couple hundred miles — till you get to New Mexico. Fort Bascom's on the Canadian. Keep goin', you'll find Fort Union this side of Santa Fe. More excitement right around here. Hunters comin' in from the north. Buffalo's shot out in Kansas, they say, and is might near on the Canadian."

He was a man of pale skin and eyes, of the same padded roundness from waist to shoulders. He seemed to size up Keith; then he said:

"Need a buffalo gun? Hide prices pretty good right now. I'm buying all the boys haul in. Two fifty to three dollars." He waved toward a rack of long-barreled rifles. "I can fix you up with the best — Sharps or Remington. Sharps .40-90, a .45-100, or the .50-90 Sharps Special. If you don't like any of them, there's the .44-90 Remington. A mighty good gun." He regarded Keith again. "Whole outfit — any rifle, with bullet mold, wad-cutter, bullet-seater, shell-crimper, loading tube" — he cocked an eye — "for a hundred and eighty dollars."

Drawn to the shiny blue barrels, Keith stepped to the rack. The storekeeper laid a rifle in Keith's hands, which sagged with the weight. It was a handsome killer: walnut stock and forearm, Vernier peep sight, double set triggers, big side hammer, octagonal barrel.

"That's a Big Fifty," the man said. "You yank down on the trigger-guard to open the breech."

Keith opened the breech and closed it. "Some gun," he said, balancing the piece a moment longer, and handed it back. "All I need today is supplies." He had a .44 Henry rifle on his saddle, and the talk of hunting had no appeal for him; in truth, he didn't know where his next destination lay, for in his wanderings he was like the whimsical wind itself. He purchased bacon, flour, coffee, and some dried apples.

"There's a fine spring south of the fort," the merchant said: "You're on the Sweet Water, which is a good place to be in this country."

Leaving the store, Keith saw a woman slouch out of the dance hall next to the store. She glanced idly along the street, and when she discovered him he saw her slack face undergo a slow turn. She fixed on him a deliberate smile of invitation.

At the same time he heard the rumble of a wagon. The woman's attention on him dulled when he did not speak. She slouched away to watch the wagon.

Keith saw a single rider in advance of a light wagon. The rider's mouth was relaxed behind the curly black beard and his eyes held a good-natured tolerance. The woman, hands on hips, played a long look on him, smiling in the way she had at Keith. The horseman touched the rim of his hat to her.

Surprise caught her face, followed by momentary confusion, succeeded by head-shaking amusement, as he rode to the store and dismounted. Behind him the young man driving the wagon stopped the team of mules, wrapped reins around the brake lever, and jumped down.

The woman strolled back, alertly hopeful for some sign. Only the young driver looked at her. As the men started toward the store, the rider jogged his head in greeting to Keith, who nodded back. A distant friendliness flowed from the man. Keith sensed it.

The young man, glancing again at the woman, said in an undertone, "Not bad lookin', is she?"

"Let's get some groceries, Andy," the older man replied, smiling.

The woman watched them go inside, bent a look on Keith, held it for a time, shrugged, and turned back to the dance hall.

Riding southwest from the settlement, Keith saw the orderly encampment of a large wagon train formed along the upper curve of the stream, and bands of mules and horses. Stout freight wagons, they were, some with great snowy covers, and others stripped to running gear and frames holding stacks of yellow lumber boomed down by chains and ropes.

He skirted the train, passing on to the south, and found the spring in a clump of willows. Camping down from it in the timber, he watered his horses in the clear, shallow creek and picketed them. Filling his coffeepot at the spring, he cooked his biggest meal in days.

This sheltered bend of the creek was beginning to work on him. The spring tasted sweet and

11

there was abundant firewood — hackberry, lo-
cust, cottonwood — and northward he could see
the wind-breaking hump of a long ridge. So far
he had escaped any of the sudden winter storms
that lashed these rolling plains, now wrapped in
deceptively mild weather; by going north to
Dodge City he would invite that hazard. In-
wardly he shied from the prospects of snow and
cold, or anything which might force him to remain in one place longer than he wished.

That afternoon he hiked down the creek, and
where it hooked southward he came upon an oblong structure of hackberry poles covered with
buffalo hides, flesh sides in. Behind, two wagons
drawn in close. A pole corral held eight lean
mules.

No sign said the place was a store, but he saw
that it was, of sorts, and dirtier even than the raw
village. Rusting cans, bottles, pieces of rotten
leather and bones littered the clearing in front,
evidently pitched there from the doorway.

A blood-red bay stirred at the pole hitching
rack. Keith looked closer. The rawhide bridle
had no bit and the saddle was a pad of dressed
hide. The gelding showed the proud grace and
spirit that only a wild horse could have. It snorted
and backed to the end of the reins, eyes walling,
as Keith approached. He admired it a moment
and ducked inside the hide hut, pausing at the
rancid stink.

A long-haired white man in a greasy red shirt
stood behind a counter of rough planks resting

12

on whisky barrels. He was talking signs with an Indian on the other side. Between them on the counter lay a tanned buffalo robe. Even Keith could tell that it wasn't an ordinary robe. The seal-brown hair was long and silky-looking and rippled with a sheeny beauty as the Indian, obviously haggling for a higher price, held up the robe and rubbed the thick coat.

Shaking his head in refusal, the white man raised his right hand and opened and closed it twice. Then he dipped a tin measuring cup into a barrel and poured brown sugar into a small sack. The Indian's dark eyes followed every motion.

Keith was examining a stack of smelly wolf hides when he heard the Indian's grunt of protest; looking, he saw the Indian pointing from the cup to the sack and shaking his head sideways. The white man kept on dipping and pouring.

Keith could not ignore the wrangling trade. From what he could tell, the little sack seemed slow filling. By the time he neared the counter, glancing at the store's few visible items of merchandise as he went along, the transaction was ending.

He saw the storekeeper plop down the cup and bring his hands together, closed, and move them right and left, a sign which Keith interpreted to mean Done or Finished; and, in smooth, quick movements, slap the robe on a pile at the end of the counter and shove the sack at the Indian. The red man stood motionless, his puzzled eyes flicking from the sack to the measuring cup. At the same time, Keith heard a man's boots in the doorway.

"What'll it be?" the storekeeper asked, disregarding the Indian and turning to Keith.

The little sack and the barrel reminded Keith that he had forgotten to buy sugar in the village. "Pound of sugar," he said.

"Jest sell it by the cupful," came the gruff reply. "Five for a dollar."

Keith got the sour stink of the man. He drew back, hesitating, and saw the careful eyes hook into him and saw the bony jaws in the stained brown beard chomp faster on the tobacco cud.

"I sell cheaper'n they do in town," the man said.

Keith's glance fell to the empty cup on the counter. He started to look up. But something sent his eyes trailing back to the cup in deepening recognition. Of a sudden he knew.

"Not that cup," Keith said.

"Same cup I always use."

"No wonder."

"Jest what d'you mean?" The man was hedging, Keith saw, not actually wanting to argue the matter.

"It has a false bottom," Keith said.

"Lookee here now!"

In swift motion, the storekeeper grabbed for the cup, but Keith clamped his right hand across the hairy forearm and held it there. At that, the other groped under the counter with his left hand. Before he could straighten up, a man spoke from the end of the counter:

"Leave the pistol be, Tobe. Don't bring it up."

Startled, Keith jerked around. It was the rider that morning in the settlement. Even now, he seemed incapable of anger, his steady blue eyes displaying only a weary disgust.

A look of recognition showed in the storekeeper's taut face, a keen pique. Keith saw him try to force a show of welcome, but it wouldn't come.

"When'd you pull in?" he asked, mouth crimped.

"Today." The blue-eyed man stepped behind the counter to the sugar barrel. He wet a forefinger, dipped and tasted and spat. "Same ol' Tobe Jett," he said. "Still puttin' sand in the sugar. Or is it the other way around — sugar in the sand?"

"Hell, a man's entitled to a fair profit, ain't he?" A put-upon defensiveness rose in Jett's complaining voice. "Merchant pays sky-high prices in Dodge — hauls everything — takes all the risks. Has to look for Injuns ever' step of the way." He spun around. "Where's that greasy buck?" His eyes bugged in fury. "Why, goddamn his thievin' red hide — he's not jest took back the robe, he's run off with my sugar!"

A horse was rushing away. The other white man began to roar and slap his thigh. Tears ran down his bearded cheeks. He kept shaking his head. "First time you ever got skinned — and dogged if it didn't take an Indian."

"Go to hell," Jett grumbled and busied himself

sorting pile of hides. "I don't see you runners sproutin' any angel's wings."

Keith, smiling, walked out. Tobe Jett, he thought, could be a dangerous man if circumstances favored him. Keith could see the Indian riding hell-bent for the fort. Now the blue-eyed white man came out, still enjoying Jett's comeuppance.

"We ran ol' Tobe off the Canadian for selling us short supplies," he said, his voice mild. "Watered his whisky, too. When we called his hand, he claimed sand blew in on the sugar when he crossed the Arkansas and Cimarron. All he did was move camp here on the Sweet Water."

"Was he going to use that pistol on me?"

"Not with a white man watching."

"I'm indebted to you. I don't believe he knew you were there."

"That trick cup," the man said. "How'd you get on to it? It fooled me."

"My father owns a wholesale business in Connecticut. He used to get calls for cups like that for the western Indian trade. Specialty items, he called them."

"Now that's interesting. Time we got acquainted. Saw you this morning. I'm Sam Massengale."

"Keith Hayden. Glad to know you, Mr. Massengale." Keith felt his hand enveloped in an astonishingly powerful grip. Several inches shorter than Keith, Massengale wore a wide-brimmed hat with a low crown, and his

16

black, wavy hair hung cropped just above his shoulders. A slightly stooped man, but deep-chested, whose clear blue eyes never wavered. His nose straight, his mouth wide, his square face well shaped and so openly friendly and without guile that Keith hardly knew how to take him.

"You have a keen eye," Massengale said approvingly. "Ever hunt buffalo?"

A courteous remark and no more, Keith saw, shaking his head no. Sam Massengale wasn't a prying man.

"Thought maybe you had."

Keith rubbed his stubbled chin. "Maybe it's the beard. I've been camping out lately."

They turned up the creek, Massengale taking high-stepping strides, the clomping tramp of a farmer accustomed to crossing rough fields, the stoop of his shoulders suggesting that likely he had toiled too hard as a boy. Ungainly and awkward afoot, yet carelessly at ease on a horse, Keith remembered.

Massengale stopped a short distance from four wagons parked along the creek. "Come over this evening for supper," he said. "We'll visit." Keith started to decline. But the other brushed aside any refusal with a wave of his hand. "That's a genuine invitation. Want you to meet my crew. We're a buffalo outfit."

Keith's hesitation vanished, on instinct as much as desire. "Thank you. I warn you I'll be hungry."

Walking on, he realized he had hesitated because he wasn't used to the open-handed hospitality of the frontier. Out here when a man asked you to share his food, he meant it in the fullest sense. To refuse would have been *gauche,* as the French said. It was, Keith considered, another little discovery he liked.

In camp he saddled up for a ride to the fort on the chance that mail from home had caught up with him. Perhaps another reproving letter from his father, such as the last one received weeks ago in St. Louis, asking why, after wandering from England to Italy, he chose to bear off into the wild Southwest? Why, when opportunity went begging at home? One woman needn't spoil a man's life. Furthermore — and Keith could imagine the wryness puckering along the firm line of the mouth and the lean hand stroking the mutton-chop whiskers — there were any number of giddy, yet attractive, young females around who might take the Hayden name in the expectation of living beyond their former means. At twenty-eight, wasn't it about time that a man of good Connecticut stock considered the future with soberness and gave thought to settling down to steady business and rearing a family?

But it wasn't one woman, Keith knew. It wasn't Charlotte. Not any more. It was himself, something he couldn't fully explain or understand. His journey into the wilderness, so to speak, meant more than removing himself from civilization. Was it the desire to see and hear and smell and feel firsthand — yes, rediscover — his own country after three years of traveling from one moldy European capital after another, and in doing so to find himself as well?

And possibly he was. He couldn't recall feeling better or more at peace with the world. He ate like a she wolf with pups, slept well, and seemed to thrive on a few hours' sleep; most times his mind swung in a placid hammock of contemplation while he rode steadily westward up the rising swells, through pristine expanses of short, curly grass.

At the post a bored sentry halted him, listened, and directed him to the headquarters building, a paintless frame box warping under the sun. There, making inquiry, Keith learned to his surprise that the date was December eighteenth, and it grew upon him that he no longer thought of time as spent or lost. It bothered him not at all that most of the year 1876 was used up.

There were only a few civilian letters, those for the merchants in the new village, which the noncom called Hide Town; but Keith didn't mind. Instead, he was relieved not to have his contentment broken.

That feeling stayed with him as he left the fort. He had it when, before dusk, he walked to the Massengale camp.

"Come in!" the hunter boomed, striding out to shake hands. "Boys, this is Mr. Keith Hayden. Fellow that showed up ol' Tobe Jett's short-sugar game," and he indicated the nearest man.

"That's Levi Oatman there. Can't even go into Dodge any more, the women hound him and pester him so."

And when Oatman, all bony corners, turned and wiped his hands on his flour-sack apron before he shook, Keith looked into a face of shocking ruin. Oatman's nose wasn't a nose, but a flattened wreckage, as though crushed and left uncared for afterward. His mouth was drawn up at one corner, which left him a permanent grimace, and the streak of a scar, white against the tan of his clean-shaven face, curved from left ear to jaw, and his long body seemed to rise out of a tortured shell. Keith forgot the painful ugliness when he noticed Oatman's eyes, the only parts of his features not visibly damaged. They were keen and bright and intelligent, alien to the rest of him, and as warm in greeting as Massengale's.

"Howdy," Oatman said. His voice had no tone. It was crushed-out and throaty, hoarse to the ear. "Supper'll be ready in a little bit."

"And over there," Massengale continued, "is Hub Stratton. Smart aleck of the outfit. Got as far as the sixth grade back in Indiana."

Keith saw a man leaning against a wagon wheel, his body turned obliquely, his lowered face in shadow under the wide hat brim. For a count or more his stare appeared to hold Keith at a distance, and in question; a thorough look, before he stepped across and offered his hand. A man neither large nor small: in between, well-knit, active, whose brown eyes squinted up into Keith's face.

"Howdy," Stratton said. "Back home anybody who could read and verity was considered an educated fool. Leastwise, I can lay claim to the last." There was more bitterness than banter in his words. Having spoken, Stratton returned to the wagon.

"Over there," drawled Massengale, "is my nephew, Andy Kinkade. A right good skinner when he don't cut his thumb, and a right good driver when he knows where he's headed."

All the older men laughed in a remembering way, but young Kinkade took the ribbing in good nature.

He was, Keith judged, shaking hands, no older than nineteen or twenty. Farm boy stood out all over him: lump-knuckled, work-broadened hands, and big feet. Although slim and somewhat gawky now, he would, however, be a sturdy figure of a man when he quit growing and filled out his frame. Beardless, a good-looking boy wearing his yellow hair long, imitative of the style of his hunter uncle, and whose eyes were a deep blue and whose strong, even teeth were a startling white.

"We're short one man," Massengale commented. "Levi's got his hands full with the cooking. Andy's our handyman. Pegs the hides, turns 'em and cures 'em. Hub's chief skinner. Need another skinner to help keep up with the runner."

"Runner?" Keith asked. "You hunt buffaloes from horses?"

Massengale's smile was considerate. "You'd never make expenses chasin' after buffalo. Oh, you'd get a few; but the rest would spook and you'd wear out your horse right quick . . . What you do is ride up within four or five hundred yards. From there you work up to about three hundred yards. Sometimes you have to do some crawlin'. Always keep downwind. Buffalo'll run from you quicker from smell than from sight . . . Get down in a wallow, or behind some soapweeds or rocks or in some tall grass. Set up your rest sticks and commence. So all the killin' is done afoot. But hunters — the real ones — call themselves runners.

"Supper's ready," Oatman called.

Keith had never tasted such food. Buffalo hump meat and buffalo ribs and marrow-bone gravy and sourdough biscuits and thick, yellow cornbread, marrow for butter, and beans flavored with salt pork, and slabs of dried apple pie and tin cups of steaming black coffee.

He felt at ease among these rough but friendly, generous men. They spoke but little. Mealtime was for eating, not idle talk. And when they did speak, it was in brief banter or to press more food on Keith. Not once did they inquire into his past or his reason for being here.

Twilight deepened and the rising wind flung its chilled breath down the long slope from the dark huddle of the fort and the feeble lights glowing

22

there like cat's-eyes.

Keith heard a horse trotting. Stratton gave an alert lifting of his head, listening for a space, and returned to finishing his supper. Keith heard the hoofs stop and pick up again, gradual sounds, as if the rider searched for a camp in the dimness. The horse padded nearer, in a walk. Horse and rider loomed and now Keith could see the man outlined in the yellow light.

It was an Indian, the one who had fled Jett's store.

Keith, seated next to Massengale, saw the hunter turn and study the Indian, his heavy brows contracting. "Come in," he called.

At once the Indian slid down, tied up at the closest wagon, and came forward, a canvas sack in one hand. He spoke, his voice choppy and ingratiating, "Friend, me — heap friend, heap friend," and he linked his index fingers in front of his body for emphasis. He stepped close to Keith and looked down. Standing, Keith felt his right hand grasped and pumped up and down like a well-handle, three, four, five times, yet formally, in ceremony; and as he met the gaze in the broad, grin-split face, he thought of a genial brown bear.

"Friend — heap friend," the Indian said, moving on to Massengale and pumping his hand. "Friend," Massengale said, with less enthusiasm. In a twinkling, the Indian cut rapid signs for Eat, always grinning. Massengale nodded.

"Sam," Stratton objected, "you gonna feed an Indian?"

An expression squeezed into Massengale's mouth and eyes, a fleeting thing. He said, "Never turn away a hungry man, Hub," and, motioning for the Indian to sit, he banked a tin plate high.

The visitor ate in enormous gulps, between deep grunts of satisfaction. Disdaining the cutlery Massengale offered him, he reached inside the sack and drew out a buffalo-horn spoon, with which he scooped beans and gravy when he wasn't wolfing bread and relishing the generous hunk of buffalo meat, held between his hands and munched, as a boy would, corn on the cob.

"He's the Indian," Massengale explained, his mouth crinkling, "that got clean away with ol' Tobe Jett's sack of sugar sand. Looks like a Cheyenne, don't he? Like we used to see in Kansas? Look at that Roman nose."

"Friend, me — heap friend," the Indian said and hooked his fingers again in the sign. Before his plate was empty, Massengale stooped at the fire and cut off a fence of ribs and passed it on the tip of a long knife. The guest's black eyes glowed. In moments he was stripping meat from the bones, drawing them through his mouth with a final gustatory sucking and smacking, and tossing them over his shoulder like sticks, cleaned of the last shred.

"Good — heap good," the Indian said when soon finished. Running greasy hands through his black hair, he belched prodigiously and held his right hand up to his chin, signifying Enough. Turning shrewd, black eyes on his host, he showed Massengale a wreathing smile, revealing strong teeth as wide and even as a horse's. He parted his hair to the crown and favored long braids on each side. But he wore white men's trousers and a faded blue shirt, its tail out, and a frayed, blue cavalry jacket, which, open, rode the bulge of his enormous stomach.

He swelled his chest and tapped it. "Savvy white man talk, me. All white man talk. Heap smart — me."

"All right," said Massengale, a playful glint in his eyes. "Talk." His hands scattered signs. "Talk white man. Big talk."

The Indian puffed out his chest again. Rapidly, he said, "Damn them mean mules — go to hell — gimme chew, Mick — who's got whisky? —"

Everybody roared except Stratton. "You can sure tell he's been around soldiers and freighters," he said. "Guess he works 'em all."

Pleased, the visitor thumped his chest harder. "Friend, me. Big Jackass, me. Heap smart." The laughter rolled again and the Indian beamed.

"Better look out," Oatman observed. "He's after something besides a free supper."

"Whisky," the Indian said, fawning on Massengale. "Whisky good. Heap good. Friend like plenty whisky."

"Now we know," Stratton said, not amused.

"No whisky," Massengale said, shaking his head. "All gone. Who are you?" he asked, using signs, too.

25

As if forgetting himself, the Indian drew on his own language and mixed in sign pictures. Massengale nodded that he understood. Now and then he threw in an Indian word or some English and signs. When the Indian had finished, the hunter said around:

"Name's High Medicine — and he's Cheyenne, all right. Says three times him trade with White-Man-Stinks — that's ol' Tobe. Three times White-Man-Stinks put sugar in little brown sack. Three times little brown sack not get much bigger. Heap strange to High Medicine, smart as him is. Close as him watch. Till Quick Eye — that's Hayden, here — found out about the bad medicine cup. So High Medicine, good Indian that he is, has come here to thank his friends for helping him get away from White-Man-Stinks."

"You mean," Stratton grumbled, "he came to eat."

"I reckon that was included. Claims, too, he scouts for the fort. Says he's one great horse thief, one great warrior. When he howls, all the wolves hunker down. When he screams, all the eagles drop their prey. When he stomps the prairie, all the buffalo bulls run the other way. Boys, he's heap hoss, he says."

More laughter, more talk, more signs, more chest-thumping by the agreeable High Medicine, after which Massengale, once more putting on his straight face said:

"I asked him why he scouts for the soldiers. Why he's not with his people. His story is he used to sell magic arrows to his friends. Each arrow cost ten ponies. For a long time whoever bought one wasn't killed in battle. One day something went wrong. Two of his friends got rubbed out . . . Bad, that was. High Medicine, him feel bad all over. But there was a reason why the arrows didn't work. Somebody in the war party had killed a skunk right before the fight started. That broke his medicine."

When the amusement ebbed, Massengale became sternly solemn again. "Now he's going to show us some of his medicine."

High Medicine was rummaging inside the sack. Keith saw him withdraw two stiff, oval pieces of hide about six inches long and several wide. There were drawings on them. For once, the Cheyenne wasn't grinning. Head up, dignified, he handed one to Massengale and the other to Keith, speaking in Cheyenne as he did.

"Hunting licenses for friends," Massengale explained. Keith made out the crude figures of a white man and an Indian, above them a sun emitting rays, and between them two crossed peace pipes; below them a running horse and a series of lines that could represent streams, and head sketches of a buffalo, antelope, deer, and bear, and a rifle, rest sticks, and four smaller suns next to the horse.

"Way I read it," the hunter said, still solemn, "High Medicine's license is good as far as a horse can run in four days. That's considerable." He spoke to the Indian, who pointed south and southwest. "He says that's where the buffalo are, which is about right. Not many left around here."

"If his magic arrows went bad on him," Oatman said, going along with the fun, "would his huntin' licenses be any good?"

"He says one Indian always respects another Indian's mark," Massengale replied. "This shows we're friends. Heap friends. Heap good white men."

High Medicine turned a fawning smile on the hunter, the corners of his thick lips curving upward like a purring cat's. He nodded faster, faster, his approving dark eyes growing brighter. "You like — you like?" And when Massengale nodded back, the Indian held out his hands, palms up, to the hunter and to Keith. "Five dollar, huh?"

Massengale froze, then let out a roaring laugh and slapped his thigh. "By God, he's another Tobe Jett — only slicker!" He faced the expectant High Medicine, shaking his head. "Five dollar too much."

The Indian's face fell slack. But he was soon fawning again. "Four dollar, huh?"

The hunter shook his head again.

"Three dollar, maybe?"

Again, Massengale refused.

"Two dollar — you like?"

Massengale nodded and held up his right hand, the thumb and forefinger crooked, which Keith supposed was the sign for dollar. The hunter did that twice. "Two dollar," he said and made the Done sign.

"The show he puts on is worth that," Keith agreed, and reached for his money. He counted out two one-dollar greenbacks, but held the money when he saw the Indian's pushing-away sign.

"He wants silver dollars," Massengale said. "He knows what they are. He's not sure about greenbacks. I've got silver in the wagon."

Everyone got quiet. Stratton looked straight at Massengale, a flicker of caution in his eyes. Oatman chewed his lower lip. Andy lost his smile. Massengale, seeming not to notice, walked to a wagon and climbed inside. He resumed after some moments, clinking four silver dollars, and Keith gave him the greenbacks.

Fawning, nodding, High Medicine took the silver and dropped it in his sack, repeated the signs for Filled and Friend — Heap Friend! — pumped Massengale's hand, then Keith's, formally, and went quickly to his horse, and rode drumming off into the darkness where the fort lay.

Bitterness ripped into Stratton's voice. "Never figured you'd feed a damned sneakin' Indian, Sam."

"He's Cheyenne. Not Comach'."

"All the same to me."

Massengale broke a twig from a chunk of firewood, held it over the fire until it flared, and lighted his pipe, his motions relaxed. He seemed to be thinking to himself. He jogged his head, understanding while not agreeing. "Andy," he said, "mind playin' us something? When we all get back to work, we'll be too tired of an evening to entertain ourselves."

Andy took a harmonica from his coat, tapped it in the palm of his left hand, blew some reedy notes, cupped his hands, and started in, swaying from side to side. After a bit, Massengale began to hum and sing, low, in a better than middling baritone voice:

"It's now we've crossed Pease River, our troubles
  have begun.
The first damned tail I went to rip, oh how I cut
  my thumb!
While killing the damned old stinkers, our lives
  they had no show.
For the Indians watched to pick us off while
  skinnin' the buffalo."

Presently, Massengale left the fire and came back swinging a brown jug, forefinger crooked in the handle, a hike in his tramping walk. He pulled the cob stopper and offered the jug to Keith, who, balancing it in both hands, tilted his head and took a swallow. It was quick and fiery: corn whisky. It sent a tingling through him.

Massengale frowned when Andy held the jug on his right shoulder and took a swig, but his face smoothed as Andy began to play the buffalo tune in a catchy way, rising and falling; and now Oatman and Stratton joined, humming more than singing. Their voices swept a feeling through Keith, who, after several more stanzas, discovered that he was following the words and keeping time, swinging his hand. Massengale passed the jug again. Andy, catching his uncle's disapproval, took a brief pull.

While his nephew rested, Massengale said to Keith, "That's Andy's favorite — 'The Buffalo Skinners.' Reckon it just about fits us all. Now give us 'Home on the Range,' Andy."

It was late when Keith rose and thanked his hosts. Leaving the firelight and striding toward his dark camp, he felt his isolation the moment he entered the darkness. Tonight, for the first time in months, he had experienced the warmth of people again. He had almost forgotten.

After seeing to the picket ropes of his horses, he looked off to the north and marked the broad blur of the fort, its low bulk skylighted on the rise. The wagons in the train sat like pale ghosts. A keener bite rode the wind, turning him ever sharply away from Dodge City. He thought: the eternal wind, the open sky, the wild scents; combined, they conspired to dim the past.

His bedroll was a tarp lined with blankets. He took off boots, hat, coat, and trousers, crawled in at the head of the bedroll, and drew the end of the tarp over his head, shutting out all but the soft roar of the wind in the grass, leaving a slit for his face; for after the Indian country through which he had passed, he mistrusted what he could not hear at night.

Next to him under the blankets lay the Henry rifle and his handgun, a single-action .44 Smith & Wesson. He stretched out; briefly, the faces around the campfire flickered in his mind, and he imagined Andy's shrill music again, akin to the wind, rising, falling.

That, and he rolled on his right side, and instantly he felt the warm mantle of sleep drop over him.

He awoke with a start, hearing the nervous stamping of the horses. He opened his eyes without moving, thinking, momentarily, that he was alone in Indian Territory, and alarmed because he didn't feel the saddle horse's rope in his hands. Gray daylight exposed the timber of the Sweet Water and the gelding faced downcreek, fox ears alert.

Keith took the handgun and sat up, bringing the weapon abruptly about.

He could see the figure of a man, unrecognizable in the dingy light.

CHAPTER 2

"Sorry to wake you up," a mild, low-pitched voice said.

Keith threw back the bedroll top, laid down the pistol and stood. It was Sam Massengale and he was saying, "I was afraid you might pull out early and I'd miss you."

"Come in," Keith called. He slipped on his trousers and pulled on his boots, feeling the damp cold of the creek bottom, and reached for his hat and coat. "What is it, Mr. Massengale?"

"Sam's the name," the hunter said, tramping forward. "It's like this: We want you to throw in with us when we go south to hunt. Kinda like the buffalo skinner song goes: *'How'd you like to go on the range of the buffalo?'* "

Keith laid a closer scrutiny on the man. The hour was too early for banter. Keith could see that Massengale meant it.

"I'm a stranger to you," Keith said. "You know nothing about me."

"I know you know a cup with a false bottom in it."

They laughed in unison and Keith hurried to start a fire, and when it was going and he had coffee and water in the pot, he said, "I'd be the greenest hand on the range."

"We all started green. I did back in 'Seventy-Four in Kansas. Man learns fast when he has to.

33

Few days'll make a big difference." He studied the grazing horses. "From the looks of your stock, you've come a long way."

"From Fort Gibson."

Massengale blinked. "Why, that's on the east side of Indian Territory," he said and trailed his approval over Keith's scant camping outfit. "You travel light. That's good. A tenderfoot would haul a passer of stuff he didn't need."

"There's a tent in the pack, though I haven't used it." A perception fastened on Keith that, while he wanted Massengale to know the truth, he also wanted to convince the hunter that he wasn't helpless. "My Indian guide turned back at Fort Reno. Said he didn't want to lose his scalp. After that, I was on my own."

"In the middle of Cheyenne-'Rapaho country." Massengale rocked his head. "You learned to take care yourself, else you wouldn't be here."

"I was lucky, too."

"It takes both," the hunter said, experience speaking in his voice. "About goin' with us. In my outfit we all share alike. Runners, skinners, handyman, cook, what have you. Now some runners take half, but they can't always hold a crew together. What I do is deduct all expenses, then split the rest. That way no man can complain. We'd like to have you go along with us, Keith."

"Tell you the truth, I've been interested in you fellows, too."

When the coffee was ready, Keith filled a tin cup and handed it to Massengale, who squatted down and sipped the scalding brew without change of expression.

"You won't get rich," he said. "Far from it. At best, you'll make fair wages — if we find plenty buffalo. I aim to quit soon as I save up enough for a farm I got my eye on back in Missouri. Wife and three little girls won't be any happier'n I'll be when that day comes, about next summer, I figure."

"I wouldn't go as a handyman," Keith told him, turning the thing over in his mind. "Nor strictly as a skinner. Though I'd help out where needed. I'd want to hunt." And somewhat amused at his own display of preference: "I know how that sounds from a man who's never been a buffalo hunter."

"First off, never call yourself a buffalo hunter. That's tenderfoot lingo, marks you as such. Always say you're a buffalo runner."

"But you said you don't run buffalo."

"We don't. Only sometimes, when a range is shot out, there's a long run before you find another herd. I've looked for days. Then one morning there they'd be: the prairie all black. I could use another runner, you bet. That would let me shift off on the skinnin'."

"Can't Stratton and Andy do the skinning while you hunt?"

"We need Andy to help Levi part of the time. Levi's kinda poorly, you know. Hub's our main skinner. Says his eyesight's not sharp enough for long-range shooting. He's an artist with a knife.

We hand-skin everything we shoot . . . None of this damn-fool yankin' off hides with a team. More times than not it just tears the skin; leaves more meat on the hide so it sours."

Keith spoke thoughtfully: "You could hire another skinner at the settlement."

"Most everybody's lined up. Them that ain't you wouldn't have. Riffraff. Thieves. Name it." Keith saw Massengale's eyes go over him and rest on Keith's hands. "Besides, you look like you'd make a better runner than a skinner. It's dirty work. I'll help Hub when Andy can't. You could pitch in once in a while." Massengale stood to go. "We all share alike. The outfit pays for your powder and lead and keep. That fair enough?"

"Fair enough," Keith said, feeling the sudden heat of excitement, and held out his hand. "When do we leave?"

"In a few days. After we rest up our stock and see what we need at the store. We been on the Canadian. Sold our kill to a buyer out of Dodge." As he talked, he was idly observing the wagon train encampment.

"A big outfit," Keith said.

"A. B. Barr's. He's the big bull around Dodge and Denver. Wise as a tree full of owls, they say. Runs freight lines all over the west. Owns saloons from Kansas City to 'Frisco."

"Know him?"

"By rep only. I respect his judgment. See all that lumber? Story is, that's for a brand-new town south of here he's going to build. Where he can get on the flank of the southern herd. Buy and freight hides to market. Sell the runners supplies and" — he winked — "some other things a man can't hand-load in a cartridge or fry in a skillet."

"Sounds as if we're all going the same direction?"

"Just about. South or southwest. I figure that foxy High Medicine knows where there's heap buffalo. And you can bet your boots A. B. Barr knows or he wouldn't be headed there to born himself a town." Massengale finished his coffee, threw out the grounds, set down the cup, and wiped the back of his left hand across his mouth.

"Last night," Keith said, pausing, "you mentioned being one man short."

"Yes. Indians. On the Canadian. My brother, Daniel."

"I'm sorry. Quite sorry, Sam."

Massengale looked down and up. "Thank you. Daniel was a right good runner. That's the chance we all take, Keith. When we go south, we'll be in the heart of Comanche-Kiowa buffalo country." The soberness left his face slowly giving way to his natural cheerfulness. He glanced at Keith's rifle on the bedroll. "I see you got a .44 Henry. Fine for Indians, but not enough kick for buffalo. The breech can't take the heavy charges an old Sharps can . . . Much obliged for the coffee. We'll talk some more."

He turned away in his clomping walk.

That afternoon Keith saw Andy Kinkade, on

37

his way to the spring for a bucket of water. He turned in. "Howdy, Mr. Hayden. Hear you're going with us."

"That's right. And why not start by dropping that mister?"

Andy's white grin flashed. On a frontier of mostly bearded men, his smooth face made him look younger than he was, and brought out his high cheekbones and the line of his firm jaw, while the brown of his skin set off the amiable blue of his eyes, as clear and steady as his uncle's. He smiled easily, and Keith saw again the stamp of his boyishness.

"High Medicine took dinner with us," Andy said, grimacing. "Looks like we got us a star boarder. Uncle Sam can't stand to see anybody go hungry . . . Guess the War did that. Rebs took him prisoner at the Battle of Shiloh, there in the Hornet's Nest with General Prentiss and his Missouri boys. Kept him prisoner a year. He just about starved to death before he escaped. You in the War, Keith? Guess you's too young."

"I ran off and joined. However, my father pulled some strings, had me discharged. By then the War was over." He was surprised at the indignation still in him and for speaking out.

Andy looked sympathetic. "Son-of-a-gun. I know you didn't like that."

"How could you tell?" Keith asked, smiling.

"By the way you said it. The way you looked. Guess you lied to get in?"

"I was considered big for my age. In those days

they were taking anybody who could bite a cartridge and stand on his feet."

Andy's eyes grew reminiscent. "I remember when Uncle Sam got home, when he walked into the yard. All us kids ran. We didn't know who he was at first. Thought he was some kind of scarecrow . . . Well, I'd better get along."

He strolled on up the creek, swinging the wooden bucket, looking off toward the hooded humps of the Barr wagons. Andy hadn't seen the likes of so many wagons since last summer in Dodge City. And never so much new lumber being hauled, and the sight of so many boxes and barrels and sacks cramming the giant freight wagons, and the swarms of mules and horses. He left the bucket at the spring and went on.

He wasn't far from the train when a woman's voice, soft yet clear, broke his fixed attention, a woman calling her dog. Curious, he looked that way, along the creek, and saw a small dog, spotted black and white. At the same moment the dog discovered him and ran yipping toward him.

Kneeling, Andy extended a petting hand. The little dog darted in, eager for attention. But not all the way. Yipping suspicion, it scurried back near its mistress and faced about with a stronger bravado. The woman laughed and shushed it

As Andy grinned and started on, the woman spoke to him. "Please excuse Tippy. He's noisier than he is brave."

"Believe he'd fight if he had to," Andy answered. "That's about all a man will do. Bet he'd fight to protect you, ma'am." At last he remembered his hat and took it off, aware that his face revealed his surprise over seeing a woman here, especially a woman like her. A lady. He saw her eyes follow the movement of his hand, as if she didn't expect the courtesy. He had spoken naturally, on impulse. Now his remark struck him as too forward. She would walk away sure. He felt awkward. He kept swinging his hat and shifting it from hand to hand, and running the brim between his fingers.

"No one," she said, instead, "has ever taken up for Tippy before. He's a terrible coward."

Again he moved to pass on, and again her voice seemed to hold on to him. "Are you with one of the hunting outfits?"

Was that loneliness in her voice? Yet it seemed unlikely that a lady like her would be lonely. "Yes, ma'am. Camped downcreek a way. I was looking at the wagon train. Never saw such a shebang of stuff."

"Yes," she agreed, not particularly interested, "it's quite a lot."

She looked several years older than his new friend, Keith, and there were tiny tracings of wrinkles at the corners of her eyes and under her eyes, which were a smoky brown; but, my, she was pretty. Enough to take a man's breath. Small but not dainty, nigh lost in the fine, dark-green coat. Her hair glossy black under the light-colored scarf drawn over her head, and her face pale and delicate, like a carving he had seen

40

once on cameo. Across the distance between them he smelled a delightful fragrance. A perfume, he supposed. Like roses or violets, maybe. He wasn't certain, it was so faint.

"Enough to build a town," he said, recalling camp talk.

"A very small town," she replied, with the trace of a smile. And just when he thought she would say no more, she added, "Do you like to hunt buffalo?" She sounded educated to him. Also she had a guarded manner of speaking, a carefulness, of holding the same even tone, never loud, of reflecting before she spoke. Yet her dark eyes, on him, showed kindness and interest.

"I'd rather raise good Missouri saddle horses," he said, and that was gospel.

Her interest was immediate. "Missouri? What county?"

"Audrain. That's fine horse country." He couldn't suppress the pride he felt. "Some say it's the best. I've seen right smart since I left home, but not any place that's up to Audrain County."

She smiled, yet in no way belittling his native pride. It was past time for him to be on his way. Andy sensed that, though he wanted to talk some more; for she gave him a feeling which he had never before experienced around women or girls. Like he was somebody. A man. Not a mere boy. She was different. And again, just as he started to leave, her voice delayed him:

"I've heard of Audrain County."

Beyond her, unseen by her, Andy noticed a

41

man moving from behind a wagon. He wore a dark suit and a brown hat. He stood still, boots planted wide, a broad trunk of a man, a middle-aged man, watching the woman as if he owned her.

Andy began to feel uneasy. "Raising horses beats the hide business," he said uncomfortably.

Still, she was unaware that the man watched her. "I never thought shooting poor, dumb animals for their skins and tongues was sport," she said in a reasoning way.

"It's not sport," Andy said, taking a departing step, while trying to appear casual. He could not tell her she was being watched without startling her, or without the man hearing him. "It's plain hard work."

Somehow her eyes seemed to speak to him. He paused. He saw the watcher bring a cigar to his mouth and blow out a puff; in a fleetness Andy smelled the drift of tobacco smoke. So did the woman and she stiffened slightly. Her pale face lost its dim animation, became inscrutable.

"Thank you," she said distinctly, enough, Andy discerned, for the watcher to hear, "for finding my little dog," and she turned and the dog followed, and Andy saw her lift her head and, in even steps, go toward the figure waiting by a flat-topped spring wagon.

"I thought I told you . . ." the man began.

Andy heard no more. He was walking back the way he had come, vaguely troubled. Why was she afraid? I should have gone on, he rebuked him-

self. But there's nothing wrong in being neighborly.

He had wanted to linger. Uncle Sam would say
that was because he was headstrong. But Andy
knew it was because she was the prettiest woman
of his brief experience. A real lady. He could see
that plainly. Different in ways he could not define
to himself, unlike the farm girls back home. As he
walked on to the spring, he kept remembering
her voice, its unusual softness, though clear and
melodious. Sweet to the ear, he thought; like a
singer's.

He wondered if he would ever see her again.

Early the morning of the day the outfit was to
pull south, Keith heard a gathering stir across the
way where the wagon train was. A welter of
voices and chain jingles and rattles, stampings
and leather-slaps. Later, he saw the caravan form
and swing downcreek.

In front rode a horseman wearing a brown hat,
heavy overcoat, and trousers tucked inside black,
glossy boots. Keith thought: that's A. B. Barr. He
rode hunched forward, a dogged cast to his
lumpy shoulders, a cigar clamped between his
teeth, and he glanced to neither side. That
looked like a compass tied to his saddle horn.

Behind the lead rider flowed armed riders, a
dozen or more, rifles in saddle boots. They impressed Keith as a sober lot, almost as grim as
Barr himself.

Behind them sturdy men rode in two open

wagons which sprouted picks and shovels. Dig-gers and shovelers, Keith guessed, to grub out crossings over streams and ravines. There was a gap to the next wagons.

Hearing laughter as the first vehicle drew even with his camp, he saw women waving at him. Some were calling:

"Gonna start us a town."

"Better come along."

"Just ask for Baby Doll."

One waved and sang in a strong, brassy voice:

"Come on down to Barr's Town,
Try the flavor of our honey
Come on down to Barr's Town,
Our whisky'll make you funny.

Another gap appeared in the long train, and Keith saw a flat-topped wagon drawn by four lively mules, an armed horseman on each side of the driver. A wide interval likewise separated the wagon from the next one behind; thus, it seemed to occupy a special seclusion in the long column, apart from the others.

Beneath the rolled-up canvas side curtains of the wagon, which resembled an army ambulance made over to comfortable civilian tastes, Keith saw a slender woman, pale of face. She was gaz-ing out at the winding creek and the hunters' camps. When she passed him, she neither waved nor called as the other women had. She had no expression whatever.

The column continued to pass as he prepared breakfast. More than fifty wagons in all; those carrying supplies had hind wheels higher than a man's head. Hunters' outfits brought up the rear.

After breakfast, Keith rode to the fort to inquire about mail. The same listless noncom shuffled through a packet of thumb-marked letters.

"Hayden, you say? Keith Hayden? Here's one for Keith Madison Hayden. You him?"

Keith nodded. Only one person had ever written his full name like that; probably, he used to suspect, because she thought it read more elegant, more impressive to others. He took the letter.

It was addressed in care of the post commander, in small precise, perfect handwriting, which he recognized immediately, with a swirl of surprise, irritation, and yet a degree of restrained eagerness. He opened it. After the great distance traveled from Connecticut and the time that had passed, the linen paper still emitted the faintest familiar scent: verbena. He was annoyed that he remembered. He read:

Keith, dear — In desperation, I am writing you at every army post in the Southwest. Although your father respectfully declines to reveal your whereabouts to me, I know you are somewhere in that vast region of immense buffalo herds, savage Indians, and lawless white men. (How like her, he thought, to exaggerate the dramatic.) You

45

may wonder how I know — that is my guarded secret, dearest.

If this finds you, as I fervently pray it does, I implore you to write me. I shall not rest until I find you. When I do — and I will — I shall come to you and things will be the same again — I promise you, for I am coming West early in the spring — and we can pick up the thread of our interrupted lives as before.

Lovingly, as ever,
Charlotte

He did not move, seeing in the eye of his mind the perfect gold head, the perfect lips, the perfect eyes like green pools, and the high, regal forehead.

"Bad news, mister?"

Keith looked up. "No — just old news."

"Mail's goin' out in a few days, case you want to send a reply."

Shaking his head, Keith refolded the letter and returned it to the envelope, tore it in half, and half again and half again, dropped it in a trash barrel by the door, and walked outside, taking a deep pull of the crisp, high-plains air.

The letter meant no change in his plans. He wasn't running any more. He was looking and searching, to find himself and his identity, the place where he belonged. At the moment he was thinking of Sam Massengale, a genuine man if he had ever met one, and the crew and the great open country that awaited them, and the new life he would lead with them, and his new .50-90 Sharps Special, purchased at the settlement store.

CHAPTER 3

When the outfit rolled out, Massengale followed upon the deep, broad rim marks of Barr's caravan, veering south where the Sweet Water crooked, and on to the cottonwoods sheltering Tobe Jett's makeshift store.

He pulled up, mildly puzzled, and Keith, beside him, saw why. Save for piles of litter and the skeleton of chinaberry poles yet standing, the grove was empty. Wagon tracks left the clearing and swung in on the column's trail A curiousness went through the hunter's voice:

" 'Pears like ol' Tobe went south with his sugar sand. Well, there'll be new outfits down there he can short."

They forded the shallow creek and struck due south, Keith riding ahead with Massengale. Young Andy drove the gear wagon, which held bedding, rope, lead, powder, buffalo rifles, nails, axes, spades, several cases of butcher knives, a grindstone, water kegs, and the crew's war sacks. Next came Oatman rattling in the cook wagon, which hauled provisions for three months and curing salt, and last, Stratton driving eight mules hitched to a stout Shuttler freight wagon, a lighter trail wagon hitched on behind. Massengale said the big Shuttler could haul 500 hides to market when the frame was fixed like a hay wagon.

Among other items, Keith had helped load onto Andy's wagon 250 pounds of lead in ten 25-pound sacks, 5000 primers or caps, six 25-pound kegs of Dupont powder, and three cans of arsenic, to be dissolved in water and sprinkled, on pegged hides for bug poison.

"We keep the bug stuff out of the cook wagon," Andy joked to Keith while loading in the village, "so Levi won't get it mixed in with the flour. Oh, I don't mean that. Levi's the best camp cook you'll ever see. He was workin' on the railroad up in Kansas when he liked to got stomped to death. Was cut up, too. Two men jumped him one payday. He wasn't able to do a hard day's work after that, so Uncle Sam hired him as cook. Levi'd do anything for Uncle Sam."

Southward, the country rolled and dipped in massive, beckoning sweeps of dun prairie. An exhilaration lifted Keith which never quite seemed to leave him. Everything lay open and uncluttered and the air was bracing. At any moment he expected to see buffalo. West of Fort Reno, he had observed scattered bunches and avoided them for fear of Indians. Now he wanted to see the shaggy creatures up close. And as he rode with Massengale, the past fell away into insignificance.

At noon, still following the broad trace of the wagon train, they halted to rest the stock and eat cold meat and biscuits around the cook wagon. A little later Keith started by where Stratton rested in the shade of the freight wagon, squatted down

49

on his heels while he nursed a stubby, black pipe.

"Sam says you're gonna be a runner," the skinner said, a sourness edging across his angular face.

Keith swung in, caught off guard, uncertain how to take the remark. "I'll need some practice," he said.

"Sports from back east come out here all set to shoot buffalo from the doors of their tents."

"I'm green — but not that green."

"Ever hunt a-tall?"

"Deer and bear."

A scoffing sliced into Stratton's voice. "Close-up shootin'. Won't work out here."

"Believe I can learn to shoot a Sharps," Keith replied, keeping his tone conversational.

"Best shot ain't always the best runner," Stratton differed, squinting off. "Give me a man that drops his kills close together. A skinner works his butt off enough as it is. Now Sam's good at stackin' 'em up. His brother, Dan, was better. *Dan was the best.*"

In that, Keith read considerable. This was a small, close outfit. Obviously, Stratton had made up his mind not to accept Keith, or possibly anyone filling Dan Massengale's boots. Keith would have to earn his place, which wasn't going to be easy.

Massengale called to roll the wagons, and Keith went to his horse, puzzling over Dan Massengale. A crack shot, yet Indians had killed him.

Keith was disappointed when he sighted no buffalo during the morning, though now and then they passed bones and rotting carcasses with the black hair still on the curved-horn heads. Keith held his nose at the first wave of sickening stench. The hunter seemed used to it. In the cool, glittering sunlight, the skinned carcass had a glassy look. A fat wolf lurked among them.

"Some runner got himself a good stand over there," Massengale pointed. "See how he laid 'em in close. That's good shooting." He rode on a bit "Idea is to knock down the leader first."

"How can you tell which one's the leader?"

"You'll know when you look over a bunch. A leader stands out in a peculiar way. I can't explain it. Sometimes it's a cow. The leader won't always be at the head of a bunch, either. Sometimes there'll be two or three leaders." He gazed around before he resumed. "Best place to shoot a buffalo is in the lights — the lungs. He'll snort blood out his nose and sling it around . . . take a step or two backward, sink to his haunches, rock sideways for a little, flop over and die. If you shoot him through the heart, he might run a couple hundred yards. When that happens, he takes the whole bunch with him — they stampede."

Massengale paused, his attention fixing in the distance. Then he rode ahead. "So you try to drop the leader in his tracks. You bet. Rest of his bunch will mill around him. They'll smell his blood, beller and paw the ground. You got yourself a stand workin'," he said, chuckling, "*if*

51

you're a steady shot, *if* the wind's right, *if* the buffalo don't see you or smell you, *if* you don't shoot
too fast and ruin your rifle barrel, *if* you knock
down the buffalo as they drift off."

"Sounds easy," Keith smiled

"This time of year," Massengale went on,
"you'll find buffalo in small bunches — from
twenty to thirty up to a hundred. Past early July
on to October, cows and bulls mingle and you'll
see bigger bunches or herds. They'll stay together
till the calves are five or six months old."

A stream slanted out of the northwest which
Massengale said was the North Fork of the Red,
and here he pulled the outfit off the caravan's
tracks and swung upstream to look for game.

It was three o'clock when he signaled the wagons to halt and, giving Keith a look, pointed
northwest.

At first Keith saw nothing in the rolling vastness. And then, as he shaded his eyes against the
sun, black shapes became visible. He felt a flare
of excitement: buffalo grazing into the wind. Just
a few. A little bunch.

"Better'n a mile off," Massengale said. "Let's
ride in closer. We sure need the meat."

About four hundred yards stretched between
them and the buffalo when Massengale drew
rein. Keith tied his horse to sagebrush. His hands
were sweating as he took the new Sharps from its
leather case, and the sack of shells from his
saddlebag, and the *bois d'arc* rest sticks, bolted together, the last a gift from Massengale.

The hunter glanced at him. "Glad you got on a brown hat. Won't be noticeable. We'll have to hoof it a way now."

He set out and Keith advanced a few paces to his left. After a hundred yards or more, the hunter motioned Keith to sink down and began crawling on hands and knees. Sweat broke in runners across Keith's temples. His knees were beginning to feel raw. Nettles tore his trouser legs. But in his eagerness he didn't mind.

Massengale did not stop to rest, did not pause until he took cover behind a clump of soapweeds and sized up the situation. "All right, Keith. See that buffalo off to the right? That cow off to herself? Notice how alert she is? How she keeps lookin' around? Knock her down. She's the leader."

Keith's pulse was hammering. The buffalo band seemed quite near. Fifteen animals or so. He studied the cow grazing by herself. Like Sam said, there was a watchfulness about her. A difference. She stood out.

"Sight just behind the shoulder," Massengale said. "Shoot for the lights."

With both hands, Keith rammed the rest sticks into the soft, reddish earth. He moved the screw on the Vernier rear sight, setting the elevation for three hundred yards, and tightened the peep cut. He cocked the heavy side hammer, rested the long barrel in the crotch of the sticks, steadied them with his left hand, and drew a bead on the cow.

All at once he couldn't seem to control his

damnable shaking.

He fired — too suddenly, too anxiously, he knew the instant he pulled the trigger. As the rifle butt slammed his shoulder, a deafening boom burst around him, and a puff of acrid, white powdersmoke bloomed.

But the cow was still standing, now faced in his direction, now drifting off, now trotting the bunch with her.

"Shoot again," Massengale said.

Overanxious, Keith yanked down on the trigger-guard to open the breech, clawed out the spent shell, rammed in another, snapped the lever shut, and eared back the hammer.

The cow was a humping target. Keith's hands were uncertain. He set his mouth, he steadied the sticks, he fired.

Nothing changed. The cow continued in that lumbering, deceivingly rapid, up-and-down motion.

In disgust, Keith emptied his rifle and met the hunter's wry understanding. "Most men get buck fever first time they level down on a buffalo," Massengale said. "I did. After you drop your first kill, you forget all about it. That bunch is spooky, too. Prob'ly shot into this morning somewhere. Well, tomorrow's another day." Keith, silent, pulled up the sticks. "Better pick up them empty cases," the hunter said. "Save 'em. When we get a batch of empties, we reload 'em. Damned sight cheaper."

They were walking back, boots scuffing the

stiff, winter short grass, when Massengale spoke again:

"You need leather knee pads. I've got some rawhide. Your rifle pulls hard — enough to throw a man off. You want double triggers set so delicate you can almost fire your rifle with a whisper."

Keith nodded sheepishly. "I forgot to set it on hair trigger."

When they rode back to the crew waiting by Andy's wagon, Stratton's alert eyes had a relishing look. "Well — ?" he began, though anyone could tell by looking what had happened.

"I missed an easy shot," Keith said, straight out.

"It's sure no gentleman's sport," Stratton said and strolled back to his wagon.

Keith scowled after him. "Never mind Hub," Massengale said, shaking his head. "He can't help it, I reckon."

On the third day of scouting up the North Fork and the clean wind blowing to them, Keith was riding with Massengale when they sighted another bunch. The hunter got down and pulled a handful of grass to determine the wind's drift.

"Remember this, Keith," he said. "Long as you keep a straight line, up to three or four hundred yards, they won't take alarm. But if you veer off of a sudden, why right away the leader and the old bulls on the rim of the bunch start gettin' uneasy."

The morning sun felt warm, and morning was always the best time for hunting, Massengale explained as they began the approach; by that time, the buffalo, their early grazing finished, were resting with full bellies. He told Keith to look sharp.

Keith could see them: black hulks quiescent on the rust-colored grass. Some lying down. Others grazing, hardly moving.

After some distance, Massengale took a long look and bent down. This time crawling came easier for Keith. The buffalo-hide pads he had stitched over the knees of his trousers enabled him to slip easily through the thick grass and take the rub off his knees.

Sometimes in a low trot when hidden from the buffalo, but most times crawling, they scrambled up a small rise. Here, Keith saw, they were close enough.

"Take your shot," Massengale said. "You'll get meat today."

Keith, peering over a patch of dry weeds, saw a sentinel bull on the outskirts of the bunch, which numbered twenty-odd animals scattered about, indolent under the climbing sun. Even from here the bull loomed enormous, his great shaggy head like a mossy boulder.

Suddenly the *bois d'arc* sticks seemed cumbersome and unnecessary to Keith, and hadn't he missed with them the first time? He stretched out to fire from a prone position, to rest on his elbows. But he heard Massengale's murmur before he could cock the Sharps:

"Wait, Keith. When you fire a buffalo rifle close to the ground, the sound carries more.

Kinda rolls. Makes more noise than when you fire higher up. Down like that, a few shots'd soon scare off the game."

Keith turned his head, his irritation fading before the hunter's patience. "Makes sense," he said, getting up.

"Now take your time."

Keith set up the sticks. Again his hands shook. Angry at himself, he bit his lip and gripped the sticks, sighted behind the bull's shoulder, squeezed the front trigger, and the Sharps bellowed.

For a tick of time the bull appeared untouched, and Keith thought he had missed once more. And then the dark beast lowered its head as if against its will. Sinking backward, it flopped down kicking.

"Got 'im!" Massengale yelled. "Now take the left side — shoot any that start driftin' off. I'll work the right side."

When the shooting was over, Keith counted eight dark shapes within a space of fifty yards. The survivors were running wildly into the wind, in the heavy, pitching motion of stampeding buffalo, yet traveling far faster than appeared to the naked eye. Three of the kills were Keith's, knocked down in seven shots.

Keith thumbed another shell into the breech, but the hunter said, "Better let our guns cool. I run a greasy rag through the barrel every four or five shots. Sometimes I carry a little bottle of water with me. Sometimes a man has to urinate down the barrel to cool it."

"They broke on my side," Keith said, blaming himself. "I missed too many. Got in too big a hurry."

"We got meat just the same. A good start."

Keith trailed his eyes over Massengale's rifle — a single trigger, .40-90 Sharps, its battered stock mended with rawhide, the initials *S.M.* carved in small, deep letters on the walnut forearm — and downward to the empty cases in the grass.

"Five shells," he said, impressed. "Five buffalo."

"You can do the same when you learn your rifle. I know what this ol' smokewagon will do. You did better when you set it on hair trigger. Lots of fellows forget to pull the back trigger first." The hunter started picking up his scattered brass. Keith did the same. Afterward, they walked back to their horses, where Massengale waved the wagons in from half a mile away. Mounted, they rode out to the scene of the kill.

Keith's bull *was* enormous. Blood had frothed out the black nostrils, as Massengale had said it would after a true shot in the lights. Keith gazed in awe at the powerful animal which he had felled with a single Big Fifty slug at a distance exceeding three hundred yards.

"Biggest doggoned bull I've seen in a coon's age," Massengale said, eyes measuring from the massive head to the wispy tail, insignificant on so huge a dark beast. "Twenty-five hundred pounds if he's an ounce. Now if you's an Englishman,

Keith, Lord Something or Other, you'd have his head stuffed and sent back to your castle . . . Better show you how to skin 'im. Man wants to take the hide the same day he makes the kill. Leave it overnight, the damned coyotes and wolves tear up the carcass. Next day the skinnin' is always harder, too."

Taking a straight knife from a sheath at his belt, he split the hide beneath the chin and down the neck and belly to the tail. Next he ripped down the inside of each leg and around at the knee and hock joints, peeling back the hide as he went.

The buffalo flesh smelled warm and sweet, a smell Keith got used to after a short while, listening to the slithering whisper of Massengale's gliding knife.

Switching to a crescent-shaped knife, Massengale cut around the neck, talking as he worked. "Sometimes I roll Mister Buffalo over on his back, cut off the head and brace it against the shoulder. Else I use a prod stick to hold him just right." He began loosening the hide from the carcass. Keith helped him cut it free.

"Some fellows get in a big rush," the hunter said. "Use a mule and chain. Jerk the hide off. Best way I know to ruin all your work. We hand-skin every time. Brings better prices, too." He continued to instruct as he worked, no motion lost, a man of endless patience. With practiced strokes, he removed the tongue, hams and hump, and bagged them in the huge hide. "You try the next one, Keith."

Keith held back a moment, took the straight knife at his belt and selected a cow. The hide proved heavy and loose and unwieldy, his hands unsure, soon bloody. He was still slitting the shaggy belly when the wagons rolled in, and Andy and Stratton got down. From time to time Massengale helped, patiently advising Keith how to cut here, how to slant the knife to avoid gashing the hide. Once the hunter handed Keith a steel and told him to sharpen his curved skinning knife. After Keith had done so, Massengale said, "See if it'll shave the hair on your arm." Keith pulled up his sleeve and took a short stroke. The hairs fell.

"All right," the hunter said.

Sweat coursed down Keith's cheeks and off the tip of his nose. He hurried when there was no call to hurry, and was near finishing when the knife slipped and nicked his left thumb.

"Man's not a skinner till he's cut his thumb," Massengale chided him. "Go on. You're about finished."

Keith peeled off the hide and stood back, breathing hard, his back stiff, frowning at the pile of prime meat that, save for choice parts, would go to waste. He glanced up to see Stratton dragging three hides toward the wagon. He tossed Keith a look that brushed ridicule.

"How you like it, sport?"

"Easy as falling off a log," Keith called back, and when Stratton had passed, he turned to

60

Massengale. "What's bothering him?"

Massengale shook his head from side to side, and stooped to take the cow's tongue. Later, riding ahead of the wagons to find a camping place, he said:

"Hub's had a hard time. Lost his whole family few years back in Kansas."

"My God —"

"They were camped out. Hub went to the settlements for supplies. Wasn't more'n eight, ten miles. Blizzard came up. Hub was late startin' back; couldn't get home. They froze to death."

Keith groaned in sympathy.

"Don't say anything to Hub. He shies away from any feeling. Another thing. Hub was with my brother Daniel that day."

"I see."

"Dan shot out a little bunch. He always rode a big gray horse so Hub could see him better. Hub saw Dan show up on a ridge a long way off. That was the signal to come ahead, to start the skinnin'. About that time Hub heard rifle cracks — not buffalo guns. It was some Indian bucks — they'd slipped out of a draw on their ponies, close to Dan.

"Now Hub's eyesight is poor. He can see a man horseback all right, but that's not shootin' at him. He carries an old Spencer carbine in the wagon. He emptied it and he heard Dan's Sharps boom a time or two — that was all."

"The Indians didn't attack Hub?"

"Just a little dab of 'em. They rode on. I figure

it was some young bucks on a raid."

The horses footed along, raising tiny puffs of dust in the dry, curly grass. "A man in Hub's position would blame himself to some extent," Keith said. "I would."

"But he still does. Which is wrong. He won't let us forget it. Says if he could see like an ordinary mortal he'd saved Dan's life. I've tried to tell him it wasn't his fault. That I don't blame him — that men with sharp eyes can't hit a buck on a runnin' horse a long way off. Hub won't listen."

"When was this?"

"Last summer. Ever since, Hub's held Dan up as God. Never was anybody like him; never will be. Nobody can take Dan's place. Lord, I know that. He was my only brother — a year younger. But Hub's wrong. These things happen. It's the Almighty's way. We don't have any say-so." They covered a bumpy slope, and Keith saw Massengale face him. "You're the first man I've asked to come in with us since we lost Dan. We need another gun — somebody who can shoot. Levi's nigh helpless. Hub can't see far. That leaves Andy and me. However, if you want to pull out of our deal, Keith, I'll understand."

Keith didn't have to think about it. "I'd be running out on myself if I did," he said, and saw the blue eyes on him narrow in thought, in depth, an expression that went away almost as Keith saw it.

"Good," Massengale said and held out his hand. "Good."

CHAPTER 4

A spring-fed branch wandered southward toward the North Fork of the Red, sparkling before Keith's eyes like a string of glass beads tossed carelessly across the fawn land. By the spring a brace of old cottonwoods stood guard, everlastingly bent by the southwest wind.

The hunter rode to the spring, stepped down and scooped up a handful of water for taste, smacking his lips. He jagged his head, approving, and pointed downslope. "Good place to cure hides, Keith. Just enough slant if it rains. We'll camp here."

As soon as the wagons rolled in and the stock unhitched and picketed to graze, all the crew but Oatman started dragging the green hides to the slope and spreading them out to dry, flesh side up.

Keith, observing Massengale, cut slits in the edges of a thick bull's skin. From a sack he took wooden pegs which he drove through the slits, first at the neck end, next the tail end, meanwhile keeping the hide taut, and finished by pegging and stretching each side.

In a few days, the hunter said, you turned the hides hair side up; after that, over every day until dried. Then, to keep out the bugs, you sprinkled arsenic water on both sides and threw the hides in the freight wagon or stacked them on the ground.

Massengale stopped pegging to view the huge hide which Andy was putting down. "Boys," he said, "you won't see many bigger than that bull Keith shot today."

"Forgot the one Dan killed last winter on the Canadian?" Stratton spoke up.

"It was a big 'un, all right," Massengale replied, skirting an argument.

"*Biggest* I ever saw," Stratton insisted. "Bar none."

Keith saw Andy and his uncle trade brief glances. Neither said a word. Presently, Massengale finished and got up. "I'd better show you about reloading," he said to Keith, and went to the gear wagon.

His strong, thick fingers were practiced and skilled. He punched out the exploded primer in a shell, brushed out the debris, put the case in a vinegar pot to soak while he and Keith set to work removing the other used primers. When the shells had soaked a few minutes, the hunter washed one in warm water and dried it with a flannel cloth.

"When a man loads his own shells," he said, "he knows where he stands. You bet I remember two fellows up in Kansas. Both in the same crew. Cap Starnes and Bill Yates. They sure didn't have any use for one another. Both stuck on the same girl in Dodge, and Cap a Confederate and Bill a Yank. One day Cap went out to hunt. He found a bunch, crawled up, got set — fired his Sharps. It just snapped, didn't go off. Same thing happened again.

"Well, he dug out one cartridge and found a big hide bug in the bottom of the shell between the powder and the base. Been two or three men doin' the reloadin'. He figured Bill did it, but he couldn't prove it. After that, you bet he loaded his own shells. Why, what if he'd shot at an Indian instead of a buffalo?"

Stratton came from the pegging ground, pulled another hide out of the wagon, and stood still, scowling, watching, while Massengale examined a shell for hairline cracks around the neck and reduced the mouth of the case with Keith's new crimper.

"Too bad we ain't as particular about everything as we are about cartridges," Stratton grumbled.

Massengale didn't speak for a moment. He thumbed on a new primer, and pressed the bottom of the cartridge against a block of wood to seat the primer below the base of the case.

"Being particular helps us stay alive," the hunter said, his voice as agreeable as a man could make it.

"Didn't help Dan," Stratton threw back. "Didn't help me see far enough. Didn't give me enough horse sense to have the wagon closer to the stand." He dragged the hide away.

Keith saw Massengale rest his hands on his knees and lean forward, a forbearance pushing into his face. A moment and he picked up one of the new, straight, 90-grain Big Fifty shells which

Keith had fired. He dipped a thimble-like cup into the powder can and poured the large, black grains into the case, curling forefinger and thumb around the mouth. He put in a pasteboard wad, and a little powder on top of the wad, and seated the paper-patched bullet, making certain not to crush the powder or to tear the paper patch. Last, he pressed the ball gently down with his thumb and the cartridge was finished.

"I'll do the others," Keith said.

Massengale, nodding, drifted off to the sturdy Shuttler and shortly Keith heard him hammering on a loose wheel rim. Awkward in the beginning, Keith picked up speed after reloading several shells. Behind him Oatman was making a path from the cook wagon to the buffalo-chip fire, talking all the while. Tomorrow, he said, be time to tie a green hide to some poles and fix up a vat, salt down some hams, leave them in there a week or more. By then the meat would be just right to hang on a rack and smoke over a greenwood fire. But, Oatman said, there'd be no big curing until Sam picked out a permanent winter camp.

Toward evening, after Massengale had entered in his black memorandum book the number of hides taken for the day, Keith sat down to a supper of hump meat and ribs and boiled tongues fried in marrow and biscuits seasoned in marrow. In fact, the crew spread the marrow like butter on the bread.

"Buffalo meat's got everything a man's body needs," Massengale vowed, wiping his beard.

"You don't need greens. Why, I recollect runners that went a whole year without a single tater or bean. Imagine that? Lived on just straight buffalo meat and marrow, mind you. Their cheeks got as pink as a baby's."

"That 'fore or after they visited Dutch Charley's saloon in Dodge?" Oatman questioned, a certain reminiscent wistfulness in his hoarse whisper.

"Now, Levi, you've done gone and shot holes in my story. Keith won't believe another word we tell him."

Contentment reached all through Keith's being. Already, he thought, astonished at his capacity to gorge on the coarse, dark, succulent meat, which tasted better than beef, he was becoming like the others. He leaned back, feeling on his face the light wind off the prairie scattering the heady scents of unfettered country, conscious of a new peace of mind. Killing his first buffalo had helped; that and Sam Massengale's company. Sam's patient guidance, his unalterable good nature. But Keith had found out today that hunting for hides was gut-busting toil, a business instead of a sport; and so, understanding, he approved of Sam's fairness whereby every man in the crew, from cook to runner, shared equally in the profits. Although there was no formality among these men, they respected the individual and did not intrude, even in banter, past a certain line. A man's private life was his own business.

Keith wondered about Oatman and Stratton,

their backgrounds, their reasons for being on the buffalo frontier; and recalling Stratton's family tragedy, he knew that he could harbor no rancor for that bitter, contentious man, even if he did resent Keith's presence in the outfit. Possibly Keith reflected, what counted out here was not what a man had been, or where he was from or the standing of the family name — but what he was now. How he stood up. Keith liked that.

"Like Levi's been sayin'," Massengale said, "we need time to cure some meat. Come a blizzard and we'd be mighty short. So might as well hunt around here before we turn south. A. B. Barr's wagon train will scare off any game in that direction for a while. Outfit that size takes plenty meat, you bet, and is noisy as a screech owl doin' it."

"Particular, them women he's got along," Oatman said, looking thoughtful.

Something impulsive quickened in Andy's face. "Prettiest woman I ever laid eyes on is in that wagon train. She's beautiful." He clamped his mouth shut and shrank down, as if realizing he had left himself vulnerable to more jesting.

"Just how'd you know?" Oatman asked, teasing.

"I saw her one day along the creek, when I went for water. She didn't look like one of them" — he searched for the descriptive term — "like one of them *other* women."

"Cowboys call 'em calico queens," his uncle said, speaking plainly. "Missionaries call 'em soiled doves. Oh, I reckon they shine in a man's eye when he's gone six months without a female around. Them all painted up, their smell a sight better than a hide camp, you bet. Truth is, Andy, they're women to stay away from."

"I said she didn't look like any of them," Andy retorted, a righteous indignation bracing his voice.

"How could you tell?" Oatman ribbed him.

"Tell? I told you why. First, because she didn't look like one."

"Would you buy a fancy saddle horse without lookin' at his teeth?"

"Second place," Andy said stoutly, "she didn't go back to the main wagon train. She went to her *own* wagon. It had springs, a side door, canvas side curtains, and a little stove pipe out the back. Mighty nice."

"Hell," Massengale said, "that's A. B. Barr's wife."

"*Wife*, you say?" Oatman asked, lifting an eyebrow.

Massengale shrugged. After considering his nephew a further moment, he said, "Who's to say she's not and who are we to ask?" He shifted position and looked around, signifying that the subject was dropped. "Keith, want to try your luck tomorrow? Hunt out a bunch on your own?"

"I'm willing," Keith said, and saw Andy's eagerness to go with him. Yet it swept into his mind that he and Stratton must resolve their odds soon, if at all, and he said, "If it's agreeable with

Hub, I'll hunt with him."

Stratton started up in surprise, but not for long. Disdain rubbed into his voice. "Why not, sport?" he said, leaning toward Keith. "Think you can gun down enough to keep one skinner busy?"

"I got a few today."

"Like hell you did. Sam killed the whole she-bang."

Keith's anger broke loose. Before he could stand or speak, Massengale rose and stepped between them, holding that position and blocking any exchange. No one spoke. Massengale, after several seconds, took a deliberate forward step and faced around, a stooped and toil-drawn man determined to prevent a row among his friends. He sighted his gaze straight between Stratton and Keith, favoring neither, and spoke in a tone which Keith had never heard before:

"Keith got three kills today, Hub. Sure, he wasted some shots. He's green. Wasted more than a man would if he had a 'scope on his rifle. Now if you don't want to pair off with him, just say so. That's all there is to it. There'll be no argument." Stratton said nothing. Massengale spoke faster, in a still flatter voice: "If we can't get along, I'm gonna break up the hull damned outfit and go back to Missouri. By God, I will!"

Keith had never seen Sam Massengale nearer to uncontrolled anger, and the sight shook him. No man stirred. No man spoke. Oatman discovered unusual interest in the low-burning coals.

Andy inspected the tip of his right boot, his mouth creased. Stratton did not meet Massengale's eyes.

Finally, the hunter's mouth relaxed. "Play us something, Andy."

After breakfast next morning, Stratton barely lifted his head when Keith rode across to the mule-hitched trail wagon. A moodiness was banked in the skinner's eyes as he slipped tapered cartridges into the tubular magazine of the Spencer carbine. Massengale, nearby, eyed the prairie and sky.

"Don't ride all over hell's creation lookin' for something to shoot at," he said. "Keep on up the North Fork. If you don't find game by noon, make a little swing and come in. Andy and me, we'll rig up that vat for Levi. He won't let us rest till we do." He left them abruptly.

Stratton's lips stayed shut. His moody eyes spoke for him: *All right, sport. Let's see you find 'em.*

Riding northwest ahead of the wagon, Keith could doubt the time was late December instead of autumn. The sun was playfully warm, the arch of the sky a clean blue and too boundless to be imagined back home, and the husking wind was faintly cool. Away off he could see the blurred suggestion of choppy country forming. Sam said if a man kept right on traveling, he'd bump into the edge of the Staked Plains, a land of no echoes and no trees, as flat as a wagon bed and nigh as dry, but with grass as rich as a miser's dream.

The sun hung past noon before Keith decided to turn back. In all directions stretched a motionless world of bright silence, an immensity that in one moment threw a man back on his lone helplessness and in the next reminded him of his freedom from restraint. The waiting emptiness caused him to think of cattle to fill it. Any man could see what was happening, with the buffalo cleaned out in Kansas and Texas next. Comanches and Kiowas held a nomadic claim to the limitless prairies, and the state of Texas claimed them in general. In his opinion, Sam said, the buffalo range belonged to any man having the spine to start himself a ranch and hold it against all comers, Indian or white.

He discarded his pondering when he found Stratton driving the mules at a listless walk. "What do you think, Hub? Go ahead or swing back?"

"You're the runner," fell the indifferent reply.

To ask, Keith saw was a mistake. He swung northward to begin a looping circle back to camp. Hereafter, he would ask no opinions of Stratton. Talking over things wouldn't work with the man. Likely Stratton interpreted asking as a sign of weakness, and maybe he was right.

Yet Keith had learned a good deal about himself while making his way to the Sweet Water. He knew he owned the faculty of direction; therefore, he could find his way to camp. Sam said some men were born with it, something nature gives you. If a man had that instinct it was better than a compass. Sam believed likewise that most Indians had it and few civilized men did. He figured a man thus gifted never got lost and relied on what lay in his mind as much as he depended on the sun and the stars and landmarks, which in this country meant peculiar buttes or peaks or a conspicuous line of hills, maybe.

The lowering of sunlight of midafternoon slanted across the prairie when Keith, keeping the location of the North Fork in mind, in relation to camp, reached the crest of a wave of land and halted.

He caught his breath, drenched in excitement. On the gradual slope stretching below him grazed scores of buffalo, so many they blackened the brown turf.

And here he was, a realization raced through him, showing himself on the rise like a fool tenderfoot. He reined back out of sight and tied his horse in a draw; lugging rifle, shell sack and sticks, he ran back toward the vantage point. Remembering Stratton then, he saw the wagon bobbing half a mile behind. He waved his hat and ran on. Near the rim, he crouched and crawled the remaining distance, his breath coming in excited gulps.

He peered over the top and saw them still grazing undisturbed. In fascination he watched the dark beasts, the golden sunlight catching the seal-brown of their thick winter coats. These buffalo seemed different in some way. Bigger.

Shaggier. Because, he knew, he had found them on his own.

And suddenly, in his impatience, he jabbed the rest sticks upright. A thought arrested him in time, before he laid the Sharps in the notch. The wind, of course. He pulled a few blades of grass and released them; wriggling, they drifted from him toward the buffalo. He flattened down at once, damning his carelessness. A shot from here would carry straight to the buffalo, might spook them. So might a man's scent. Sam said they'd run from you quicker from smell than from sight.

Scrambling down out of sight and going in a crouching run, sometimes sinking past his ankles in the loose, reddish soil, he bore to his left, aware that the bend of the slope was taking him flankwise to the buffalo. When he checked his position and looked again from the crest, the shaggies grazed to his right and the range was very short, close to two hundred yards.

Drunk with excitement, he set up the sticks, eared back the hammer, pulled the rear trigger to set the front one on hair trigger, and searched for the leader. So large a band as this could have more than one leader.

A particular bull captured his eye. A bull that seemed to stand out from the others. Why, comprehension rushed over him as he took a swinging look, the entire bunch was made up of bulls. Mostly stub-horns, which Sam said were old bulls, their hides an inch thick around the shoulder and neck. Some spikes: young bulls whose horns were straight; at five years old their horns would begin to curve inward. Sam said matured bulls usually left the cows about November and ranged by themselves until rutting time, which he called the "running" season, which started about July and lasted into late September or early October. But often a few active bulls stayed with the cows as defenders.

Keith's hands were unsteady again. Lips compressed, jaw taut, he drew down on the bull, behind the shoulder, squeezed, and the shaggy shape lunged and fell as if axed. Nearby animals looked up, others continued to graze. Keith reloaded and chose a bull on the outside. When he fired, it lurched and whirled in Keith's direction, more stung than hurt, and Keith knew his bullet had struck high into the hump. He punched in another shell, took aim on the lights — fired. The bull made a startled leap, wobbling, and stood like stone, a frozen black image. A second later it crumpled.

Keith's ears roared. Watching left and right, he spied an animal drifting off. He knocked it down, but the killing required two shots; and as he came ready again he detected a restlessness. Shaggy heads lifted from the short grass, turning where Keith crouched. He hesitated, watching two bulls lumber up to sniff those on the ground. One hooked a downed buffalo; now other bulls threw up their heads and bellowed. Some started off. If he didn't stop them, the whole herd would move off.

He worked faster, hurrying his shots. After three rounds the next buffalo arched up its back and staggered, head swaying, and fell on its side, kicking violently. Although Keith was hitting, his first shots were missing vital parts.

His bullet took another bull too low, because it humped away, one foreleg flapping.   damn his hurry! It was cruel to cripple an animal and let it live.

Savagely self-reproachful, he cradled the Sharps in the crotch and sighted. At the rifle's boom the bull shook its head balefully, bewildered and hurt; it went on in jerks. Keith jammed in a cartridge. He aimed higher. The bull turned sideways at the roar, took several rocking hops, stopped, struggled forward, and fell with a dusty flop.

Keith's rifle was hot, and an overheated barrel caused the bullet to wobble. So he slipped a greased rag in the eyelet of the wiping stick, swabbed out the barrel and left the breech-lock open to cool.

But the excitement of the moment was too much for him and he prematurely jammed in a new cartridge. A bull came into his sights and he squeezed off a shot. At the impact of the bullet, the bull lurched wildly toward him, in rage, head lowered. By the time he had reloaded, the buffalo was a charging dark hulk only thirty yards away. Willing himself not to run, Keith fired again. The beast paused and sat down on its haunches and glared at him hatefully, the massive, curved-horn head weaving back and forth.

More and more of the shaggies were bellowing and moving off, and Keith saw that he could no longer hold them. By impatience, by gambling for a stand instead of a fair number of kills, he had lost a big day's hunting. And as he realized what was happening, he heard a low rumble and the entire band, a hundred or more, swept off to his right, jamming and crowding. Ravels of yellow dust drifted high.

He overcame his disappointment and stood up to watch the headlong flight of the dark mass, as intrigued as though he saw buffalo for the first time. In his ears the drumming hoofs sounded like the roll of spring thunder. His hunt was over.

His chest was soppy with sweat. He rubbed his sore arm and shoulder, reflecting on his unsatisfactory marksmanship. He counted thirteen empty cases in the curly grass. On the slope lay six dead bulls, counting the nearest one, which was dying, still weaving, still on its haunches. It was wasteful to use a shell on an animal that would be dead in moments. He remembered using three shots on two animals; in all, it was the poorest shooting he had done. More times than not, a veteran runner like Sam required but one bullet, only two now and then, and seldom three.

Keith asked himself what had gone wrong? After starting off with a one-shot kill? Was it because he was trying to impress Hub Stratton?

As he finished gathering up the empty cases, he

saw Stratton coming along the spine of the grassy rise, the short-barreled Spencer in one hand. A springy-legged man whose squinting face was already framed in derision.

"I been watchin' back there," he said, with a fling of his head. "You let the outside bulls drift off. Let 'em draw the whole bunch."

"I know," Keith said.

"You had a stand, easy. Any greenhorn that could hit the side of a barn would 'a' had a stand."

"Sam would have," Keith agreed, feeling that covered the issue, yet resenting the skinner's superior manner. Keith picked up the shell sack and the sticks and his rifle. "Better get busy if we make camp before dark."

Stratton's scorn jumped to a touchy anger. "Don't order me around. No eastern sport can tell me what to do."

"You're the skinner, aren't you? I don't even have to lend you a hand. I've done my part."

Stratton sneered. "Anybody with a lick of sense would 'a' had a stand."

A stinging nettled Keith's face. "Anybody? You mean Dan Massengale, don't you?"

"Dan?" The skinner's lean face shifted swiftly from surprise to a moody techiness. "You — you couldn't carry Dan's rest sticks."

Keith wasn't aware that he had dropped the sack and sticks until he found his right hand clutching Stratton's shirt. But in the flash of that knowing he saw something indefinable behind

Stratton's ill temper, a going back, a deep and terrible hurt, unhealed, which left Keith feeling wrong.

His anger went dry. And, strangely, Stratton had lifted no hand. Keith let go and stepped away, not looking at him, not wanting to. Because Keith had the sensation of having seen Stratton bare his innermost self, an intrusion from which no man could excuse himself.

Picking up his gear, he turned to walk out to the closest bull. It was still crouched on its hunkers, in a dozing attitude. A rather curious position for a dead buffalo, he thought. Keith's mind was yet on Stratton. He hardly gave the buffalo a second look.

He wasn't far away when he felt the first rise of fear and shortened his stride, seeing the shaggy head move slightly and the small, black eyes suddenly taking notice of him.

Keith dragged step, froze, and all at once saw the bull stagger up bellowing and flinging blood, stumpy tail raised, eyes bulging hate, and on its feet to charge. Keith dropped everything except the Sharps. He cocked the hammer and turned rigid, staring at the empty chamber which he had neglected to reload.

A heartbeat and he was stooping, groping for the shell sack. But he was out of time. And as he whirled to run, he saw Hub Stratton swinging the carbine.

Two shots banged, so close they seemed jammed together. Keith, glancing backward, saw the bull bow its massive head, and sink down and crash over.

Keith brushed a hand across his forehead. Reality, which had seemed so remote moments back, returned as vivid impressions: the bull twitching on the tufted grass, the blood running out its black nostrils, the brisk crunch of Stratton's boot steps.

Keith turned. "Great shooting, Hub. Needless to say, I'm obliged to you."

"Luck — plain luck," Stratton growled, dismissing, ridiculing. "And let me tell you something, sport. Next time you come up to a buffalo with an unloaded rifle — next time you hunt without a cartridge belt —" He was, Keith saw, not only still contemptuous, but also furious.

Muttering, Stratton tramped off for the wagon.

Keith labored awkwardly, by himself. By the time he had skinned two of the old stub-horns, Stratton had peeled the robes off the remaining four and taken the meat.

Now, impatient, arms folded, lower lip pushed out, the skinner watched Keith, who expected to hear his grumbling criticism. But the next he knew, Stratton, without a word, fell to helping him finish, his dirt-crusted hands as deft as a woman's.

At last they were loaded — hams, tongues, humps, all the choice meat of the bulls, packed in the soggy, green hides, the light wagon sagging. Keith, mounting to ride ahead, drew rein when Stratton motioned him.

"Don't say anything in camp about what happened," Stratton said, in what for him was a mild voice. "I mean about killin' that bull. Plain luck was all it was." He climbed to the wagon seat and took up the reins.

Keith followed him with his glance. "You saved my life, Hub. I can't forget that, and I wouldn't call it luck."

"Aw, you eastern sports talk too much. I don't want the crew rawhidin' me about them lucky shots, is all. Happens I don't like to be joked with. Maybe you've noticed that? So let's keep it just between us, huh?"

Keith had no choice except to shrug agreement. Riding on, he reviewed what had happened. Reliving those moments brought the shrinking coldness far down again in him, in step-by-step detail. The bull shaking dust as he heaved to his feet. The black chin-mop almost brushing the short grass as he charged. Hub Stratton flinging up the carbine. Only a lung shot could slam a buffalo dead in its tracks, or possibly a neck shot. A bullet in the heart or head wouldn't have stopped the bull in time.

So it wasn't luck.

Exceptional shooting, in fact, for any man. Shooting which bordered on the remarkable for a man with poor eyesight, even more so with a carbine.

CHAPTER 5

Thereafter, Hub Stratton's hostility toward Keith seemed to settle, though never wholly disappear, at a point between grudging allowances for a greenhorn runner from "back East" and conditional acceptance for a man determined to learn the hide game. Never talkative, Stratton communicated even less around camp after the bull-shooting incident. He did not remark on it and neither did Keith, who had given his word. And when Sam Massengale, as if to humor an old friend, began hunting with Stratton, Keith paired with Andy Kinkade, whose cheerful company he found to his liking.

During a noontime rest, Andy said, "What about them French girls, Keith?"

"A woman's a woman."

"What does that mean?"

"All women want about the same things — husband, family, home, security. But —"

"But what?"

"Some want too much. They're the selfish ones. They think mainly of themselves. They take and they give little in return. They'll destroy a man — if he'll let them."

Andy was chewing on a blade of grass. He rested and let the stem float from his long, brown fingers, and the shadow of a question grazed his eyes, stood still a moment, and passed on. Again he became musing and questing, the open face of a young man groping to discover himself.

"What about the English girls?"

"A woman's a woman, remember."

"Doggone you, Keith, you talk in riddles. Are they uppity?"

"The ones I met were fair of skin and pleasing to the eye. But —"

Andy groaned good-naturedly. "Yeah. But what?"

"They regard most Americans as uncouth fellows fresh out of the backwoods — unwashed, untamed."

"Stuck up, oh?"

"No more than easterners in our country who look on westerners as unruly wild men."

"Son-of-a-gun," Andy said, sobering, "I keep thinkin' about the lady I saw that time on the Sweet Water."

Andy, Keith could see, was smitten hard. An older woman, poised, well-dressed, experienced, versed with graces, impressed and attracted a green boy. A dreamy state which Andy would emerge from when he met a pretty girl near his own age.

"She's married, Andy."

"What bothers me," the boy said seriously, "is the way she looked. Like she was afraid. I'll swear she was, Keith."

"Afraid of what?"

"Him — A. B. Barr — I reckon."

"Why him?"

"He was the only one around. I saw it on her face when she found out he was there."

"There'll be other women in your life — young women."

"You mean," Andy said, his mouth pouching in a grin, "a woman's a woman?"

"I mean forget her. She's trouble."

Into late January the outfit hunted out of what the crew called the Twin Cottonwoods Camp, continuing to range up and down the North Fork of the Red, and sometimes swinging northward as Keith had the day he found the big band of bulls. The cured hides, which Massengale now described as "flirted," and which he sorted as to bulls and cows and packed flat, continued to grow in the freight wagon.

Keith's kills mounted. One day he shot eight; another day twelve; another seventeen, and darkness caught him and Andy before they reached camp as a light snow fell. But there were days when he sighted not even a lone buffalo. These days doubled up, grew more frequent, and when the outfit went three days without bringing in a hide, Massengale decided to pull out.

Below the North Fork the crew kept due south and pitched a new camp every night, killing and skinning straggling shaggies, and crossed the Salt Fork of the Red on the fourth day. The nights were crisply cold, but not hard-freezing, and the sky varied from dull gray to teasing winter sunshine, more sunshine than not. The lengthening stretches of dull-brown prairie, dipping and cresting, tumbling to roughness along the winding courses of the shallow, sandy streams, put Keith in mind of riding the undulating back of a tranquil sea.

And he was discovering a new tranquility within himself. He called each man in the crew by his first name. At ease with all around him, he had lost his earlier dislike for Hub. How could he feel otherwise after what had happened to the man, losing his entire family, later blaming himself needlessly for Dan Massengale's death, and after Hub had saved him from a goring, and likely his life?

Keith's mind was keener. His energy astounded him. He ate buffalo meat three times a day, steak for breakfast fried in marrow. He wondered if the altitude contributed in part to his new strength. All day he rode and crawled and stalked, over ridges dotted with yucca, up and down reddish gullies and draws, and pelted the black beasts and helped Andy with the skinning. Moreover, when the shaggies took to drifting on him as they inevitably did — and he had learned that buffalo tended to be restless on windy days — he would trot after them and throw the lever down on the Sharps and hold the rifle so more cooling air passed through the barrel. That procedure, even Hub agreed, relieved an overheated barrel from bursting the half stock. But at no time, the skinner amended, his moody face revealing not the scantiest reference while he regarded Keith, should a man approach a wounded buffalo with an unloaded rifle.

"Hub's dead right," Sam said. "Buffalo take a heap of killin'."

And Keith nodded, playing the game with Hub to gratify him, though not convinced he should.

Save for the trotting, which Sam pointed out might be dangerous at any other time of the year except winter, when Indians didn't prowl much, Keith hunted as he had learned. Also he wore a cartridge belt, cut and sewed from a tarp, a ready complement to his shell sack. And next he fancied leather pants to wear over his trousers. Following Levi's exacting instructions, he selected a stub-horn's thick hide and scraped it free of blood, fat, and flesh before it dried. He soaked the hair side with a mixture of wood ashes and water to make lye, afterward scraping the hair off against the grain. Of a morning, using a round stone, he rubbed and beat a tanning mixture of brains, marrow, soapweed, and water into the rawhide and left it out in the sun. Of an evening, he rubbed and stretched the hide some more, folded and laid it inside the supply wagon overnight.

"Keith's got it all scraped off," Andy reported early in the tedious process. "When he puts on that rawhide, it'll scrape him."

"Nothing cold as rawhide," Hub dropped in. "When hard freezes come, sport'll think he's got on icicles."

After about two weeks — "and a year's work," Sam said — Levi pronounced the leather pliable enough, and he and Keith cut it to size, using buffalo sinew for thread, and slit openings at the top for belt loops.

Keith held up the britches triumphantly, showing them around, though admitting to himself their natural light color was too visible for safety.

"You're big medicine," Sam jested. "You'll stand out like a white buffalo on a ridge."

Keith looked obliquely at Levi, whose fixed grimace stretched tighter in thought. He pulled on his chin and said hoarsely, "Never you lazy fellows mind. Go ahead and get your shins all skint up. Rawhide's supposed to look white at first. We'll smoke it darker, Indian style. That's what we'll do." And he told Keith to dig a smoke hole, to fill it with green wood, which smoldered best, and to prop the pants over the hole.

At the end of a week the results resembled a cowboy's yellowish brown chaps more than pants, but Levi said never mind, they would make crawling as much a pleasure as crawling could be.

On the eighth day south of the North Fork, Keith saw the widest river since departing Fort Elliott. Sam, referring to a rough map which he said a runner on the Canadian had drawn for him, said it was the Prairie Dog Town Fork of the Red. Not that it mattered. They were going to cross it, anyway; but a man liked to know his general whereabouts. A runner drifting 'way eastward into Indian Territory, now, which was out of bounds, might get himself arrested by U.S. marshals.

Camped on the south side of the Prairie Dog Town Fork, just west of the broad trail made by Barr's wagons, they knocked down twenty-five buffalo the first day. Here, Sam said, was the place to fix another pole-and-hide vat and to build Levi a big smokehouse, since a man could sell cured meat for three to seven cents a pound in the settlements. And so they stretched hides over a framework of hackberry poles, cut from along the river, and dug firepits in the center of the floor. Before many days Levi's first batch of cured hams and tongues were ready, cured meat a man could eat raw.

Early in March, after a run of warm days, just when Keith thought spring was about to pop, the wind switched ends from south to north like a kicking mule, the warm sunshine changed to surly grayness, and freezing gusts hurled a late snow upon the camp.

About dark the crew gathered behind a hackberry lean-to, under a hide roof supported by poles, watching Levi cook supper. Keith heard a shout off the trail and saw a rider among the swirling flakes, his strong voice hailing across the wind, "Hello the camp! Hello there!" Sam, cupping hands to mouth, called back.

The heavy voice out there sent ahead the impression of a big man, and a big man dismounted, encased in buffalo coat, thick cap with ear flaps, mittens, and Wellington boots. As he led his horse in, the firelight touched the planes of his ruddy cheeks, and Keith saw the clipped bush of a luxuriant mustache and genial eyes.

"Come in," Sam said again. "You're in time for supper."

"Thank you, friend." He tied his mount on the lee side of the freight wagon and advanced to the fire, removing mittens and loosening the great coat. "Lads," he said, his brogue thickening, "I'm Mike Cassidy — better known as Hard Cash Cassidy. Tonight your fire is like the light in me old mother's eyes." He shook hands all around, and a firm grip he had. "If you're wonderin'," he said, "what a sensible man is doin' out such a night as this, I'm agent for W. C. Lobenstein of Leavenworth, Kansas. Possible you've heard the sayin' — *Lobenstein, Lobenstein and His Forty Irishmens?* Well, I'm one o' them. At Barr's Town, dealin' in hides, spreadin' good will for me generous employer."

"Barr's Town?" Sam asked. "Where is it?"

"Due south. On the North Wichita River." A liveliness rolled into Cassidy's hearty voice. "Never talk business on a dry stomach." And, in a twinkling, Keith saw a bottle whisked gleaming from underneath the great coat. "You lads care for a taste of heather-honey?" Cassidy was uncorking as he spoke, and he offered first to Levi, saying, "To his honor — the *chef dee cuisine.*"

Eagerly, Levi tilted the bottle. Keith saw him pause in mid-swallow, blink, flinch; he swallowed, his eyes watering, and passed the bottle back. "That's right good," he whispered.

"Pass it around," Cassidy said.

Except for frequent pauses to commend Levi's cooking, the Irishman said little more until after the meal. Keith got up and rustled wood for the insatiable fire. The flames soared higher, biting at the wind and snow. The lean-to felt fairly snug.

"Yes," Cassidy started over, raising his voice above the wind's roar, "A. B. Barr built his town on the North Wichita River. He's got the bulk of the hide business, he has, which is why I'm out in such miserable weather makin' the camps — to reach you fine lads first — to make you some foldin' money."

"How's that?" Sam asked.

"Pay you half now for the hides on hand — the remainder when you haul in, plus the guarantee to buy *all* other hides you take that are in salable condition — no rips, no tears, no kip hides."

"We hand-skin everything," Sam said.

"All the better. Later on, when the weather moderates and you lads are closer to town, I'll send wagons to haul in your kill and pay you hard cash on the spot."

"How much?"

An impetuous benevolence appeared to drive Cassidy. "Three dollars and fifty cents for prime hides." Sam's eyes brightened. Levi whistled in surprise. "Lobenstein ships thousands of hides to Europe," the Irishman said expansively. "The English Army uses buffalo leather for accouterments. It's more pliable than cowhide. What don't go across the briny waters, Lobenstein sells back East. A buffalo's hide is good for saddle trimmings, luggage, coats, leather buffers. Everybody wants a sleigh and buggy robe. I tell you the country's gone buffalo crazy."

"Three-fifty," Sam said. "That's good."

"I'll even pay seventy-five cents for any kip hides."

"We don't shoot yearlings or calves."

"You might as well. Wolves get 'em."

"No," Sam said, frowning. "There's enough waste as it is. What's Barr paying?"

It was characteristic of Sam, Keith thought, to ask Cassidy and to accept his word without question.

"About the same," Cassidy said, sounding honest enough. He steepled his hands over the swell of his paunch and swayed his head sadly from side to side. "Far be it from me, lads, to run down me competitor when he cannot be present to defend himself. As me old mother used to say, rest her soul: 'It ain't Christian.'" Again the lugubrious head-swaying. "But now you've asked me a straight question, I'll give you a straight answer. There is a rub, lads, there is." Again he delayed, as if averse to continuing.

"How's that?" Keith urged him on.

And, at once, the Irishman's disinclination evaporated. "A. B. Barr likes to have the runners take part of their money out in trade at his store . . . if you get what I mean? Like a company store. It's handy, he says, and it is, for him. By the time a good lad's paid twice for his supplies, had himself a whirl or so with Barr's Dodge City girls, been drunk a week on Barr's cheap whisky, which I am sad to say is what we're drinkin' here tonight — he's dead broke and ready to chase the shaggies again."

"A tough town," Sam nodded.

"Not in the way you think. Barr runs the place. He's got men who never turn a tap of honest work; they just stand around to keep an eye on business. He calls 'em marshals." Cassidy winked broadly. "You can be sure there's no destroyin' of A. B. Barr's property, and no layin' on of hands of A. B. Barr's girls, and no drinkin' of A. B. Barr's whisky unless a lad can pay his way."

A question formed in Sam's face. "Smelled a slippery storekeeper down that way named Tobe Jett?"

"Not in Barr's Town. Barr won't let an outsider come in to sell a ball of string. Buyin' hides is different. Me and my drivers, we spend money in town."

Sam scratched his beard. "That's funny. Ol' Tobe followed on Barr's trail down from Fort Elliott."

"There's a new hangout on the South Pease River," Cassidy said. "Robbers' Roost. Tough as bull's hide. Dugouts, hide tents."

"That's more to ol' Tobe's likin'."

By next morning the snow was melting under a capricious sun. Mike Cassidy paid Sam cash for half the 396 hides stacked and drying, and agreed to pay the balance on delivery at Barr's

Town in a few weeks.

"Don't forget, I'll buy every hide you haul to town and pay four cents a pound for cured meat — hard cash!" Cassidy shook hands on the deal. After he rode south, the great coat tied behind his saddle, Sam climbed inside the gear wagon to put the money away.

"Uncle Sam's gettin' closer to that black-bottom farm back home," Andy remarked to Keith as they turned the pegged wet hides. "That tin box will be full of money by end of summer. We can all go home then. But before we do, I aim to take in Barr's Town. You bet your boots."

"What if Sam says no?"

"I'll draw my share — go anyway. Nobody's gonna stop me."

Although Keith and Sam averaged fifteen kills a day each while the greening country swelled with early spring, Keith could see this part of the range was thinning of game. Bunches came fewer and smaller and those he found feeding into the warm wind were farther south and southwest each time. Cows were dropping frisky little yellow calves; in two months, Sam said, their humps would begin to show. To protect the calves the bulls stood guard against gray wolves larger than farm dogs. The bulls walked around and around their cows and calves, bunching the tawny little ones toward the center; and when the bands grazed on to new grass, Keith saw the beaten circles where the guardian bulls had walked their beats.

One afternoon Keith and Andy, watching three wolves stalk a small band, cheered when a bull horned a wolf and tossed the writhing gray figure high. It bounced on the sprouting grass, twisted violently, broken, dead. But more times than not the wolves proved too sly and quick for the bulls.

Spring, Keith soon learned, was the season for shedding. The buffalo became a tattered-looking beast. Except for the long black hair covering his head, hump and forelegs, his brown hide hung in ragged patches, and to rid himself of flies and vermin, he pawed the grassy sod and rolled and dusted his hide in saucer-shaped wallows, some as wide as thirty feet, and rubbed on boulders and trees.

As the days passed and the hides piled up and the prairie around the camp resembled a checkerboard of brown and flesh-colored patches, depending on which side of a pegged hide was turned up, Keith wondered why Sam delayed the long haul to Barr's Town. A decision must be made soon. There were almost more hides than could be hauled now in one trip. No hides could be left when they broke camp. Keith said nothing yet. It was Sam Massengale's outfit.

Besides keeping tab of the kills, Sam kept track of the days. Every now and then he would say what day of the month it was. "Boys," he announced one morning, "it's April the fifth."

"— and time we pulled out," Hub countered, squinting hard at him. "We got all the hides we can get on the wagons and the teams can pull."

"I know. I just dread goin' south. Country'll be crowded down there. Cassidy says guns are poppin' all over."

Hub didn't understand. "That's where the main herd is, Sam. Not here. We came to hunt — to make ourselves a stake, didn't we?"

"We can make it here, off to ourselves. Slower, maybe, but we can make it. We can haul in from here."

"Hell of a long haul. Look at the time it'll take."

An unusual reluctance seemed to grasp Sam. "You, Hub. You and Keith — and Levi — make the trip. I'll hold down camp with Andy." He looked away from Andy when he spoke, and Keith saw Andy jerk as if Sam had laid a quirt across his shoulders. Feelings tangled in his face — surprise, hurt, desire, indignation, raw anger — all at once.

"Don't I have any sayso, Uncle Sam? I'm nigh nineteen. I earn a man's share in this outfit."

"That's got nothing to do with it, Andy. I promised your mother I'd bring you back safe. I've already lost Dan. I don't aim to lose you." He paused, a sudden understanding in his eyes. "It's not what you'd do there, son. It's the place. The rough crowd. Cassidy says the country down there is fillin' up with all kinds."

"I've been to Dodge City. It's bigger."

"Barr's town is tougher. Maybe you didn't get what Cassidy meant. Barr's *officers* are all gunslicks. They rule the town."

"I won't look for trouble."

"You don't have to to find it."

"I can take care myself."

"Every man thinks he can. Hardly a day goes by there's not a killing in Barr's Town. Sometimes two or three. A runner sells his hides, goes to the saloon for a drink. Likely as not he'll get a knockout drop in his drink, come to in some alley or get his head bashed in. No, Andy," the hunter said firmly, yet with sympathy, "you can't go."

Andy whipped his arm in a dashing motion, elbow bent. He was trembling. His voice lashed out in jerks: "I quit — right now — I want my share of th' money — money I saw Cassidy pay you — I know you got it!"

Sam Massengale winced, astonished, left speechless. He stared at Andy through a sheet of sick pain, while still understanding him. Andy rubbed the thighs of his trousers. Although his expression said he might wish to call back what he had just said, his mouth remained locked.

"Why can't we just move camp on to the south?" Keith said. "We can haul from there when we please."

Sam sat another moment, his lips foraging for a decision. He looked up and his clear-blue eyes took in everyone. "That agreeable?" Levi nodded right off, for he was an impulsive man, quick to settle a thing one way or another. Hub nodded assent, without expression, as if nothing could surprise him anymore. Andy was turned away, looking at nothing in particular.

"That all right with you, Andy?" his uncle asked.

"Guess so," Andy said, not turning, sounding unconcerned. At once everybody became busy. Levi cleaning up after the meal. Hub seeing about the picketed teams. Sam tramping to the freight wagon.

All but Andy. He couldn't seem to straighten up. A consciousness of shame stamped his clean, tanned face. But he said no word to his uncle.

Keith went toward the pegging ground, knowing that nothing had been settled, only postponed.

Three days later, finding a good spring, the outfit camped in sight of the breaks of the North Pease River, where on the dark humps of the hills across the valley Keith could see buffalo marching single file to water, others resting after watering, others lazily returning to their feeding grounds. Buffalo trails spread over the country like the branches of a tree, back and forth, linking the buffalo to water and grass. Close-by rose a lookout hill. Riding up it, Keith saw game scattered in three directions.

No one spoke, that evening, of hauling to Barr's Town, though Keith was aware that stood uppermost in every man's mind. Sam, while thoughtful, was in his usual easy nature. Andy showed an occasional forced grin. Levi and Hub seemed to wait.

"There's turkeys roostin' below camp," Levi said presently. "You fellows like some for supper tomorrow?"

"Too bitter," Hub said. "They been eatin' chinaberries."

Keith got up to move his saddle horse nearer the wagons for the night, and dallied over the small chore. Andy, he reflected, was merely young. He only wanted to investigate life, to see what it was like — that was all.

Keith was leading his horse back when he saw Sam waiting for him, a blocky shape outlined against the pale of the wagon covers.

"I just told Andy it was up to him," the hunter said cheerfully. "So he'll make the haul to Barr's Town. Leave in the morning." His low laugh had a remembering in it. "Back in 'Sixty-Two when we all went off to the War, we used to say a boy had to see the elephant. Still holds, I guess."

"You can't fight all his battles, Sam. Why don't you go, too? I'll stay in camp; in fact, I'd rather."

"Me? I'm not goin'. I want you to go with Hub and Andy. Keep an eye on Andy. He's head-strong."

"Why me?"

"You've seen the world. I can tell."

"Seems to me a rough-and-ready runner would make a better guardian." Keith had no relish to go; in that, he understood why the hunter, perhaps unconsciously, had delayed moving south. The outfit was entering country into which all sorts of people, not just professional buffalo runners, would be swarming, now that winter had passed. Riffraff, drifters, men on the dodge, fortune-seekers. Barr's Town was the hub between here and Fort Griffin, and the great southern herd, even now dying in its primitive helplessness, was the magnet. So the quiet days on the streams and prairies of the upper country were already relegated to memory, placid times when you rode out and played a kind of unhurried stalking game, when you shot just what you could hand-skin for the day. Be no leisurely killing down here. Instead, a frenzy of slaughter and skinning and spoilage. The best times were behind the crew. The realization was saddening.

"You can be rough if you have to, Keith."

"What makes you think so?"

"I can tell that, too."

"My father wouldn't agree. His opinion of me isn't much. He thinks I'm a wanderlust — not a man. A man, he says, wouldn't tramp around. A man would stay home and tend to business."

Sam put a hand on Keith's shoulder. "I know you better than your father does. Now, will you keep an eye on Andy for me? No tight-reining, no snubbing — just an eye?"

"Sam," Keith laughed softly, "I'll be the quietest watchdog in town."

CHAPTER 6

Even before noon of the first day south, Keith knew the country was changing. As the tumbling roughness of the North Pease valley fell behind the jangling eight mule teams pulling the creaking lead freight wagon and the coupled trail wagon, he saw tracks coming up from the south and southeast and angling westward, and the deeper rim marks of loaded wagons trailing in from the west and heading down Barr's old caravan trace.

And west and southwest the big-caliber rifles rumbled like strong-voiced men in a shouting match.

Next morning the outfit wound through broken columns of grazing buffalo, the robes of the bulls and cows changing from the dark blue of winter to spring's moult of yellowish-brown. The wind was blowing from the southwest — they ranged straight into it, veering curiously to give the wagons passage. About them clung a wild pungency, keen in the April sunshine, a moist gaminess of hot dust and trampled grass and warm breath and fresh droppings. Not an unpleasant smell to Keith. Strong but clean.

Early the afternoon of the third day he saw the clutter of Barr's Town scattered on the nearest side of the North Wichita River. A larger settlement than he had expected. Two blocks of frame and picket buildings facing across a broad street that pinched in to a trail running down to the river crossing, the way to Fort Griffin. Acres of stacked buffalo hides formed dark lumps behind the buildings on the east side of the street.

"Son-of-a-gun," said Andy, sniffing as they rolled down the noisy stretch. "Smell that?"

"Just town stink," Keith said. "You'll soon get your fill of it."

Hub, driving the teams, turned his head and sniffed, making a face. "That saloon smells like an old cellar where the water's stood."

"Hear that music?" Andy went on, unabashed. "That woman singin'?"

Hub winked at Keith. "Music — is that what that is? And so that's singing? I thought it was a lost calf bawlin'."

There was, Keith observed, a rampant vigor to Barr's Town, an unrest, a high hum in the air of bees swarming. A line of freight wagons was moving up from the crossing, the mule-skinners popping their whips and cussing their teams up the grade. Men milled in and out of the one saloon, the greasy-smelling eating places, and the one general merchandise store, and stood around the parked wagons. Cowboys in high-heeled boots and pants that hung snugly on their lean hips. Long-haired hunters and grimy skinners, their clothes earthstained, the look of the buffalo range in their steady eyes and unkempt faces. And greenhorns smitten to go buffalo hunting, in shiny boots and buckskin jackets, new shirts and new britches, some ostentatiously carrying their new rifles on the street. And farmers in chimney-pot hats, their plain-faced women, their swarms of coltish kids.

Keith's attention swung back to a brisk little man — bowler hat, checkered coat, double-breasted vest, Wellingtons — who, apparently sketching the street's traffic, closed his sketch-book and went over to a dismounting hunter and spoke questioningly. The hunter turned away with a laugh.

A short way on Keith saw a wagon yard, sheds and corrals, an array of huge wagons on which buffalo hides were piled like hay on the stout wooden racks, and more stacked hides, like ant hills, extending the yard eastward. The painted plank sign on the street side read:

W. C. LOBENSTEIN HIDE YARD
Mike Cassidy, Agent

When Hub pulled up, a man came out of the picket-house office at the entrance, and Keith said, "We're Sam Massengale's outfit from up north. Got meat, too. Where's Cassidy?"

"I'll fetch him."

The man hurried across the street and in a few minutes returned with Cassidy, who waved and called, "Drive on in. We'll count and weigh the meat right now. Tomorrow I haul out for Fort Griffin and Dawson." Afterward, Cassidy said, "You lads win do better to unhitch and sleep here in the yard tonight. Not a spare bed in town — if there was you wouldn't like the cozy bugs. Now let's stroll over for a little heather-honey and settle up."

He led the way across and down the street to the Texas House, a square, two-story frame hotel whose new planking was weathering fast under the southwestern sun and wind, and upstairs to his quarters.

Hub drank, then Keith. Cassidy, in the act of passing the bottle to Andy, glanced in question at the older men.

"It's up to Andy," Keith shrugged and Hub nodded.

Andy took the bottle and poured himself a man-sized drink, downed it in a gulping swallow. His throat muscles contracted and a sudden flush flooded his face, but otherwise he showed nothing. After which he stuck in his shirt tail, took a hitch at his belt, hooked his thumbs in his hip pockets, and waited impatiently for the tally to be completed.

More than three thousand dollars in on the table when Cassidy finished settling up. "Andy," Keith said, "you want to carry part of this? It's yours, too."

"Not me. You an' Hub worry with it. I want to see the town."

"You saw it all when you rode in," Keith smiled, and divided the greenbacks with Hub and stuffed his half in his money belt.

"When you lads feel the urge for a drink, which

you will," Cassidy cautioned them, "buy a fresh bottle from behind the bar or stick to beer. Don't let them slip you anything from under the bar. When you go into the Buffalo Bull, which you will, go together. Never one man alone. Well," — he shoved to his feet and shook hands — "tell Sam Massengale I'll be sendin' wagons up in the Pease country before long."

Coming down the hollow-sounding stairs, Keith saw a man scanning the register on the clerk's desk. He turned at the boot racket and Keith recognized the bowler-hatted man seen earlier on the street. The sketchbook was gone. There was a brusqueness about him. He wore his hat at a rakish angle. His full, black beard, v-shaped, seemed affectedly debonair. He all but blocked their path to the door and spoke in an ingratiating voice:

"Afternoon, gentlemen. How's hunting? I'm Nate Ives, artist-correspondent for the *Kansas City Star*. Checking on new arrivals off the buffalo range. Maybe you've read some of my dispatches?"

Irritation creased Hub Stratton's angular face. "Can't say I have."

"Have you encountered any war parties this spring? Fort Sill reports Black Horse's Comanches have left the reservation."

Hub, in the lead, stepped past Ives, who then turned to Keith. "Mind giving me your names and where you're from, gentlemen?" In his hands pad and pencil appeared suddenly, drawn

104

from an inner pocket.

Something restrained Keith: the man's loudness, his insistence, his plain bad manners, even for the frontier. Keith brushed by him, and in doing so saw the man's intentness quicken instead of lessen, and he heard Ives begin, "Surely, sir, you can oblige me —"

A flurry of gunshots on the street broke Keith's attention. A hard drumming of hoofs. He checked himself, as did Andy and Hub ahead of him, and saw a knot of whooping riders charging up the street from the river, cowboys leaning low in their saddles and firing revolvers over their heads. They raced midway up the street, sending the farm families scurrying to one side, and got down in front of the Buffalo Bull, the raised fog of reddish dust settling about them.

Cowboys, Keith thought. They'll be here after we're gone with the buffalo. Cowboys and cattle. He went out after Andy and Hub. Ives did not follow. Andy was sniffing upstreet. "Son-of-a-gun, I'm hungry."

"Supper's on me," Keith said.

For a dollar each, paid in advance, amid hordes of circling flies, they ate greasy buffalo hump steaks, beans and sourdough biscuits. Men were waiting to take their places even as they sat down.

"Levi would get rich in this town," Hub said outside. "Reminds me. We'd better get him and Sam a bottle of good whisky apiece. None of Cassidy's heather-honey."

They joined the stream of men flowing into the Buffalo Bull. After the street's brilliant sunlight, the place was dim and smoky. Keith blinked, inhaling the muggy odors of tobacco, damp sawdust, spilled whisky, beer, and sweat. Men jammed the bar and the rough tables and crowded the gaming tables, and leaned against the walls, laughing, talking, swearing. At the rear of the long room Keith saw a small stage, its red curtains depicting a bosomy nude reclining by a waterfall. On the cramped dance floor couples danced to the racehorse music of a tired-looking piano player and a head-down banjo picker.

Finally reaching the plank bar, Keith and Hub bought bottles of whisky to take back to camp, then Keith ordered beer. They were drinking it when the music ceased and a dapper individual appeared on stage and raised his hands for silence. His stagey voice was as audible as a bugle call:

"Now . . . gentlemen . . . for the feature of the afternoon . . . Brought all the way from the Rocky Mountains — at great expense by the friendly management of the Buffalo Bull . . . In her one and only performance of the afternoon — beautiful Tess Thompson — the Denver Songbird! Here she is!"

He was applauding as he slipped off stage, his departure the signal for a storm of whistling and stomping and whooping. The red curtain rolled upward, the musicians began playing. A pause while the crowd gawked and grew still. And then

106

a slender woman glided gracefully out from the left wing, a half-smile on her pale face. The crowd whooped louder. One hunter, black hair dangling down his back, reeled toward the stage.

Instantly, two burly figures loomed. They seized him like a steer and threw him to the floor. He reared up flinging sawdust, fighting like a wounded buffalo bull. Keith heard a series of solid whacks. The hunter fell senseless and the pair dragged him to the swinging doors and pitched him headlong into the street. No one raised a hand. No one seemed to mind.

As the racket subsided, the woman's clear voice floated over the crowd: ". . . if you'll quit acting like little boys, I'll sing you a song."

Another storm of whooping and stomping. As the first musical notes sounded, the crowd hushed, save for those struggling to see. With all the neck-craning and jostling, Keith saw little of the singer. Her voice, however, reached him in warm and sentimental tones:

> *"The years creep slowly by, Lorena,*
> *The snow is on the grass again."*

Beside Keith, Andy was also stretching to see her. At first, during his maneuverings, all he heard was a pleasing voice — not strong, but distinct and sweet and full of feeling, and all he saw were glimpses of a pale face and jet black hair and a glittering green costume as she moved about, her white arms outstretched to the stilled crowd:

"The sun's low down the sky, Lorena
The frost gleams where the flowers have been."

Suddenly the parts — the compelling voice, the pale face, the dark hair — seemed to come together, to form a whole, and a curious and delightful elation swam though him: the woman on the Sweet Water. That's who. *Her.*

All too soon the song ended and the music faded, she left the stage and the red curtain dropped. For minutes the whooping crowd carried on to bring her back. But she did not return and presently the racket wore off, the hum of voices and the clink of glasses and bottles took over, and the crowd spilled out into the street.

Outside, Hub squinted at Andy and said, "You're mighty quiet. That beer make you sick?"

Andy's manliness was offended. "The beer was fine. Think I'll get me a haircut."

"Case we don't recognize you on the street," Keith said, slapping him on the back, "better meet back at the wagons before supper."

Hub wandered into a saddle shop, and Keith moved idly along the street, feeling an impatience to leave town. But the afternoon was spent, the teams needed resting, and he had a long list of supplies to be filled at the general store in the morning. Besides, it was good for a man to come to town and smooth off the rough edges. Andy, he could see, was enjoying himself. Hub seemed in better spirits.

Farm families were still gathered in front of the

general store, the men off to themselves, their plain, toil-worn women visiting in tired tones, while the kids ran here and there.

One man's voice carried above the others. He was leaning against the tailgate of a wagon, his weight on his left foot, his right leg across his left shin and the toe of his heavy shoe burrowing the street's sandy dust. A fleshy, bearded farmer whose knowing voice overrode those around him:

"I calculate the best buffalo country's west and northwest o' here, say on the South or Middle Pease," he was telling the little group. "I figure a man needs to get 'way off where he can hunt by himself, where other folks won't scare off the game."

"Cal, you git off out there by yourself with no neighbors about, an' some wild Comanche'll sneak up on you, sure," a voice differed.

"Not if a man's on the lookout."

"What if they's a hundred of 'em? What then?"

Cal's bulging jaw ground once. He spat into the dust. "By grab, I got through the War. Calculate I can hold my own with any sneakin' heathen."

"How you aim to haul your hides to market, Cal?" a new voice queried.

"Easy. Contract for some buyer to pick 'em up."

There was a snicker. "What if he won't come out? You don't have airy freight wagon, either."

"You tellin' me what I don't have? Me — a man that's grubbed all his life. I tell you what I'd do: I'd haul in on drags. What the Indians call travaways."

"You mean travois, Cal."

"Means the same. What's the difference?"

"Well, we've all decided to pull out for Gainesville. Gonna look for farm land to take up. You Dockums are welcome to come along. We'll all stick together; help each other. Same as we did all the way down from Kansas. Cal, I'd think twice 'fore I took Coralie and little Lenny out there. I sure would."

"Calculate I'll hire me a skinner," Dockum said, unswayed. "Lookin' for a good man right now. We'll have all the help we need."

Keith turned away. He concluded that Dockum was a foolish man, a braggart to boot, too high on his own opinions to take sound advice when he heard it, and too heedless to survive in buffalo country.

"Papa, are you ready?"

Keith looked around. The speaker was a young woman who hadn't been there a moment ago. She held the hand of a blond boy, about seven or eight. Apparently the two had just crossed from the other side of the street. Dockum started to resume his conversation. Before he could she interrupted. "Papa, it's time we found a camping place. Lenny's hungry."

"Plenty time," Dockum answered and said something in a lowered voice to a farmer, jabbing an argumentative forefinger to reinforce his remarks.

Keith saw weariness heavy in her eyes, not a physical weariness but a long-enduring patience,

110

though she smiled reassuringly at the restless boy while they waited. She was tall, yet without the gaunt boniness of most frontier women he had seen, though perhaps that was because she was young; and her face was plain, like the other farm women, and she wore her light brown hair swept back, unparted, and knotted on her neck.

He was, he found, openly observing her and admiring her. He saw her become aware of his gaze. She turned her head and he saw that her eyes were a rich hazel. Thus caught, he touched the brim of his hat to her, and saw her instant of surprise and saw her look away, and then he was turning to step by her.

That was when he noticed her shoes, heavy and blunt-toed, a man's workshoes, the high ankle-tops reaching to the hem of her long dress. A quick protest went through him. No woman should have to wear such brogans. And no, he thought, walking on, her face wasn't plain after all. There was a quality to it he couldn't describe: the look of a young woman who had experienced hard times, who would experience more, but who wouldn't whine or cling or give in to her harsh surroundings. Another face that stayed in a man's mind for a long time, until finally, not seen again, it blurred and passed.

Keith entered the general store, left his list of supplies, bought a pipe and tobacco for Sam and a new belt for Levi. At the hide yard, he and Hub grained the mules and sat outside the office shack to wait for Andy.

On the street a team of bony mules pulled a light wagon whose wobbling and shaking produced a chattering of pots and pans and the high squeaks of dry axles. The wagon was bowed in the middle from overloading and patches held the cover together. Cal Dockum drove, the boy between him and the young woman. Coralie was her name, Keith remembered.

"A mighty poor outfit for buffalo country," Hub said, falling into his old mood. "You need the best out here if you make it at all. But not havin' it won't stop 'em. Why, I knew a fellow that tried to hunt buffalo with a shotgun."

More than anything else, Keith thought, it was the hoping that took people west, the expectation of beginning over again. Across the next river or the plains or the mountains always glowed in the mind's eye, no matter. Partly for that same reason he found himself here, in the drowse of late afternoon, at peace with the world while he watched the Dockums turn off at the north edge of town to camp.

Andy was grinning self-consciously when he arrived, looking a couple of inches taller and coming at a crimping walk, in new cowboy boots, red shirt, a cigar jutting blackly from his mouth, his long yellow hair a bit shorter and the reek of bay rum preceding him.

"Whew!" Keith said, wrinkling his nose. "You'll spook the mules if you come any closer."

Andy removed the cigar, spat with evident relief, stuck almost the entire length of the cigar

112

back in his mouth, alongside his jaw, put down his old shirt and shoes and opened a box of Pittsburgh Stogies, which he held out to Hub and Keith.

"I had to tell that barber not to cut it too short," Andy said, talking around the cigar. "I want folks to know I'm a buffalo runner — not a danged sodbuster."

"There's another way you can tell a runner," Hub observed.

"How's that?"

"By the smell."

"Well, this stinkum takes care of that, and we all took baths comin' in, didn't we?"

They ate again in town and sauntered back to the hide yard and watched dusk settle like a purple veil over the rolling dark green of the hills. With evening, the town shook off its late-afternoon lethargy. Music hummed. Another bunch of cowboys raced in from the south, yelling and shooting. At the north edge of town Keith could see the cone of the Dockums' small campfire. He pictured her preparing supper while Dockum sat and talked, just sitting, doing nothing.

When darkness fell, Hub yawned and went off to bed. Later, Keith got up and said goodnight. "Believe I'll stay up a while," Andy said.

Lying in the open freight wagon, listening to the town's din, Keith watched the milky sky glitter. It had to be his imagination, but he would swear the stars had seemed nearer when the outfit was farther north. And his last consciousness before he slept was of their camp on the Prairie Dog Town Fork, and the open, uncrowded country and the balm of contentment and strength given him there, and which he still possessed.

CHAPTER 7

Andy sat on the porch of the shack, watching light from the Texas House and the Buffalo Bull fall yellow on the dusty street and lay a sleek shine on the rumps of the tied horses. His interest kept going back to the saloon and to Tess Thompson. How she looked; the sound of her voice. How it made you feel lonesome inside, and you thought of home and your folks.

He just watched and listened, content not to move. But when the night turned cooler, he realized time had passed and the evening was gone. The outfit would be rolling tomorrow. Hub was an early riser on the trail. Crossing to the trail wagon where his bedroll was, Andy could hear Hub and Keith snoring in the freight wagon. After a tussle, he tugged off the new boots, peeled down to his long underwear, and crawled into bed.

He rolled over to his side and closed his eyes, but sleep would not come. Music and voices from across the street frolicked in his ears. More riders rushed into town, the clatter of their horses rolling along the street. Above the racket, he heard a woman laughing, laughing, laughing, and a man's frustrated shout; the two voices quit and all Andy heard now was the town's throaty undertone.

Unable to sleep, he sat up and studied the

blurred buildings beyond the yard. A woman was singing in the Buffalo Bull; however, he was too far away to recognize her voice. An impulse caused him to sit up. He would go over there and stay a little while. He dressed fast, pulling on his shoes instead of the tight, new boots, slipped to the ground and went silently to the street.

He wasn't exactly certain why he was going; partly in hopes of seeing Tess Thompson again, partly because he was leaving tomorrow and he knew the same gut-busting work waited for him on the North Pease. But mainly because he was young and yearned to see and hear and smell and taste and feel something of the wild night whirling over there in the Buffalo Bull like a million lightning bugs turned loose.

He hesitated before the swinging doors, pushed in and paused again, giving his eyes time to adjust to the murk. A drunk weaving through the smoke came between Andy and the stage where the woman was singing. Andy stepped around the man to see, for the din was so great he couldn't tell who was singing.

His expectation withered as he looked. It wasn't Tess Thompson. It was a much older woman, large-bosomed, fleshy-faced, and she was singing something about "Good-bye, old Paint, I'm 'a' leavin' for Cheyenne," her voice roughly weary and unfeeling.

Disappointed, he was ready to leave when a voice spoke behind him:

"Hello, kid. How about a drink?"

Andy turned, recognizing the brisk little man who had asked questions at the hotel. The only man in town Andy had noticed wearing a bowler and checkered coat.

"Just leaving," Andy said.

"So was I. But, first, I want to buy you a drink. I'm Nate Ives, the well-known artist-correspondent. Here to cover the Great Buffalo Hunt. Believe I saw you earlier today."

Andy shook hands and gave his name.

"You must do me the honor of having a drink with me, Andy."

Ives had a way of saying a first name that sounded flattering and confidential, a way of making himself friendly before you knew it. Andy didn't know whether he liked that or not. Ives was a forward little runt. Still, Andy found the man interesting and he didn't want to offend him.

"All right," Andy said. "Much obliged." He was thinking that anyhow he wasn't sleepy and Tess Thompson might sing later.

At the bar Ives made a sweeping gesture. "What'll you have, Andy?"

Andy slid his hat back a notch and surveyed the array of long-necked whisky bottles behind the bar, some embossed with roses, others wearing on their labels the whiskered likeness of the brand's founder.

"Old Green River, there," Andy said carefully, mindful of Cassidy's warning about under-the-bar drinks.

"Ah, good boy," Ives praised, slapping Andy's

shoulder. "You're a judge of fine whiskey. Otto, open a bottle of Old Green River for my young friend here."

Andy poured his own, downed it determinedly, and although it burned like fury, he controlled his face and knew he did not give himself away as he saw Ives watching him. After a few moments, he was beginning to feel pretty good all over.

Ives took his drink neat and slapped Andy again on the shoulder. "What was your name in the states?"

"Same as now," Andy replied seriously, "and I thought Texas was a state?"

Ives' chuckling laugh rolled out. "Just joking. That's the name of a song which applies to a great many of the West's new citizens who left home in a hurry. Another drink, my boy?"

"Believe not. Thanks."

"Might as well. Tess Thompson's gonna sing in about ten minutes."

"She is?" Andy swallowed over his good luck. "You're sure?"

Ives turned to the bartender. "Isn't Tess singing tonight at the usual time, Otto?"

"Yep. Ten o'clock sharp."

"Good. Slide that Ol' Green River back this way for my young friend."

Before Andy quite knew, he felt the bottle fill his hand and he was pouring himself another; it burned less this time. With the excitement and all, he felt grand. Nate Ives was a mighty generous and sociable man, you could see that, and the story he was telling about the Traveling Salesman from Pittsburgh was a dandy. Even the straight-faced Otto was smiling behind his waxed mustache.

Otto guffawed outright and Ives, braying at his own joke, coiling up his wiry shoulders in convulsion, hugging himself, the button eyes in the narrow face watering, pounded the bar again and again with his right hand.

Andy laughed also, though not wholeheartedly, not positive he had caught the exact point of the story.

Now Ives drew pad and pencil. "Have to earn my keep, Andy. Same as you do on the buffalo range. Let's see. Your name is Andy Kinkade. K-i-n-k-a-d-e. Right?" Andy nodded congenially, and warmed by the drinks and the cheerful atmosphere, he was glad to oblige when Ives asked. "Now what are the names of your friends?"

"Well," said Andy, speaking expansively, "there's Hub Stratton," and saw Ives show an attentive interest as he wrote that down. "He's from Indiana. As steady a man as you'll ever see. Fastest skinner I ever saw, bar none. You oughta see him —"

Ives' brusque voice interrupted: "And the other man?"

A soft body smelling of perfume and powder brushed against Andy, and he saw a girl whose lips were too red and her skin too dark under her gray eyes. She looked up at him, partly shuttering her eyes, and took his arm.

"Come on, sonny. Let's dance a round."

"I . . . uh . . . I ain't very good at dancin'." Speaking, Andy felt his face flushing hot. Here he was taking and holding his whisky like a man, yet talking like a tongue-tied hayseed.

"I'll show you. Just a dollar a throw."

That, Andy thought swiftly, was something else. He was just of a mind to try it, however, when Ives' voice lashed out at her: "We're talking business. Go on."

She lifted a bare shoulder and flashed him a scathing look, but before she could speak, a hunter grabbed her and they went sailing off to the dance floor.

Andy's eyes followed her. She was pretty, all right, and just about his age. Son-of-a-gun.

"Got to watch these girls," Ives said in a confiding tone. "They're all on the make. You were telling me about the other man with you and Hub Stratton."

"He's new to the outfit. Good shot. Not scared of work. He's one of us."

"What's his name?" Ives' voice contained a hint of impatience.

"Keith Hayden."

"Hayden, you say? H-a-y-d-e-n?"

"Guess so."

"Does he have a middle name?"

"Don't know."

"Where's he from?"

"Back east."

Ives looked amused. "I mean the state."

The little man sure could ask a flock of questions. Andy thought a moment, remembering that Keith seldom talked about the past. "Connecticut," Andy said. "Yeah, that's it. I don't know the town."

"Where'd you meet Hayden?"

Andy told him, and also about Sam and Levi and how the outfit had hunted south from Fort Elliott, and was now camped on the North Pease and, like other outfits, hoped to find the flank of the southern herd.

In turn, Ives said buffalo hunting interested him, and he began asking a slew of questions. What was the outfit's daily rate of kill? Did the Army patrol the ranges? What was the top price for prime hides? Were supplies high? Was English gunpowder superior to American? Did Andy think the buffalo was being exterminated? And since Andy and his uncle were Missourians and Ives represented the *Star*, did Andy mind telling him more about their families?

Andy, answering, felt more customers jam in along the bar and heard the shuffling and gabbling of more men crowding inside, obviously for Tess Thompson's performance. Finally, he heard the music wear down. Through the smoky light he could see the girls and their partners leaving the floor to gang the bar and the tables. A minute or two passed. Ives was still asking questions. Andy turned as he saw the dapper fellow step out on the lamplit stage and waggle one hand for attention:

"We know what you're waiting for. But try to be patient, gentlemen — if you can. Give the Professor time for a mug of beer before he returns to tickling the ivories, and likewise Little Ned on the banjo. The management —"

"Shut up the palaverin' an' bring on Tess!" a bull voice shouted.

"Now gentlemen . . . now gentlemen. Patience, if you please!"

"Where's th' Perfessor? Git 'im out there!"

A garter-sleeved figure, swiping at his mouth, scurried out from the end of the bar and to the piano, and a shorter figure took up the banjo.

"And now gentlemen . . . for her only performance of the evening . . . the Nightingale of the West — Tess Thompson!"

The Professor ran the keys, Little Ned strummed his banjo like mad, the master of ceremonies disappeared like magic, the crowd whooped like Comanches, and Andy edged forward to see.

Tess Thompson, her pale face composed, took graceful steps to the center of the stage, the gleaming spangles on her dress as blue as Texas sky. Her lovely dark eyes swept over the crowd; they seemed for every man there, even Andy, and without preliminary her clear voice lifted in "Green Grow the Lilacs."

Her pale face fascinated Andy. In the smoky, yellowish light, dim at best, she looked unreal and mysterious; and although the tone of her voice registered on him with waves of feeling, the words of the song escaped him almost as she sang them. And seeing her, and the hungry stares on her, Andy experienced a doubting. Would a married woman sing in a dance hall and saloon? Would A. B. Barr, a man everybody said was rich and wise, let his wife sing here? No, Andy decided. No man would. And hadn't the man on the stage called her Tess Thompson? Didn't everybody call her Tess Thompson? No, he reasoned, she wasn't Mrs. A. B. Barr, and yet she sure wasn't any ordinary dancehall girl either.

She finished the song and the Professor tinkled in the fadeout. She inclined her dark head, bowing graciously, like a true lady, Andy thought, and clasped her hands to her bosom. Before she could turn away, the crowd was shouting

" 'Lorena!' Sing 'Lorena!' "

Andy was also shouting. It seemed that everyone was shouting. She took a step toward the wing, a provocative motion that drew groans and cries of "No! No!" and then she turned back, smiling the half-smile, and the crowd whooped and cheered and stomped. She held up a quieting hand, and Andy marked again the marble whiteness of her skin.

"Professor," she said, after some moments, her warm voice sounding small and intimate over the hubub, "are you ready?"

With a swaying flourish of his right hand, the Professor softly rippled the keys and swung into the slow, tender notes. Andy knew it was a song from the War. Uncle Sam had sung it around the campfire at Shiloh, and judging from the wildcat Rebel yells and the Yankee cheers heard just a while ago, men from both sides were in the crowd tonight.

Too soon the show was over. Andy looked around for Nate Ives. To his surprise, Ives was gone. So was the bottle of Old Green River. After glancing up and down the bar, Andy joined the others tramping outside.

Never had he felt so good and he guessed he was a mite tipsy. But his feet felt light and his hands sure, his whole body kind of feathery, all his senses extra keen. Being in town, he thought, sure beat skinning shaggies.

Stepping outside, he strolled to the end of the building, drawing in the cool night air, not yet ready to go to his bed in the wagon. Stairs ran steeply up the side of the building to a landing where light spilled through an open doorway. Andy knew that was a whorehouse up there. He'd heard talk in the Buffalo Bull and he could hear the muted laughter of men and women and the low strumming of a banjo.

Standing there, looking, listening, he felt young and out of place, inexperienced in the ways of this raw frontier world, conscious of a simultaneous pull and tug going on within himself. For the first time tonight he sensed an actual fear — the fear of venturing up there into such a place.

A woman came out on the landing and gazed over the humming town. The light was unkind, revealing her over-painted middle-aged face, her heavy-set body, as thick as a blacksmith's across her bosomy front. She discovered Andy about the same time.

"You, down there," she called, a good humor in her voice. "Want to come up and listen to the music?"

He was, after several seconds of indecision, climbing the wooden stairs, his bootsteps uncertain, hardly thinking what he was doing.

When he moved into the doorway's light, he saw her surprise. "Sonny, you're hardly wet behind the ears. You'd better go on."

He didn't like her manner of talking down to him. A strong perfume, too sweet for his liking, hung about her like a musky cloud.

"Oh, I guess you can come in," she said, seeing his affront, "if you want to."

He followed her a short distance along a narrow hall, down which he could hear voices, and into a room fixed up like a parlor. A beefy-shouldered man was strumming a banjo now and then, only playing at making music. From the sizing-up look he measured Andy, Andy figured him as the bouncer. A frizzy-haired woman sat on a red sofa. She looked tired to Andy, and she wasn't young any more, though not so old as she looked, either. When she glanced his way, working up the beginning of an old smile, he saw a scrawny face, a lifeless mouth smeared red, and thin shoulders.

She got up and took swaying steps toward him,

a kind of mincing dance. She smelled like the other woman, of a sickening sweet perfume and too much powder. Andy stopped. She sent her hand brushing up and down his left arm, and he saw her face full-on for the first time. He saw a numbness there that struck him as pathetic. He shrugged off her hand, a revulsion rising in him, yet tinged with sympathy for her.

Boots jarred down the hall and to the parlor. Turning, Andy saw a hunter staggering through. He waved a bottle and his eyes were glassy. "Where's Maude?"

The scrawny woman moved like a cat. She flung Andy her scorn and slipped one arm around the weaving hunter, her nasal voice like a purr. "Why, Buck, I thought you left town?" She turned him through the door and down the hall.

Andy caught the first woman's grin. "Like I said, sonny. You can listen to the music if you want to."

It was the kindness in her voice that really angered him, like he wasn't grown up. A hot flush branded his face; he could feel it like shame.

"Reckon not, ma'am."

He almost ran down the stairs, relieved to reach the semi-darkness of the street. He strolled on and passed the dark general store, the harness shop, the barbershop, and the cindery stink of a smithy's. Other small buildings and sheds were strung along the street. No lights showed between him and the Texas House. Sounds fell off.

Gradually a sense, a faint noise, a wrongness,

something warned him that he was being followed. He angled away from the shadowed buildings and out into the street, and when he picked up the faint sound again, he took a whirling look. He saw no one near, only the indistinct figures milling in front of the Buffalo Bull. He heard no threatening sound, not a single following bootstep. A sort of recklessness affected him. Let 'em try to jump him. Hell, he wasn't afraid

He stood waiting, tense, watchful. Nothing happened and he turned back toward the Texas House, intending to cross the street there and make tracks to the wagon yard.

Ahead of him three people stepped from behind the broken line of buildings on his right and started east across the street. A woman, he saw curiously, and a man on each side of her. As they walked between Andy and the lights of the hotel, he slowed step, momentarily forgetting what might be behind him.

He sensed movement too late. A blow hurled splintering pain through his head and shoulders, and as he reeled forward, he managed to cry out sharply before the spinning lights went out. He felt rough hands clutching him, digging into his pockets, and he heard quick-running steps fading away, and dimly, before all feeling left him, he thought he heard a woman's voice . . .

He flailed upward toward the cone of muddy light. But his arms were too heavy for him to reach it. He kept slipping back, dragged down by the stone of his body.

He heard the scrape of a match, and dimly he made out a man's pitted face over him.

"He's just a boy." That was a woman's voice.

"He's been slugged."

"He's bleeding," the woman said. "Take him to the house."

"To the house?"

"You heard me, Quinn. *Take* him to the house."

Strong hands groped under Andy, lifted him. He tried to see who was helping him, but the pain-driven blackness smothered him and he knew no more . . .

Andy opened his eyes, seeing a glow of light somewhere above him, as of sunlight shining behind a gray cloud. Nearer, little by little, he made out a pale face looking anxiously down upon him. He lay in complete silence, on the softest of beds, in a pleasant-smelling room. He'd never smelled anything so nice. The room reminded him of his sister's back home, only fancier: light-blue curtains, a wooden clothespress with a full-length mirror on one side, a rose-patterned carpet, a little slipper rocker, and a dainty dresser laden with perfume bottles and powder boxes.

He stirred to speak and instantly a thunderous throbbing smote his head. He shut his eyes against the pain and brought his right hand to his head and touched a cool, damp cloth, feeling beneath it a lump as big as a goose egg.

"Don't move." It was the woman's clear voice again, the one he thought he'd heard on the street and maybe once before sometime. He couldn't be certain. Mere thinking wearied him.

"Where am I?" he heard a voice say. It sounded odd and far in the distance, a stranger's, yet recognizable, a voice which finally he realized was his own.

"Don't talk," she said.

He was thinking better. "What time is it?"

"Past midnight. You'd better rest a while."

He reared up, anyway, only to have the ruthless pain knock him back. His helplessness annoyed him; and with it, deeper than his physical weariness, a wave of punishing remorse. He'd got himself in a peck of trouble, all right. Going into the Buffalo Bull was his first mistake. Next, taking those drinks with Nate What's-His-Name? The newspaper man. Now Hub and Keith would be looking for him, and he didn't want to worry them.

"Ma'am," he said, forcing himself to pull his thoughts together, "I got to get back to the hide yard. We're camped there. My outfit."

Her voice reassured him. "There's plenty of time for that. You were beaten and robbed. We brought you to my house. Fortunately, you're young and strong."

He was too weary to talk any more. He shut his eyes and lay still, drifting off. Vaguely, he thought he heard her rustling movements out of the room; but when he opened his eyes again, she was bending over him. He could feel himself slipping away, dozing. When he awoke, she was still there and the blur around her face had disappeared. He saw her clearly for the first time: the smoky brown eyes, the unusual fairness of her coloring.

"You're the lady on the Sweet Water," he said.

She touched a slim forefinger to her lips, puzzled. "The Sweet Water?"

"That's the creek below Fort Elliott."

"Oh. I believe I do recall that name."

But, he saw, she still didn't remember him. "I saw you one day along the creek," he said. "How's your little dog?"

"Yes! I remember now." She touched his arm impulsively, and then he saw her animation wane. "Tippy's dead," she said simply. "I remember you — you're the young man —" She did not finish, and he saw her withdraw from any show of feeling, the same expression he remembered seeing that day on the Sweet Water, when she had discovered the man watching her, the man Andy knew had to be A. B. Barr. "You're from Missouri," she said. "You like to raise horses."

"That's right," Andy said, flattered she would remember. "I heard you sing this afternoon and tonight. Mighty nice."

Color brushed her cheeks. "Anything sounds good out here."

"It was the best singin' I ever heard, miss —" he said, stumbling over the proper way to address her.

"Thompson," she supplied. "Tess Thompson."

That, Andy realized, told him no more than he knew before. Well, it wasn't important right now. He was getting tired again, and he would like to rest here for a long, long time. Except he couldn't stop thinking about Hub and Keith. Suddenly, before she could prevent him, by sheer determination he forced himself to break through the band of pain holding him down and sat up in bed, causing him to reel with dizziness. He couldn't check a low groan.

She reached out instinctively to help him, and when his head swayed against the tip of her shoulder and her arm went around him to steady him, he felt her slenderness and he breathed the faint scent of violets he remembered.

Bit by bit, Andy got a grip on himself and was able to sit up without falling. She took away her arm and handed him a glass of water, which he drank in long gulps, dulling the sour whisky taste still burning his mouth. He set the empty glass on a little marble-topped table by the bed, peeled the damp cloth off his head and stood up, unsteady on his feet, head lowered, enduring the pulsing pain.

At last, he knew he was all right. Seeing his hat on a chair, he picked it up and turned to her. She was standing, visibly doubtful of his readiness to go. A while back, he had no difficulty talking to her. Now he felt ill at ease.

"I'm obliged," he said, making an aimless gesture with his hat. "You didn't have to help me."

"Are you sure you're all right?"

"I can make it."

She said no more. He kept noticing her face. She was, he thought, a very quiet, deep woman. A very kind woman. A fine-looking woman to boot. He turned. She went with him to the door, where he glanced at her again. She stood very straight and composed, almost expressionless. He was caught off guard, when, without any intimation of her intention, she asked abruptly:

"What is your name?"

"Andy Kinkade."

"Well, goodnight. Quinn will see you out." She was hurrying him, which he could well understand. Her face changed, mask-like, in the half-smile he had seen in the saloon. "Never turn your back, Andy, unless you know what's there."

He passed into a hallway and down it to the front door. A man stood on the porch. Andy went out and as he reached the steps, the man spoke:

"Don't press your luck, kid."

Andy, surprised, swung around so fast his head started banging again. "What do you mean?"

"Don't come back here."

Angered, Andy let his retort go unsaid, figuring he'd been fool enough for one night.

He entered a scattering of trees, following a path which took him some hundred yards to the main street. Looking eastward, he could see the small house standing in lonely isolation, alone in a clump of black timber. A ringlet of light burned there in the bedroom where he had laid. It went

132

out as he watched.

A hot rebellion churned in him as he turned north toward the hide yard, dreading the long days ahead, the backbreaking chores in the hot weather to come, the dull sameness that older men seemed to dote on.

And he could see another shape: as soon as he could, he was coming back to Barr's Town, hell or high water, he was.

CHAPTER 8

Soon after daybreak, Keith rode to the lookout hill. A squad of loose clouds quick footed across the changing sky, shedding tatters of woolly gray. It was going to be another good day for hunting. Grass smell freshened the cool wind, bringing a headiness that always seemed to clean him out and leave him eager again. As the sky cleared and the sunlight poured dazzling over the rolling country, he looked north, then slowly, all around, surprised rather than disappointed.

Everywhere the country was motionless. Not one lone buffalo. Not one sound. Not one bawling calf sound. Overnight the buffalo had vanished. An odd emptiness, he puzzled, after yesterday, when the outfit could have dropped three times as many as it could skin in one day, when last evening buffalo grazed upriver within four hundred yards of camp.

He searched his mind for the explanation. He and Sam had hunted the fringe bunches so as not to disturb the main herd, trying not to cause a general movement away and force moving camp again. A man given to superstition might say that nature, weary of the shooting and skinning, had sent a summons by some mysterious telegraph during the night and the dark, patient beasts, complying blindly, had disappeared. Whatever the cause, it was strange and fascinating.

He rode back to camp.

"Wind shifted last night," Sam said, mulling over Keith's news. "I felt it. Woke me up. It's out of the southwest now, you bet." A resisting admission filled out in his eyes, as much as saying he had held back as long as he could; now the outfit had to strike out southwest.

By ten o'clock they were across the North Pease and rolling the wagons southwest, the only signs of life around them circling vultures and coyotes slinking among the rotting carcasses. The stink seemed to stick in a man's nostrils; in that connection, Keith was like Levi, who said he never got used to the smell, but guessed he could put up with it.

When a low stream crooked out of the broken country to the west, Sam looked at his map and said it was the Middle Pease. Later in the day, keeping to the north side of the river, Keith heard the first heavy mutterings of buffalo rifles.

The sun was going down when Keith and Sam, seeking a camping place, found a sweet spring which formed a series of pools below it. As yet there were no buffalo. They rode to a hogback ridge and looked southwest.

Keith's jaw went slack. As far as his eye could reach, he saw buffalo. More buffalo than he had ever seen. Not a solid mass, the impression one received from reading about millions of animals on the grassy plains, for he knew better now. Buffalo didn't pack together unless they migrated or stampeded, in which latter event they charged as one solid, swerving, jamming, unpredictable herd, never continuing on the same course they had started on. He turned his head slowly, seeing buffalo in small and big bunches as far west as he could sight, on and on, and northwest and southwest. An image formed in his mind, picture-clear. He stood on a high shore and that was a dark and restless sea out there, the lowering sunlight catching the swirl of eddies and the roll of waves, formed where the shaggies stirred indolently in the cup of a draw or grazed on the slopes and over the crest of a rise.

Sam broke the silence softly. "There's one side of the great southern herd, Keith. Some day you can tell your grandchildren you saw millions of buffalo."

Next morning they were edging in on the flank of the vast herd, stalking, shooting, skinning, butchering what they could use. On in the day the crew constructed another vat and a hide-and-pole smokehouse for Levi. As the busy days held, Keith saw that the sheer number of buffalo available was increasing the outfit's daily kills, forcing Sam and him to double up to help Hub and Andy do the skinning. Often darkness fell before they could allow time for supper. With the warming weather and the heightened slaughter swarmed hordes of flies, food for the horned frog; and before the men could eat their meals, they built smudges of buffalo chips and smoked the pests away.

After a week, two hundred and eighty-three

fresh hides were stacked and drying. Every morning Keith rode to the hogback ridge, spotted the day's game, and the work commenced.

And every day, like distant peals of spring thunder, Keith heard big guns bellowing in all directions but east, a constant bombardment that went on until dark, like a battle. He sensed a frenzy, a hurry down here that drove men, leaving no time around the fire for Andy's harmonica A man fell in bed dead tired, asleep at once, got up feeling he'd been dragged through brush, an exhaustion that even Levi's breakfast of strong coffee, biscuits and buffalo steaks, fried in marrow, was slow to remove. Tempers shortened. Too, everyone knew that "summer hide" wasn't the best, that late fall and winter were the best seasons for prime robes, when the shaggies were "in the blue," their hides a rich brown and bluish cast. But as Mike Cassidy had told the boys in Barr's Town, "It makes no difference — leather's leather back east. Price is the same, winter or summer, unless you bring in silks, and you know how rare they are." A silk, Keith knew, was like that long, sheeny beauty of a robe which Tobe Jett had tried to short High Medicine out of on the Sweet Water. And there wasn't a silk in camp.

Thus, everyone was working too hard, rain or shine. Yet — and Keith felt in himself, besides seeing it — they couldn't seem to slow down. Sam called it "buffalo fever."

Today the buffalo had drifted farther southwest than usual, following the feed along the valley of the Middle Pease, away from the roughness straighter west, grazing into the wind. Presently, as Keith rode on, a new range opened before his eyes. The country rippled in long ridges sheathed in an abundant matting of grass, wrinkled with buffalo trails, veined with the dark curve of a good creek wriggling across a broad mesquite flat rich enough to pasture God knew how many cattle. He pulled up, still thinking about cattle, watching the May wind ruffle the short grass. Just below that ridge, and some two hundred yards from the creek, occurred to him as an ideal location for a house and corrals. He thought: grass, water, cows, and came to himself with a mild start and looked back. Lost in his daydreaming, he had delayed so long that Andy, trailing him in the wagon, was catching up. Keith waved and rode ahead.

He was well past the creek and still jogging along the flat, on the lookout for buffalo, when, picking up a different rifle sound, he turned curiously. A sharp, quick snap, lighter than the deep-toned boom of a Sharps. Sam said that was one way you could tell Indians' rifles. Indians had Winchesters and Spencers as a rule, and once in a while an old army Springfield; seldom a Sharps, unless they had killed a runner and taken one. That's why the Sharps was so vital. With it, you could outrange an Indian several hundred yards, fend him off like a long-armed man in a wicked barroom fight. Unless, Keith amended, you made Dan Massengale's mistake: let Indians get in close. Then a one-shot rifle wasn't fast enough.

He passed numerous saucer-shaped buffalo wallows pocking the flat. All held water from the hard rain three days ago. He saw the new gouged-out depressions where buffalo had pawed the turf and rolled to dust their hides and shed their ragged winter coats, and, in the old wallows, the sundried muddy places where they had plastered their hides for relief against flies and vermin.

One pool-like wallow, larger than the rest, pulled Keith's eyes a second time. Green grass grew down its sides, except for a small outcrop of red rock rubbed smooth by buffalo. The water looked clean enough for a bath on the way back to camp. A thorny old mesquite tree overlooked the wallow. Buffalo scratching against a tree gradually killed it; this one showed a broad ring around the trunk, rubbed smooth and oily, with balls of loose, brown hair on the ground and a deep trail circling the base. As stubborn as the mighty beasts that punished it, the mesquite was bravely leafed out for another spring, its boughs a sheen of light green.

Half a mile onward a familiar sensation ran through Keith — buffalo. There they were again, as dark hummocks on the green floor of the rolling flat, ringed by low, broken hills. Bulls, cows, calves all mingled. Several thousand head, many more beyond that gap opening to the west. Backtracking to where he could see Andy, he took the Sharps and held it over his head with both hands and brought it down and up. When he saw Andy wave his hat, Keith rode on again and tied his horse to a mesquite, scanned the hills for Indians, and advanced into the wind.

He walked in a straight line, careful not to veer sharply. He was about two hundred yards from the herd when he stopped, surprised that he could come so close. As he started to set up his sticks, meanwhile watching, something in the herd's inertness told him he could move still closer. He took up the sticks. Bending, crouching, taking a few steps, waiting, pausing, motionless, crawling a little stretch, peering, he approached as near as he dared and set up.

Never, he realized, had he been this close, and he wondered why. Many animals were lying down, chewing their cuds, hoofs cupped under to escape the heel flies. Those standing seemed in a trance or dreamy slumber; when one moved it was more a stirring of contentment. Cows and calves bawled in a low, guttural undertone. Small, black cowbirds, which Sam called the buffalo's friend, sailed back and forth over the flat, hovering over the bemused animals, perching on a reclining buffalo's back, walking about and feeding, holding their tails high, chattering shrill, sociable squeaks.

The wind on Keith's bearded face was no more than a faint murmur. The day was still and warm, as languid as a blue pool; a growing day, the burgeoning earth softly alive under Keith's boots. He took note of the wild flowers, everywhere in cloaks of white, purple, brown, yellow. Sweet scents filled his nostrils. He fed no hurry and he understood why. It was the drowse of spring. Full, bursting spring, the scented air and the passive sun lulling his senses as it did the buffalo.

He could sense his resistance against breaking the spell, but he fixed the Vernier scale for one hundred yards, tightened the peep cup, cocked the hammer, and picked out a bull standing sleepy guard.

When the Big Fifty roared, the bull merely crowned up his back and froze, enormous, statuesque, as motionless as if turned to brown stone. A moment later he crashed to earth. Not a nearby buffalo as much as moved. Keith shot another outside animal, a cow, and few got up, more curious than disturbed. One cow strayed off to Keith's left. When she turned broadside, he knocked her down with a bullet in the lights. A few others came standing, faster now, and restless. They got up like a horse, on their front feet first. They commenced to drift. Keith felled the leading bull in his tracks. The rest paused and lowered their heads to graze.

Keith thumbed in another shell, but held his fire. A lassitude settled over the others, over the entire flat. He shot another bull.

A taut knowing clutched him. Five bullets, five easy bulls. He had the beginning of a stand, a big kill, something Sam and Hub had often talked about, but which Keith had not seen. Tense, his movements deft and swift, he ran a tallow-greased rag in the eyelet of his wiping stick and swabbed out the hot barrel.

Then, methodically, in the grasp of an excitement which he had never quite experienced before, pausing every four or five shots to clean and cool his rifle, sometimes pouring a mixture of water and urine down the barrel from a whisky bottle, he slammed away at the uncaring herd, amazed at the shaggies' indifference. They would drift over and just stand by the dead ones, seeming puzzled or unwilling to leave, perhaps held there by a herd instinct; or they would nose or hook the furry hulks or paw the ground beside them, as if trying to bring them back to life.

By now he knew it was more than Keith Hayden, professional hunter: it was the day, the placid, perfect day, the lack of stiff wind, the belly-filling new grass, the enervating sun, the buffalo all mingled. These many things combined and rarely found. Most times he was dropping a buffalo with one slug. His own senses were likewise extraordinarily alert, for whenever an animal sidled off, drifting, he saw it at once and shot it down.

Keith couldn't seem to miss. He broke a bull's left front leg. Before it crow-hopped six steps he killed it with a neck shot. A sense of devastating power fastened upon him. He breathed a heady blend of acrid gunpowder and dry grass, soapweeds and fragile flowers.

He heard something. A whistle. Behind him. He looked and saw Andy crawling on all fours, dragging a shell sack and canteen, and bringing an extra Sharps, the .40-90 that had belonged to Dan Massengale.

"I knew you had a stand goin'," Andy panted, staying low. "Was afraid you'd ruin your gun."

"It's all right. But the barrel's getting too hot. I'm out of water."

Andy handed Keith the lighter rifle and took the Big Fifty and poured canteen water down the muzzle. After a little bit, while Keith rested, he opened the breech and let the water run out. He couldn't keep his eyes off the littered flat.

"Son-of-a-gun, why there must be forty-odd down already. All laid in close, pretty as you please. Dan couldn't 'a' done any better." He turned. Excitement burned in his eyes. He slapped Keith on the leg.

Keith's eagerness was wearing off. His head pounded. His right hand, arm and shoulder were soring up. His senses felt dulled. "You finish it, Andy."

"Go ahead. Shoot till the stand is broken."

Keith drew a shell from his belt. Grinning, Andy plopped his sack in front of Keith. That's a Big Fifty you took. Better use these."

Keith loaded the .40-90 and laid it in the fork, drew down on a bull. At the rifle's boom, it switched around wildly and broke down in front. Keith's second shot stopped the beast's broken lunging.

There were little pauses while they switched rifles every few shots and ran the wiping stick, cooled the barrels and talked in low tones and watched the buffalo, still milling and pawing around the dead ones, many still lying down, in the strange torpor of self-destruction.

It was so gradual, Keith didn't know when he first began to lose his hold over the herd. A missed broadside shot, taking two shots more often than he was one. Once he used three shots. He was tiring and falling into his early bad habits, firing too fast, trying too hard, driven by a singleness of mind in which the excitement had burned out long ago. A blurred and shimmering haze hung over the flat; maybe it was the heat or his straining eyes. Deafened by the steady firing, he couldn't hear a word Andy said. They conversed in signs.

Keith acted by rote: loading, aiming, firing, opening the breech, time after time. The exchange of rifles and again the repetitive motions. All meaning left him; still he kept on.

A shape edged into the rim of his vision. A bull. A prime bull, unafraid and alertly suspicious. A monstrous bull lumbering this way. Keith, reloading, felt Andy's touch and saw Andy point to the same animal. Keith nodded. The bull was advancing straight toward them, and a head shot was seldom effective. Keith continued to wait, hoping the bull would turn so he could place a shot into its vital parts.

It kept coming, somewhat faster now, in the

dogged, nodding gait of the buffalo. One hell of a big bull. Surly. Ragged-looking. Winter coat hanging in brownish tatters.

Now Keith knew the bull saw them. In a moment it would charge.

Keith fired, intending to break the bull down in the forequarters so it could neither charge nor spook back into the herd. He saw the bull flinch and instantly, enraged, whirl around twice, hooking wildly, and bob back toward the others. Keith jammed in a shell and fired, knowing the angle was chancy. He saw the bull lurch and swerve with the bullet, saw it continue lunging ahead. And as Keith reloaded and looked up, he saw it breaking into the herd, and buffalo springing up and scattering, the bull's wild charge and the surge after him creating a wave of sudden movements rolling across the calm surface of the resting, grazing animals, gathering force, faster, faster.

Keith heard a rumbling and the prairie seemed to tremble. A dense haze of dust flamed up. All the buffalo were in headlong flight, up crowding and jamming. A dusty, solid mass ramming toward the gap. There was yet time to knock down a few stragglers; instead, kneeling behind the sticks, he just held the Sharps and rested the butt on the ground, relieved the killing was over, dully observing the dark tide rushing away under the clouds of yellow dust.

Keith rose stiffly. Arms, neck, shoulders — his entire body ached. For a moment the flat swam before his eyes. He shook off the dizziness and looked about. The sun had taken a long stride across the clear sky. It was afternoon. Dully, he stopped to gather the pile of empty shells.

A sensation of shock hooked into him as he and Andy approached the kill and he could see the full extent of the slaughter. The flat was like a battlefield, the huge carcasses lying in a remarkably small area about a hundred yards square. The way you were supposed to kill buffalo: lay 'em in close for the skinners. In some places he could step from one carcass to another. It was wrong. By no judgment could you excuse such slaughter. You shot out a little bunch; that was different. But this, so many at one time, just for the hides . . . And he and Andy couldn't possibly skin all these today. By tomorrow the carcasses would be bloated and the hides torn by wolves and coyotes. He began counting, and as he wandered through the field of glassy-eyed creatures, the rebuke circled in on him again. He had killed too many. In his confusion he lost count.

Andy was calling. Keith's ears still rang. He turned his head and cupped a hand to his right ear. Andy walked in closer and called a second time and Keith got it:

"Seventy-eight! Some shooting! Wait'll we tell 'em back in camp!"

They turned back, Keith to his horse and Andy to his mules and wagon. Afternoon heat seemed to admonish Keith as they bent to skin the first animal. "Hereon," Andy said; "I'll just call you Buffalo." Flies buzzed around them while they worked, and the steamy smell of the fresh meat, made keener by the hot sun, was a sweet and sickish stain on the sultry air. Beyond the carcasses, Keith saw coyotes already sitting haunchwise, red tongues lolling.

After an hour, both skinners had to rest. "We're out of water," Andy said, "Used it all up during the stand. Son-of-a-gun, I could use a drink."

"Give me your canteen," Keith said. "There's a clean wallow half a mile back. Got to have water. You stick around the wagon. Keep a sharp watch on the hilltops."

"Say, Buffalo," Andy said as they walked slowly back, "I'm obliged to you and Hub for not tellin' Uncle Sam about my little set-to in town."

"What good would that have done?"

"None, for me. Except Uncle Sam could say he was right — an' he was."

"Not necessarily. You got jumped."

"One thing sure," Andy laughed, "I plumb got myself in trouble."

Keith climbed to the saddle. Before he could rein away, Andy stepped in and stood at Keith's stirrup. In place of banter, Keith saw now the strained seriousness of a young man who needed to talk to an older man who would listen.

"Her name really is Tess Thompson," Andy said earnestly. "She told me so."

"Singers use stage names. That way they always sound single. It's good for the trade."

"Wouldn't she 'a' said her name was Barr — Mrs. Barr — if she was married?"

Keith held back a quick answer. He and Andy had grown close, as close as brothers and more so than many. Andy was young and too trusting. Although Keith didn't want him badly hurt, Andy had to grow on his own and take his own disappointments. And so Keith said:

"Whether she's married or not, the facts remain the same. She rode in her private wagon in Barr's train. She's got her own house in Barr's Town. You saw her bodyguards. She gets special treatment. Seems to me that makes everything pretty clear."

Andy was scowling and biting his lower lip, his deep blue eyes troubled. "I ain't sure about that."

"It's plain enough. She's under A. B. Barr's wing. Barr's wife, Barr's woman — it adds up to about the same either way."

"Not if she ain't married," Andy vowed, shaking his head. "Maybe she'd like to get away from Barr an' can't."

Deliberately, Keith let Andy see his disgust before he swung away. All the well-meaning talk in the world, he thought, wasn't going to change Andy's mind about Tess Thompson.

The low-growing shape of the mesquite, alone by the wallow, grew in the distance, farther than Keith had thought, or so it seemed in the afternoon heat. He no longer heard the light crack of the rifle noticed earlier. His throat was like sand,

and he kept thinking of the cool water in the pool by the stubborn old mesquite.

His horse, traveling in a running-walk over the spongy footing of the grassy flat, threw out hardly more than an audible drumming as Keith approached the wallow. He rode hunched in the saddle, tired eyes watching just above the gelding's twitching ears.

A flash of white forming unbelievably before his eyes straightened him to astonished attention. He gaped as a clean-limbed creature emerged glistening below the rim of the wallow, from the pool's greenish depths. A frozen image half-turned away from him. Tall, full-bodied, dark hair glistening wet below the white roundness of her shoulders, the graceful back, the tapering long legs, and the rapt face gazing pensively off.

In almost the same flick of time, she heard the muffled beat of his horse. Whirling, she discovered him. Shrieking, she whirled away in a faltering run, looking in desperation for shelter.

By then, somewhat overcoming his astonishment, he reined in, aware of a shapely, incredible white figure vanishing from the rim of his eye, left unable to believe his senses.

"Go away! Ride on!"

That voice high and indignant and not a little fearful, rose near the outcrop of red rocks. He could see a dark head sticking up behind the rocks. On the grass lay brown shoes and a mound of gray and white clothing.

"Didn't mean to ride up on you," Keith called. "I came for water."

"Plenty of water east of here! Please, ride on!"

He turned the gelding around the wallow, not looking directly at the rocks, though without shutting his eyes there was no possible way he could miss the crouching whiteness.

His thirst sent him loping away. After some hundred yards, he found a clean wallow and dismounted, and while the gelding drank, he hand-skimmed the buggy surface, took his fill, washed his smeary hands and face, and filled the canteen.

He was riding back when he saw her leave the wallow. She was hurrying south, almost running, holding her skirts going in the general direction where he had heard the light rifle, on a course that would cross his. If he kept riding, he would intercept her.

He hesitated, then rode slowly ahead, moved by the hungry wish to look upon a woman again. He would apologize if she would let him, though what had happened was no fault of his.

Farther on he saw her upflung apprehension. She picked up something from the ground and hurried on. Even so, neither could avoid the other unless one changed directions. He held his horse in, not wanting to frighten her.

"I apologize," he said.

She continued straight on, her stride becoming more and more a militant march. She held her right hand stiffly to her side.

"It's dangerous wandering so far from camp," Keith cautioned her. "Could be Indians around."

"— and dirty-looking, spying white men," she accused, swinging about. She held a rock ready, her right arm back to throw. He scratched his whiskered cheek to hide his amusement. But an angry flush heated her face. Her mouth was determined, all her body poised tensely to repulse him.

He tried to give her a reassuring smile, and he took off his hat; possibly he caught a slight lessening in the taut face, perhaps a start of surprise. He seemed to be looking at a totally different young woman from the lovely white creature of the green wallow. Save for the glistening dark hair, still wet, pulled back and knotted loosely on the nape of her neck, he found scant visible likeness in the plainfaced, resolute person wearing the simple, faded gray dress and the men's ugly workshoes.

His mind flicked back and he realized that he had seen her before. Her face, plain yet not plain. She was the Dockum girl of Barr's Town. The face and the shoes. Those damned clodhopper shoes, which angered him to see on a woman, a young woman like her.

"My partner and I are hunting just west of here," Keith offered, for conversation, and saw that it revised her set distrust of him not one whit.

"Our camp," she informed him, and her voice sounded steadier than moments ago, "is just over

151

that hill yonder. There are many men there. Any one of them would shoot you on sight."

She marched away, head up, but canted sideways, as it she expected him to overtake her.

He said nothing more. She was embarrassed and angrily humiliated, suspicious and afraid of him; rightfully so, he admitted, running a hand over his face, in view of the circumstances and his murderous appearance. She gave him cause to think how he looked: untrimmed brown beard, hide pants, flat-brimmed hat, the big Sharps on one side of his saddle, the Henry on the other, revolver and skinning knives at his belt.

Watching her, he marked the approximate location of the Dockum camp, divining the "many men there" to be an invention of hers, a brave pretense which he must admire, and one he might believe had he not previously sized up Cal Dockum in town as a shiftless mover.

He played a careful look over the hills, lying emerald green under the glassy sunlight. Heat haze was building up toward the river. He loped hard for the stand.

CHAPTER 9

Keith awakened from a troubled, work-drunk stupor, the ache of fatique weighting down his body like a log. He was breathing hard, his chest shallow, burning from exertion, as if he climbed an endless slope, exhausted from the fitful dream out of which he was struggling.

He rolled over and shoved up on the flat of one hand, teeth clenched, eyelids squeezed, scowling and squinting, bits of the dream yet clinging to his straining mind: Charlotte — the mist of light on her perfect face, light which touched her alone. A figure attempted to share that brightness, and he saw Charlotte's face stiffen and dispel some of her beauty. She pushed suddenly and the figure toppled out of sight into the darkness. Then she turned so Keith could see her, clad in a gold dress whose luminosity hurt his eyes, and her full, classic visage, the perfect lips on the brink of pouting, and the perfect eyes beckoning to him.

He felt vastly eased when the last particle of the dream went out like a spark and he saw her no more. He hadn't dreamed of her in a long time. He wondered, in a hazy kind of bewilderment, what had brought her back.

He lay on his bedroll under the big hide wagon. He peeled back the blanket and looked eastward. Daylight crouched beyond the patchy blackness.

Way off, he heard the high, drawn-out falsetto of coyotes howling, far-scattered around the camp, crying to one another, a singing, a sort of sing-song talking. One, he thought, sounded on the first rise east of the wagons. Sam said Indians were seldom around if coyotes were close. Keith could imagine them on their haunches, slim noses raised to the starred sky. There was hardly any wind. Every noise was distinct. He heard the muffled stampings of the hobbled mules and horses night-grazing the short grass. Sam and Levi snored under the cook wagon. Farther away, Hub slept under the trail wagon. A few feet from Keith lay Andy, snoring softly.

But none of these usual noises or the restless dream had awakened Keith. It was something else. He pulled on his boots and sat on the blanket, listening, distrusting the mealy darkness.

After a wait, he heard a loud and persistent *kill dee, kill dee,* off northeast, the trilling of the kill-deer, which circled screaming when an intruder approached its nest on the prairie. Had that shrillness aroused him? It might mean a prowling coyote or skunk, and it might mean Indians.

The shrillness passed. On the rise the wailing, four-footed singer hushed, and the following stillness turned the night heavy and uneasy.

A strangeness swelled in Keith, fixing him where he was. And again the killdeer's circling cry carried to him and spent itself, suddenly going away. Keith turned slowly, bringing all his senses to bear. He took up the Henry rifle and cocked it and watched the eastern murk where the killdeer had voiced its last cry, not trusting the stillness there. Suddenly, lightly, he touched Andy awake. Rising, then, Keith stood by the wagon and watched the swart darkness change to a tallow hue.

Something blurred to his right near the stock. Something wrong. Keith snapped a shot at it. A startled cry of pain came. Before Keith could fire again, he heard an eruptive whooping and the vibration of hoofs. Whirling, he saw a solid wall of horses piling out of the east's breaking dawn. He put two rapid shots into the mass. At once he saw light open as the wedge split, one knot of yelling riders tearing for the hobbled stock, the others shooting and slamming and whooping through camp. At that moment Andy's Sharps boomed from the other side of the hide wagon.

When Keith glanced again, the horses and mules were crow-hopping in all directions. The Indians, unable to drive the hobbled stock fast enough, were rushing on to the west and milling about. Everybody under the wagons was firing, though Keith couldn't tell what effect the shots were having. Once more, taking advantage of the filmy light, the Indians darted back at a hard run and began circling the camp, shooting and yelling as the outfit kept up the firing.

All at once the Indians drew off out of range. Keith lost sight of them.

Only now did he feel the quivering of excitement catch up with his body. He was trembling and unsteady, his throat constricted. The whole thing had taken less than a few minutes, yet it seemed much longer.

As daylight broke, Keith saw the hobbled stock scattered south of camp, and he understood Sam's insistence on leather hobbles instead of picket ropes. Walking over the trampled ground with Sam, he found blood on the grass where the teams and saddle horses were grazing when the Indians attacked.

"You hit one," Sam summed it up. "They carried him off. He slipped in here to cut hobbles."

Keith and Andy, taking ropes, caught the stock and removed the hobbles and led the animals in and tied them to the wagons. Except for chafed front feet, they looked unhurt. All were accounted for. Meanwhile, Levi, as cheerful and unconcerned as if nothing had happened, was fixing a whopping big breakfast. Sam and Hub watched for Indians.

"We can't hunt in pairs," Sam said at breakfast. "Not any more. Not safe to leave Levi here by himself. From now on one extra man stays in camp. Three go out together. We'll take turns on guard every night. We'll hobble and picket both."

"Wonder if them Indians'll take another sashay at us?" Andy said, watching off as he ate.

"Who knows what a damned Indian will do or when he'll do it?" Hub flashed out. He finished his meal and started cleaning the Spencer carbine. "I can't see us goin' out today. Maybe that war party went on west; maybe it didn't."

A belated realization shook Keith. "My God —" he said, rising, "there's a family upriver from us." He looked at Hub and Andy. "The one we saw camped outside Barr's Town the day we left."

Hub's hands on the carbine became still. "Woman an' kid, wasn't there?"

Keith nodded gloomily. "And just one man in the outfit." He hadn't mentioned the Dockums to Sam and Levi.

"Only a damned fool would bring his family out here," Sam said, shaking his head. "You sure it's a family, not a bunch of rawhide runners, able to take care themselves?"

"I saw the young woman the day Andy and I got the stand," Keith said, seeing Andy's surprise. "She was walking out from camp. Their name is Dockum. She's the man's daughter. The little boy is her brother." He said that, then left to gather up his gear.

Keith bridled his horse, slapped on blanket and saddle. Andy strolled over. "I'll be ready when you are, Buffalo."

Keith held back a reply. He was, he realized, waiting for Sam's reaction and not wanting Andy to know why he hesitated. But all Sam did was pull on the flank of his jaw.

"You may be needed around here," Keith said to discourage Andy.

"You just said the Dockums might need help," Andy reminded him and went for his horse.

Keith finished cinching and slipped the loaded

157

Henry and Sharps into the long leather boots slung from the pommel, not the most comfortable arrangement to carry rifles horseback, but the handiest, with the butts slanting forward.

Andy led his horse across and when he and Keith mounted, Sam clomped deliberately out. "Stay away from the breaks. Ride only where you can see around you. If you spot Indians comin', bombard 'em. They'll likely veer off. A good old Sharps will bore a new belly button for the smartest buck in the world 'bout as far as you can see 'im." A severity toughened his mild blue eyes. He checked Keith's equipment without comment, then Andy's.

"Andy," he said roughly, "get another sack of shells."

"I got one," Andy said, with a near-larking tone.

" damnit — are you stone deaf?"

Andy straightened. He ducked his head and swung away, bringing back a sack which he started tying to his saddle strings.

Sam's gruffness chopped him still. "Put all you can in your pockets. What if your horse ran off with your ammunition sacks?" After Andy had filled his pockets to Sam's satisfaction, his uncle nodded; without a word, he tramped over to the tin cup of coffee he had left on the wash bench.

They followed the crisscross bands of their old wagon tracks, yet plain in the short grass after several days. The disturbing thing, Keith saw, was that the unshod prints of the war party went the same way, upriver, following the meandering valley.

"How many Indians you figure?" Andy asked, frowning over the cluttered marks.

"Twenty or so."

"You cipher tracks better than me."

"I'm going by how many they looked this morning — in the dark."

Andy's laugh was not amused. "You mean a whole cussed army. That's how many they looked to me. Son-of-a-gun, I was scared stiff."

"So was I."

"It's their heathen whoops and yells that get me. My hair was straight up, plump against the underside of the wagon bed."

Later, Keith was relieved to see the Indian trail changing course, cutting west where broken country formed, toward a studding of low, rocky hills. The exact kind of terrain which Sam had warned them to avoid. He saw the same thought in Andy's eyes.

"We won't go into those hills," Keith said. "But I'd like to know if the tracks come back to the river."

"Maybe back toward camp again." Andy had quit his funning.

Keith rode after the tracks, expecting them to swing back in the direction of the river after a short distance, but the broad trail continued to move on a line for the first rocky hill. He and Andy looked at each other and followed on to the foot of the hill. Here bent grass revealed the deeper pocks of horses stamping during a halt.

While Keith studied the ground, Andy was observing the rock-slabbed hillside. He upped the Sharps suddenly and spoke in a hollow gulp: "Keith — you see that man 'a' sittin' up there?" He eared back the hammer to fire.

"No — Andy! No!"

Andy eased off, a sheepishness coloring his face. "It's a dead Indian buried up there. If he was alive, he'd shot us sure by now."

Keith stared. A narrow crevice opened about three-quarters up; loose rocks in front, rocks that looked piled at the entrance, not natural. Some had rolled down a way. Behind the rocks closing the entrance, just visible, Keith made out the image of a coppery face.

"Hold the horses, Andy. Keep a lookout around."

Scrambling up, carrying the Henry, Keith saw holes of fresh earth where rocks had been removed. The crevice looked more like an old wash up here. Gray water stains ran down its rugged face.

He peered in and saw a paint-streaked face, the eyes closed with red clay. Streaks of red and yellow and black. Otherwise, the broad, high-boned face, that of a young Indian, was plucked clean, including eyebrows. The black hair was parted in the center and braided on each side. One black feather adorned the scalp lock. Against the body stood a bow and quiver and an old carbine of a make which Keith did not recognize. The body

faced the east in a sitting position. Facing the east
— facing the sun — that meant medicine of some
kind, Keith decided.

A deeper curiosity prompted him to pull at the
rocks, digging until he could see the upper half of
the Indian's body. Next he saw a hole in the chest
and dried blood. He thought: *the hobble-cutter.*
Seeing the dead face gave him a confused feeling,
separated from elation; seeing the young Indian,
dead like a coyote in a hillside den, made a difference. But Indians had killed Dan Massengale,
and they would wipe out the camp if they could.

He started piling back the rocks. A little of that
and an awareness of lost time thrust through him.
He took a sweeping look. Up here he had a clear
view in an directions. Nothing moved. Not even
buffalo. He hastened down.

"Want a look, Andy? Hurry."

Andy dropped to the ground and went legging
up the hill. He didn't say anything when he came
down, but he looked kind of sickish.

Keith followed the pony tracks around the hill
and when he saw the trail narrowing and string-
ing out toward humped-up country, on westward, he rode no farther.

More than an hour passed. They watered
horses in the small creek east of the wide flat and
rode among the buffalo wallows hugging the
green sod like huge, scratched-out nests and
turned south. Keith retained a picture of the
Dockum girl striding away, controlling her fear
and distrust of him. In the remote distance, heavy

161

rifles boomed. Nothing close. Missing was the light snap of the rifle he remembered hearing the day of the stand; likely that was fortunate today with Indians around. No buffalo in sight, either, and he wondered if the bombarded herd had shifted farther west on its shrinking range.

About half a mile onward he heard the *chock* of an ax. He and Andy rounded the shoulder of a hill shaggy with shin oaks and cedars, and then Keith saw the top of a wagon — more patched than whole, its pieces remindful of an old quilt — among the green mesquites; and a crude, two-wheeled cart piled with hides. A leanish man chopping wood. Another whittling in the shade by the wagon, his back resting against the spokes of a wheel. Two mules grazed out on the flat, easy pickings for the first Indian that wanted them.

Keith and Andy were within fifty yards before the whittler took notice. He closed the knife against the palm of his left hand, held it there a moment, cupped, while he studied the approaching horsemen, and seemed to draw himself up by slack degrees, standing by the wagon, a fleshy man, an air of idleness about him. It was Cal Dockum.

"Good morning," Keith said, riding in. The woodcutter ceased his steady chopping to walk toward the wagon.

"Morning," Dockum said. "Get down."

"We're in a hurry. Indians ran through our camp at daybreak. Thought we'd better tell you.

We're downriver about ten miles."

"That's neighborly of you," Dockum said and chewed his tobacco a mite faster. "Indians, you say? Ain't seen a redskin since we come out here." He regarded Keith, minimizing the threat. "Reckon they shy away from us hunters."

"They didn't from us." Keith could sense his first impression of the man redoubling. Dockum was not only an idler, he was a fool. "At least twenty, maybe more, in the war party, Mr. —" Keith held back purposely, not wishing to feed Dockum's boastfulness by speaking his name.

"Dockum's the name. Calvin H. Dockum."

"I'm Keith Hayden. This is Andy Kinkade." Keith trailed off, seeing the second man. A man younger than Dockum, in his thirties, wearing a chimney-pot hat, as lean and raw-boned and work-hardened as Dockum was rolly and soft and shiftless. His tawny eyes butting into Keith's stare, were unsmiling glints under outcrops of thick, sandy brows. His spare, laconic mouth was a mere slit in the stern escarpment of the bearded face.

"Been Indians around," Dockum told him.

"Where?"

"Upriver. Run through their camp this morning. Wiley — this is ah — Hayden — this is Kinkade."

Wiley appeared to roll the news around in his mind like a pebble, all the time nodding, the trap of his angular mouth shut tight.

Voices — light voices, a woman's and a child's

— were coming through the mesquites, and Keith glimpsed the Dockum girl carrying a bucket of water and the boy swinging a stick. She passed behind the wagon, and Keith heard her set down the bucket.

"You figure it's bad?" Wiley asked Keith.

"It'll get worse. We're killing off the Indian's meat supply."

"We'll be on the lookout," Dockum said, as if that would solve the problem. He stopped when the girl and the blond boy walked around the wagon. The man called Wily watched her, watched her closely, as she made a gesture of concern.

"What is it, Papa?"

"Been a few Indians upriver — that's all," Dockum explained offhandedly. "These here fellows rode down to tell us. Mighty neighborly."

Seeing her and Dockum, Keith was struck by the lack of family resemblance between them; none at all, in fact. She turned and Keith saw her questioning give way to surprise when she recognized him; in another moment she avoided his eyes and a rose pink crept up her throat and into her face, but in the next instant she showed him an expressionless face.

Keith spoke his name and touched his hat to her, a gesture which he saw her take note of and which he saw also she was unaccustomed to, and which he remembered he had noticed that day in Barr's Town; then he said, "Andy Kinkade — my partner," and Andy's white grin eased the awkward moment.

"Now, Coralie," said Dockum, mistaking her confusion for upset, "there's nothin' to get all ruffled up about. If that war party was headed this way, we'd know it by now."

Keith's patience came apart. "Look folks, we followed the Indians' trail. They went on west of here, maybe to hunt. Maybe they'll be back — we killed one." He was being blunt, knowing he had to be. "We found where they buried him in the rocks. I said they rode west. This gives you time to get out."

"Get out?" Dockum looked puzzled.

"Back to the settlements — to Barr's Town."

"No work in Barr's Town for an old soldier," Dockum complained, self-pity taking over. "Less he's a barkeep or cardsharp."

"Safer than here. If not there, you can move close to another camp."

"Big outfits don't cotton to a little man crowdin' in on their range. We been run off two places on the South Pease."

"Indian trouble makes a difference," Keith said.

"I come out here to make a stake," Dockum said, slapping his leg.

Keith was running out of words, and Dockum was a bigger fool than he had thought. The only spark needed here to touch off tragedy was for a war party riding along the valley to hear Dockum's rifle.

"You can camp near us," Keith said. "You

won't be crowding in."

Dockum fished a plug of tobacco from an overall pocket, bit off a sizable chew, wallowed it around in his jaw and spat reflectively, a stubborn slope to his mouth. "That's neighborly of you, like I said. But no, by grab, we're gonna stick it out." He seemed to speak with a blind bluster, yet with a hopefulness, too, that somehow everything would turn out all right. "And Wiley's with me."

Wiley nodded to that, and turned to watching Coralie Dockum.

"We can look out for ourselves," Dockum added.

To a certain extent, Keith could understand Dockum. He had never had much. Killing buffalo was his last chance. He was after the same thing Sam Massengale was, except Sam was better organized, not stuffed with his own importance, knew how to go about the business of hunting, and had a competent crew. Dockum's operation was not only too small, it was hardscrabble and ill-equipped, hit or miss, doomed to failure by his idleness. Wiley was an unknown quantity.

Seeing Coralie Dockum's absorbed look, Keith thought she was going to argue against her father, for she was strong, and she had intelligence. She took a long-drawn breath. Her lips moved. She expelled that breath with a sigh. A thoughtfulness grew over her.

"Papa's right," she said. "We can look out for

ourselves. We always have. There's nothing to go back to. We thank you." Keith was seeing her weariness again, her worn patience.

"Good luck," Keith said, and turned his horse around.

Riding off with Andy, he wondered about her. His mind wouldn't let go of her and the contradictions she posed. For she was aware of the danger, if Dockum was too heedless to acknowledge it. She was strong enough to sway her father, if she wished. And Wiley? He was sticking because of her.

CHAPTER 10

That night an enormous thunderstorm rolled out of the southwest over the buffalo country, bringing savage flashes of light and crashing echoes like the fury of artillery salvos. From under the hide wagon Keith watched the lightning slash the sky; forked lightning, leaping tongues of fire linking heaven and earth. Under him the prairie was shivering. Hardly a breath passed between one racketing charge and the next.

He felt like a small boy again, crouched in wonder and fear, watching the dark turbulence over the Connecticut River of a late spring evening, the darting flashes lighting up the ghostly white church spires and the rounded hills, so green and tranquil-looking beneath the storm. He had not experienced such a thunderous display as tonight's since joining the outfit. The rising wind carried to him the nervous trampling of the mule teams and the saddle stock Andy was up, too, listening to the furious bombardment.

Rain spattered the wagon like bird shot. A lantern glowed into life across from Keith.

"We'd better get over there," Andy said suddenly.

"What's wrong?"

"It's Uncle Sam."

Pulling on his boots, Keith heard the rain sweeping upon the camp, in silvery sheets when the lightning flashed, the thunder firing point-blank. Wind gusts rocked the wagon.

Struggling toward the cone of yellow light, Andy a quick step ahead of him, Keith saw figures beneath the cook wagon and he supposed Sam was sick. An unusual occurrence if so, though Andy had seemed to sense it at once.

Levi, kneeling, held a lantern. He was crouched protectively beside Sam, his hand on Sam's shoulder while he spoke low to Sam. Sam sat on his bedroll; he appeared to be gazing down in deep thought. Rain drops trickled off his curly black beard, coating it with a sparkling gloss, and wind-driven rain pecked his cheeks and forehead. He seemed not to feel or notice around him.

"Let's get him inside the wagon," Keith shouted, questioning Levi's vague attention to a sick man.

Levi with a shake of his head, said something in reply, a hoarseness which Keith lost against the roar of the storm. Levi's ruined face seemed to say that Sam was as well off here. It was disconcerting to Keith. But when he looked at Andy, he saw that Andy concurred. Hub leaned in, and like Levi and Andy, he did not show alarm.

Levi kept patting Sam's shoulder gently.

"Uncle Sam," Andy said, getting down beside him, his voice raised but calm and assuring. "You're all right. Hear me? You're all right."

Sam raised his head and gazed around, blinking, as a man might blink after climbing from a dark cellar into light. He had a crumbled look, an anguished look, and Keith saw that wasn't all rain on his face. He was crying, the way a person cries in his sleep, in his bad-dreaming, traces of it soon gone after awakening.

"Uncle Sam, it's Andy. We're all here with you."

Sam seemed to grope and discover Andy's face all at once, out of the troubled fog from which he was breaking free. Unmindful of the rain slanting under the wagon, he looked in turn for Levi and Hub and Keith and found them. Relief relaxed his face. The last of the nightmare slipped away.

"Now," Andy said, "we can put him in the wagon."

Although Sam understood, he couldn't seem to move, and so they helped him out and up and led and guided him to the front of the cook wagon. Levi climbed in first with the lantern, while the others boosted Sam up over the hub of the wagon box. Levi threw a blanket around Sam and told him to lie down. Sam obeyed like a tired child, after which Hub uncorked a jug of whisky and held it up, humoring, and told Sam to drink. He drank like a sleepy child, spilling the whisky down the corners of his mouth.

Levi and Hub wrapped him up, stretched him out on a pallet of thick quilts. He regarded them dreamily, through shrouded eyes, smiling faintly, and fell into a relaxed slumber.

They watched him until his breathing became slow and steady.

"He'll be an right now," Hub said, softer than

170

Keith had ever heard him speak.

Keith, standing on the wheel hub, realized that he was drenched. He and Andy ran back to the hide wagon and ducked underneath. The thunder and lightning marched on, leaving a wake of hard, steady rain that would prevent hunting tomorrow.

"It's the thunder that bothers Uncle Sam," Andy said, dragging his bedroll away from the slant of the rain. "Sometimes when it gets bad, mighty bad, like tonight, he dreams he's back in Shiloh. In the woods. In the Hornets' Nest; time the rebs lined up their hull artillery on the Missouri boys . . . He hears the cannons and he dreams he's back in prison camp, too, seein' all them sick and starvin' boys. He'll be fine in the morning."

Next morning, save for a haggardness and that Sam was quieter than usual, his nightmare might not have happened; no one spoke of it or asked how he felt The sun came out and the spongy prairie turned hot and steamy bright, like crystal, and the rainwashed air had the sweet fragrance of wild flowers and grama and buffalo grass.

After breakfast, Sam saddled his horse and rode alone for the buffalo range; no one cautioned him. Before noon he returned. Satisfaction shone through his drawn look.

"Buffalo's drifted back," he reported. "Big bunches again, far as a man can see. All the way back a couple miles this side of where Keith got his stand. Whole herd seems to be movin' north as usual with new grass."

"Any Indian sign?" Hub asked.

"All old tracks, made before the rain. That war party is fillin' up on fresh liver and hump meat, you bet."

By the second morning the boggy prairie was dry enough to bear a wagon; therefore, Keith, Andy and Sam pulled upriver to hunt. Everything Sam had reported was true. The country teemed with life again, as it had when Keith first sighted the southern herd from the hogback ridge: masses of buffalo covering the rolling green swells, as dark clouds settling over the hills and ridges and filling the valley down which Andy drove the wagon, as a dark, sluggish current flowing slowly northward over the spring-fresh grass.

"You do the shooting," Keith suggested to Sam, thinking he would be more up to that than skinning. Sam agreed and rode ahead. In a short time the mellow boom of his Sharps carried back. They hauled in two loads of hides before dark, not counting meat for Levi's smokehouse; and that evening Sam bent over his memorandum book and said:

"Thirty-eight today, boys. Cassidy had better bring a long string of wagons when he comes."

"What's the tally?" Hub asked him, not greatly interested. Keith wondered where Hub Stratton would go when the hunting ended; without a family he had no ties like Sam.

"Let's see." Sam figured on the back of an old envelope. "Comes out twelve hundred and nine.

We'll have couple thousand hides when Cassidy gets here."

"Your bottom farm is lookin' better an' better," Andy said, and Sam seemed to nod to please his nephew. It turned over in Keith's mind that Andy was thinking ahead when the back-breaking skinning and camp chores ended, when he and Sam returned to Missouri with their pockets bulging; yet when that time came, the quiet rural life would seem dull indeed after times in buffalo country. Going back, Keith reflected, was never quite like the viewer saw it through the gloss of time and distance. It was a trick the mind played, rising out of yearning for an easier way of life, and of thinking the past was always better, a perfection that existed only in the longing, impracticable reaches of the mind.

Keith turned his thoughts elsewhere, not liking his cynicism. He was working too hard — they all were — but the unspoken dread he had sensed in Hub and Sam nagged him also: that was the inevitable breaking up of the outfit.

Sam put away his memorandum book and stuffed his pipe. His voice was sober: "Way the buffalo are, I figure we can hunt around here or on west through the summer. There's a little over twenty-eight hundred dollars in the tin box, boys. We can stack more'n a thousand hides a month. We could average fifteen hundred if we had another skinner or two. When we settle up, say September, there'll be better'n three thousand dollars for every man."

From Levi's misshapen mouth hissed a tune-less whistle. His voice was like a happy croak: "Gals'll sure love ol' Levi then, won't they?"

"For a while," Hub growled. "Till you're dead broke."

"It's my money," Levi argued mildly.

"Won't be long."

"Be my worry."

"I just hate to see you whoop it all off on a bunch of no account bar-room women. Hell, we've all busted our guts for that money, Levi."

"The more to enjoy it, I say."

Hub shook his head, too disgusted to say more. Sam knocked out his pipe and yawned, stretched up to his feet. His low laugh was chiding: "Boys, we've got to make it before we spend it. Who's on first guard tonight?"

"Me," Hub said and got up and left.

A week afterward the outfit was taking hides on the great grassy flat where Keith had shot his fill. There was no end to the tide of buffalo. Solemn and deliberate, their massive foreheads seeming to bow, the bulky creatures streamed north after watering in the gyppy Middle Pease and its creeks, leaving scarcely any grass behind them. Keith marveled that the herd, under almost constant attack from here to the Double Mountain country, some hundred miles south, could continue to pass in such solid numbers. They seemed insensible to their own slaughter, unconcerned so long as they grazed and drifted and lumbered *en masse:* that very gregariousness, Keith had reasoned many times, was causing the buffalo's doom.

On this day Keith and Sam flung the last green hide on the wagon and Sam slumped against the tailgate, all the strength sucked out of him. He took off his hat and mopped a blue bandanna over his grimy forehead, and slapped his hat at the swarms of flies. Buffalo blood flecked the black hair on his thick forearms. Keith saw his haggard eyes rest on Andy and himself.

"Tomorrow's Sunday," Sam grunted, speaking from the pit of his body. "Time we took a day of rest."

Winding around the wallows, riding behind the wagon, Keith heard the infrequent popping of a rifle, and he smiled at Cal Dockum's luck of having a world of hides within walking distance of camp. Keith's weary mind, revolting against the tedium of a day that had begun before sunrise, touched on Coralie Dockum. He had, he realized, never quite put her out of his thinking. And, like Sam said, wasn't tomorrow Sunday?

After breakfast next morning, he carried water from the spring and heated it in a kettle, scrubbed and dried himself, then hung his hand mirror on the side of the hide wagon, lathered his face and started shaving, wincing at each pull of the razor.

Andy strolled over to watch. He held his right hand behind him. "Where you headed, Buffalo?"

"Visiting." The somewhat pale, clean-shaven face Keith saw in the mirror was a stranger to him. Older and stronger, the eyes far-looking, as if used to great distances, crinkled at the corners. His brown hair hung down his neck.

"Visitin' or callin'?"

"Won't know till I've been there a while."

Laughing, Andy displayed his bottle of bay rum. "Smear on some of this stinkum. It's big medicine. You'll need it the way that Wiley fellow was eyeballing Coralie Dockum like he owned her."

Keith, applying the stinging liquid, found that he had attracted a further audience.

"By golly," Levi said, "a stranger's slipped into camp."

"Another beardless boy," Hub commented, cracking a smile. "Where's your hide pants?"

"Keith," Sam said, feigning concern, "you'll catch cold. Better bundle up."

It was good, Keith thought, to hear jesting in camp for the first time in days. Especially from Sam, who hadn't quite been himself since the night of the storm. Keith scraped and knocked the mud off his Wellingtons. He found a pair of unsoiled trousers and a clean gray flannel shirt. He combed his long hair, brushed the dust from his hat and crimped it, ready to go. As he stepped to the saddle, Levi favored him with a mocking bow:

"Can we ordinary mortals expect your honor back for supper?"

"Sooner than that if I'm not invited for dinner. So long."

The morning sun stood high against the blue wall of the sky when Keith, nearing the Dockum camp, saw a span of mules pulling a cart and one man leading the team, another man walking alongside. Keith waved and rode for them, recognizing Wiley and Dockum. The older man, a carbine across his arm, was poking along beside the cart. He stopped the moment he saw Keith, openly welcoming the opportunity to rest and palaver.

"Come on with us," Dockum invited. "Just goin' in. Got ten hides this morning." He slapped the stock of the short-barreled carbine. "Had this old Peabody for years. Handy to carry. Wouldn't swap it for airy Sharps I've seen."

"Isn't a carbine a little light for buffalo?" Keith ventured.

"Just right. Knocks down all we can skin."

Dockum was bragging, any weapon he had would be the best. Keith knew that the Peabody was a very old carbine, of Civil War vintage, short-ranged and lacking the killing power of the Sharps. Common talk was the Peabody had a tendency to jam. Keith let the matter pass.

Wiley did not speak. He gave a curt nod and turned his back and led the mules toward camp, annoyed at the holdup.

Dockum fell behind to chin with Keith. "Frank Wiley, there," he said, "works too hard. Man can kill himself overdoin'."

"There are five of us," Keith said. "We all have to work hard to keep up."

"Oh, we get our share right along. Not like you big outfits, maybe. But we got us a big pile of hides. I'm a right fair shot, if I do say so. Bein' in the War helps a man out here." He slanted a sly look at Keith. "Say, would you boys happen to have some extra caps? I'm a little low right now."

"I think so. I'll bring you some in a day or two."

"Ah, fine. That's neighborly of you. I'll swap you some flour."

Rounding the hill and sighting the camp in the stand of green mesquites, Keith saw Coralie Dockum by the wagon. She was watching alertly, hand-shading her eyes with her left hand. She indicated no recognition when Keith followed the cart by to the pegging ground. He saw her place a double-barreled shotgun in the family wagon and resume her cooking. Blond Lenny came skipping and calling in his high, excited voice, "Papa — papa!"

Dockum patted him and tickled him in the ribs and the boy doubled up laughing. Forthwith, Lenny sprang up and ran to see what Wiley was doing. Wiley halted the team and took a two-bladed ax off the top of the load, peeled back the first hide and dragged it away, the boy watching him, silent, in fascination, mouth ajar, his eyes enlarging on the furry hide.

Dockum idled by the cart. "Sun's gettin' hot," he observed to Keith. "Man ought to do this of an evening so he won't get sunstroke." With a giving-in sigh, he laid the Peabody on the tailgate of the cart and tugged off a hide and loitered out to a pile of newly cut wooden pegs.

Keith dropped down to help. He saw the jagged tear the moment he pulled the hide free, and hesitated. Dockum and Wiley had taken this skin the easy way. A lazy skinner drove an iron picket pin through the buffalo's head and into the ground, rope-hitched his team to the buffalo's neck, and the team jerked off the hide. Sometimes the practice worked, more often not. The robe Keith held was all but torn in two.

He raised his voice. "Want this one pegged out? It's ripped."

"Might get two-bits for it," Dockum replied doubtfully, looking up where he was driving pegs with a wooden maul.

Wiley was watching. "If it's worth two-bits, it's worth pegging."

"Dinner — it's time for dinner. Mr. Hayden, will you eat with us?"

Keith hadn't seen Coralie Dockum come up behind him. He threw the split hide back on the cart, aware that Wiley was primed to argue the pointless issue.

He thanked her. She was gone as he spoke. His eyes followed her. The whipping wind flung her long skirts tightly against her and revealed the rounded lines of her body.

He turned around to find Wiley's eyes on him. A staying look and Wiley finished pegging the hide and rose to unharness the mules.

"When Coralie calls dinner," Dockum said, "she means right now. Come on, Hayden." He took Lenny by the hand, his walk noticeably faster than his idling by the cart on the prairie. Wiley was leading the mules out to picket. "That's Wiley for you," Dockum said, disapproving. "Can't take time to enjoy his vittles. Works from sunup to sundown. If he can't find a chore around camp, he'll go out and chop down some trees or dig a hole. We got enough firewood around here to roast a buffalo herd."

Everyone was waiting when Wiley, in long, straightaway strides, came in and laid his ax out of the way under the wagon. He took off his hat and began washing at the bench, finished by scooping water in his hands and dashing it over his face with noisy splutterings, and dried on the flour-sack towel. At the table, a plank arrangement resting on kegs over which Coralie had placed a checkered cloth, Wiley sat and started to reach for the meat platter.

"You know," Coralie said, in her voice a graciousness that stayed Wiley's hand, coupled with an instructive look for her father, "it is Sunday. Will you give the blessing, Papa?"

Dockum bowed his head. He mumbled so fast and so low that Keith was unable to catch all the words. Finished, Dockum stretched for the biscuit plate, ignoring Coralie's disapproval.

Eating, Keith thought of that first great meal with the outfit at Fort Elliot. Coralie served the customary fare of the buffalo camp — stewed dried apples, coffee, biscuits, buffalo roast and brown gravy — but what set the dinner off were the wild things she had gathered: polk salad, wild lettuce, dandelion greens.

Keith complimented her. She was caught off guard. Pleasure and surprise brushed into her eyes and mouth, an expression quickly transitory. She drew her lips together in a manner she had when deciding not to speak, when holding herself in. Part of her hard acceptance, Keith thought. She could meet his eyes without embarrassment now, but, he saw, she still did not trust him.

"Wiley," she asked, turning her gaze from Keith's, "where did you find the buffalo today?"

"On the flat." His tawny eyes stared at her. Behind their sternness a steady interest stirred.

"Were there many?"

"Plenty."

"I hate to think of those motherless little calves. It's cruel." In the pause that followed, Keith asked Wiley, "Any fresh Indian sign?"

"Not a track," Wiley said. His rebuttal struck straight into Keith. He was finished eating. He rose and picked up his hat and strode straight to the pegging ground.

"There he goes," Dockum said, "back to work 'fore his dinner has time to settle. I tell you that's hard on a man. Shortens his days."

"I never heard of work killing a person," Coralie said, a certain reproof in her voice.

"Wiley works too hard. No imagination. It was me, remember, that figured out the cart to haul the hides in on."

"Except the cart is too small, Papa. You can't haul enough hides on it."

"I know that. We need another wagon. Wiley says he'll buy one when we sell our hides. Wiley's been a farmer and bullwhacker," Dockum said for Keith's benefit. "I made a deal with him in Barr's Town. He didn't like the place. Said it was too wild. Too sin-ridden, he called it. He's all against whisky — even tobacco. Won't touch 'em . . . To make a long story short, he didn't have much to come in with as a partner. Not even a gun. But if hard work will make a man rich, Wiley will be another King Midas."

Glancing off, Keith saw about a hundred or more hides stacked; counting those on the pegging ground, maybe two hundred in all. Some of those would be ruined, judging from what Keith had seen. It was quite clean around the wagon. Poor-clean, his father would say. Coralie Dockum had swept the hard-packed ground with a broom he saw made of mesquite branches tied together. Men's shirts and trousers were drying on a rope clothesline. An air of feminine order pervaded here, and of making do with meager possessions.

Dockum planted himself on the stump of a mesquite cut down to make room for the wagon, bit off a chunk of tobacco, and eased back, his hands cupped under the sag of his paunch.

"Hayden, how long you calculate the buffalo'll last?"

"A few years. Not long."

Lenny hung on his father's arm. A cheerful little boy, his blond hair cut short and neat, his hands and face clean, his eyes a soft hazel like his sister's. He tugged on Dockum's knee. "Papa, how many did you shoot today?"

"Ten."

"Where's your big gun?"

Dockum sat up. "Durned if I didn't leave it on the cart." He rose with a grunt, and Lenny, finding a new interest in Keith, said, "Papa was in the Battle of Gettysburg, he was." His large eyes were wide, in them a glowing worship.

Dockum turned at the words and, with a sidewise look at Keith, gave Lenny an urging pat on his bottom, saying, "Run along — help your sister," and idled to the cart for the carbine.

Coralie Dockum was clearing the table, moving back and forth, paying no heed to Keith, her heavy shoes making light, even clumps. Although Keith loathed the shoes, he concluded that she wore them with as much grace as a woman possibly could; for all their ugliness, they were a practical necessity here. She looked neither toward Keith nor away from him, though now and then, when she turned he saw her eyes stray across him. "Lenny," she said of a sudden, "fetch me a piece of wood for the fire. Look out for snakes."

There was no hurry in her voice and Lenny seemed to sense it. He turned a curious appraisal on Keith and started off on a roundabout course, glancing back as he did, still curious.

"Papa's not used to watching every minute for Indians," she told Keith, her gaze on her father coming back from the cart."

"I think you should all get out of here."

"We've been over that, and we are careful."

"It's not just being careful," Keith said. "You're a small outfit. You're underarmed — that shotgun and one old carbine. A war party would ride right over you, which they almost did us. I believe you could talk your father into moving downriver, if nothing else. Why don't you?"

Dockum came back before she could answer. He laid the carbine in the wagon, carelessly, motioned to Keith. "Want you to take a look at my hide stack."

There, to please his host, Keith removed the top hide and looked at it. While hand-skinned and not split, its ragged and irregular shape showed trashy cutting and ripping. Small stirrings on the hide took Keith's attention. He peered closer.

"What is it?" Dockum demanded.

"Hide bugs."

"Bugs! How come?"

"Didn't anybody tell you? You have to sprinkle poison on hides to keep off the bugs." Keith examined two more, one a split hide. Each was infested. He laid them back on the pile.

"Hell," Dockum sputtered, taken back, "I don't have any poison." Wiley was striding up

184

from the pegging ground. Dockum waved him over. "Wiley, we've got bugs in these hides."

Wiley, a scowl clouding his eyes and ridging his brows, pulled off the top hide and studied it, swinging his head from side to side, his lips bunching. With a sudden movement, he flopped the hide back on the pile.

"What about it?" he asked of Keith.

The question was like a slap. "In time," Keith said, "bugs ruin hides. All your sweat goes for nothing." He told Dockum: "I think we can spare some poison." And he began to explain how the poison was mixed and how the sprinkling was done, suggesting that the infested flint hides be sprinkled on both sides and left out in the sun for a day to dry, turning them once in the morning and once in the afternoon, before restacking.

He wasn't finished when Wiley, suddenly, went to the wagon and picked up the double-edged ax; in those straight, lengthy strides, he headed toward the wooded hill.

Keith visited with Dockum a while longer, then took his leave, promising to bring caps and bug poison in a few days or sooner. Coralie was washing dishes and Lenny was drying them. Keith thanked her for the dinner. He drew a nod and no more, for he saw that she had donned her face of reserve again.

"Come back," Dockum invited.

Keith caught the steady *chocking* of the ax from the hillside. The cadence of those blows slack-

185

ened as he left camp, died before he reached the hill. Keith heard them no more.

When he rounded the wooded hill, out of sight of camp, he saw Wiley waiting for him, blocking his way, his jaw set at a stubborn angle. He was breathing fast from his descent of the hill, and he held the double-bladed ax across his arm, the way most men cradled a rifle or carbine. Which told Keith the ax was more familiar to Wiley than a rifle. Hence, Wiley was placing himself at a dangerous disadvantage in Indian country. That he had no visible weapon other than the ax particularized the man's unyielding nature, his refusal to change.

Keith gathered in the reins, waiting.

"Stay away from here," Wiley said.

"What's bothering you?"

A brittle sheen coated the tawny eyes. "You got everybody stirred up about Indians."

"If Indians come, you'll wish you had more than that ax."

Wiley's mouth thinned to a flat crease. "You throw it up to us we ain't huntin' right."

"You're not. You jerk off the hides — that ruins 'em. Any damn fool knows that."

Wiley stiffened and went on, enumerating in his methodical, obstinate way. "You got old Dockum worried about bugs. We'll market them hides before they spoil."

"Hauled in on a cart?"

Wiley gripped the ax handle tighter, his long fingers alternately coiling around and releasing the smooth wood. "We'll get 'em to market somehow. And," he continued, "you come in here with your fancy talk and parlor manners. You upset things. Stay away."

As Keith strained for Wiley's meaning, a little wave rolled through his mind and, in a rush, he understood, seeing the print of the whole truth in Wiley's hostile face. The other things didn't count. It was Coralie. Wiley didn't want any man around.

"I'll be back here tomorrow," Keith said and heeled his horse forward. Wiley stepped out of the way, but Keith saw no fear in Wiley, and he had the insight that Wiley feared nothing on earth.

CHAPTER 11

Preoccupation seemed to ride Sam Massengale next morning. Not just the physical weariness they all felt, but something more. A dejection. A brooding. For him, a likable, congenial man, to fall into silence had an effect on the others. Keith knew what Hub or Andy would say. That War — it was always the War. But was that all?

Not until Keith had saddled up and Andy hitched the mules did Sam speak. His voice sounded unusually tired:

"Hub, you mind goin' out with the boys today?"

When they reached the flat not long after daylight, Keith left his horse at the wagon, a departure from his usual practice of riding out, because the buffalo were resting and feeding nearby, undisturbed. Scattered here and there lay the groupings of previous kills, the thick, shaggy hair still on the enormous heads, the flesh on the skinned bodies turned dark and drawn tight, dried by sun and wind, torn by wolves and coyotes and vultures. A wall of putrefaction enclosed the plain, fouling the air, a sickening stench which made a man grateful when the wind switched in his favor.

After these days on end of almost unbroken repetition, of killing buffalo and watching for Indians while the skinners toiled, of giving them a hand when he could, of pegging and turning and stacking and reloading brass in the evening, Keith moved doggedly to his task, as a farmer would go forth to plow or reap. For the fun, the pure fun, had worn off long ago. And yet, when he first set up his sticks and the warm wind purled around his face and his experienced eyes swept over the sunny plain and he saw the buffalo, he never failed to respond with excitement.

Now, once more, he was ready, kneeling behind the forked sticks, the Sharps in the crotch. His senses quickened, all in tune. That bull out there, the big one. Always a big one. It seemed there were no little bulls except the spikes, which you passed over. He took aim. He squeezed the trigger and saw the hindquarters rise clear off the ground. The bull lurched and jumped awkwardly, jerking its bushy head, and broke down. Keith got the sulfureous stink of gunpowder . . .

By three o'clock, under a sun that sent heat waves shimmering across the flat in smoky waves, they were trailing for camp, the wagon squeaking under the weight of thirty-some green hides and what meat could be salvaged. At the wallows, everybody washed off the buffalo blood and the dirt and sweat, though the buffalo stink would remain; then Keith cut away to the south, a box of caps and a can of bug poison sacked on his saddle.

He passed the stumpy little hill where Wiley had come down to warn him off, and saw the cart was gone, which jibed with the light banging he had heard minutes back west of the Dockum camp.

A flurry of movement told him that he was discovered. He called out and rode up to the wagon, knowing what to expect, in the next moment seeing Coralie Dockum holding the shotgun ready, and Lenny a step behind her, all eyes. A book lay open on the table, beside it a pencil and a sheet of paper, which suggested she had been teaching the boy.

"You should call out sooner," she said. "You might get shot."

"An Indian wouldn't call out at all," he said, and untied the saddle strings from around the sack and held it out to her.

She did not raise her hand. "Papa can't pay for it. Why did you bring it?"

"You know what's in it?"

"Yes."

"He's short on primers and if he doesn't use bug poison he'll lose the hides."

She accepted the sack with reluctance, set it on the wash bench. He saw a good deal more: she didn't intend to ask him down. She did not trust him or know how to assess his purpose here or what he actually wanted or what he was. Beyond her he saw mules drawing the cart across the prairie, bound for camp, and two walking figures.

"I'll have to tell your father how to use the poison," he said.

"You told him yesterday."

"I'd better show him," Keith said and dismounted and tied up.

She stared at the shotgun in her hands and laid it away in the wagon. Lenny ran to the edge of the mesquites to watch the hunters.

"Before long," Keith said, "Wiley will ask you to marry him."

She whipped about and he saw the rush of feeling through the tan of her high-cheeked face. "Why did you say that?"

"I think he will. I know he will."

"How do you know?"

"I can tell when he looks at you."

"And what if he does?"

"Well, would you be happy with him?"

"I won't let you talk about Wiley!"

"*Wiley?* Why do you call him by his last name?"

She withheld her answer, her composure shaken. Finally, she said, "He's a hard-working man — a good man."

"I didn't say he's no good." Keith glanced away again. Wiley was leading the mules, Dockum ambling at the rear of the cart. "I asked you if you'd be happy with him."

Her fingers toyed with a button on the front of her long dress, the same gray dress he saw her in always, yet a dress that was clean always. She was so poor he doubted she had another. She looked at him, speaking with a naturalness he hadn't heard before:

"I've decided a woman like me takes a man or she goes to Barr's Town and works in the dance halls or is a waitress. I tried to be a waitress there, hoping Papa could find work, too, but there wasn't anything. So it's that, else she stays close to the wagon and nothing ever happens to her."

"How would you like to live?" Keith spoke faster, hearing the screech of the ungreased cart wheels coming closer.

"I'd like to hear the voices of neighbors again," she said, "and live in a white house with a little picket fence, painted white, around the front yard, and the yard full of red and yellow roses, hollyhocks, phlox, and periwinkle."

"Periwinkle? What do they look like?"

"You've never seen them?" she asked, as if he should know. "The kitten-eyed blue flowers? There's periwinkle on my mother's grave in Kansas."

"When was that, may I ask?"

"Last year."

"I'm sorry to hear that."

"Papa tried to farm there, but it didn't work out. The year before that we tried Iowa."

She wasn't, Keith saw, blaming Dockum. She was merely recounting in her loyal way.

"A woman can have a flower garden in the country as well," he said. Take that big flat where we hunt, and back this way, where the creek comes across. Be an ideal place for a house just below the ridge."

"I guess," she said, and he could sense her caution taking over again, and he could hear her loneliness, "it's wrong to talk about things you can't ever have. Wiley says it's a sin to daydream because it wastes time."

"It's all right to hope. We live on hopes and dreams. That's why we're all here, looking for something we feel we need. We don't know for certain what it is, but we're looking. There's music out here if people will just listen."

He saw her response, a new sensitiveness, hitherto hidden, as he decided she managed to hide most of her feelings. She regarded him thoughtfully. "Wasn't there music where you lived?"

"Very little — for me. But possibly I wasn't listening."

She smiled, almost. "No girl?"

He wasn't expecting that, and the answer which he thought lay near and ready eluded him.

She clasped her hands in confusion. All at once he had to laugh at her seriousness.

"It wasn't mannerly of me to ask," she said.

"It was womanly," he smiled.

"I just wondered," she said, "why a man like you would come out here to lose himself." Piercing, the screech of the cart bore down upon them; as if reminded who she was and where she was, she turned from him, and as she did he saw the hidden liveliness leave her face.

The boy ran out, his high voice shrilling greetings.

For a hanging moment, Wiley pinned his narrow attention on Keith. Then, jerking on the line, he led the mules by toward the pegging ground.

Dockum hastened out of his slack walk and

over to Keith, content to put off the pegging chores. "Have supper with us, Hayden."

Keith declined with a swing of his head.

"Papa," Coralie said, not insisting, "Mr. Hayden brought the primers and bug poison."

"Neighborly, neighborly," Dockum said, dipping his chin. "How about me sackin' up some flour for you to take back?"

"Later — if we need some." Now was the time to ride out, to skirt trouble. But, if Keith did, Wiley would think he was afraid. Thus, after showing Dockum the proportion of poison to water and punching holes in an old bucket for a sprinkler, Keith helped him sprinkle the piled hides. They labored for half an hour.

"Dad-burn," Dockum panted, pulling another robe off the flint pile and dragging it to an open place, "this puts a crimp in a man's back." He wiped his face. "Boogered mine up in the War."

Wiley, through pegging, paced over to watch. His stern, humorless eyes followed their motions. He voiced no approval, no disapproval. At the same time, Keith was aware of Wiley's dislike for him piling up. When it reached the breaking point, all the dammed-up hostility in this grim and overworked man would come helling out.

"Wiley," Dockum said, across his sprinkling, "we can save every hide."

"Guess so," Wiley replied, tight-lipped. He turned away abruptly, his stringy arms swinging stiffly, and led the mules to camp, unhitched and picketed them. In moments, Keith noticed him around the wagon where Coralie was fixing supper.

Before many minutes, when Keith looked again, Wiley wasn't there or anywhere in camp. A slow certainty spread through him. And directly, as if he were an actor moving to his place on cue, he took leave of Dockum, who ambled beside him to his mount. Dockum turned his head.

"Where's Wiley? I need him to help."

Coralie was stirring something in a black pot. She tapped the long spoon on the rim and laid it aside. "He went off," she said, turning her eyes on Keith instead of her father.

She knows it's coming, Keith thought.

He stepped to the saddle and reined for the hill, struck by an insightful self-judgment. Things had come to a low state when he, a stranger, went around advising country girls on matrimony. Maybe she was truly fond of Wiley? And it occurred to him further that he had hunted buffalo too long without pause. A woman — almost any woman — looked good out here. His father, in one of his pithy New England aphorisms, would say, perhaps, that sometimes the scarcity of an item outweighed its true value.

He rode around the hill. Fifty yards ahead, beyond sight of camp, Frank Wiley waited, the double edges of the ax in his hands shining wickedly. Wiley shifted position, planting himself directly in Keith's way.

"I told you to stay away," Wiley said.

Keith stopped. "Put the ax down."

Wiley clutched it tighter.

"Throw it down and we'll see about this."

Contemptuously, Wiley tossed the ax to one side, his hat after it, and dragged the back of his left hand across his stubbly chin. "Fancy talk won't help you now."

Keith swung down and dropped the reins, searching for the anger he did not feel yet. Wiley, advancing, brought up his long arms. His determined face looked like pitted rock. He loomed lean and hard-bodied.

A swift respect cautioned Keith. He raised his fists. He watched Wiley's eyes.

Wiley's left fist shot out suddenly, a looping blow that caught Keith on the side of his face and jarred his hat askew. He swept it off and drove his fists against Wiley's solid chest. At once they began hammering each other, neither giving ground, Wiley willing to take two blows to land one. His longer reach made it difficult for Keith to work in close. But Keith punished the man's body twice, heard his explosive *uhh* and knew that he had hurt Wiley.

A moment after, he saw Wiley lunge out with his tremendous length of arm and felt Wiley, by sheer strength, break past his guard and try to clamp a hold around Keith's body. Wiley was like a long-pawing cat, and Keith felt the powerful hands catch and lock and tighten as Wiley's body bunched, crushing, hugging.

A shock fled through Keith: Wiley was trying to break him in two. Pain shot up Keith's arching back. His wind was going. He was fighting for his life. Wiley squeezed harder, a ropy strength in his whip-like arms, and Keith bowed his body against the tightening pressure. They struggled in that stalemate for a run of moments, neither gaining nor losing. Keith felt Wiley fill his lungs for an even greater effort, and again Keith met the strain and struggled to break free. He could not, with his hands inside the band of Wiley's grasp. He twisted right and left and they rocked sideways, like two bears in an awkward dance.

Their scuffling feet tangled in the short grass. Keith drove with his right shoulder and Wiley lost his balance and they were falling, Wiley underneath. He struck on his back with a soggy impact that knocked the breath out of him. His arms loosened. Before he could clamp the hold again, Keith tore loose and rolled to his knees. From a crouch, he caught Wiley coming up. It was a short smash to the mouth, the weight of his shoulder behind it, and he ached to break Wiley's jaw.

Wiley's head snapped back. He sat down, stunned and bewildered, a slackness on his face as Keith rose.

Keith stared down at Wiley, amazed at himself. For the first time in his life he knew the desire to break a man up. But he thought it was over then, and he pulled back, sucking wind into his burning lungs.

Instead, Wiley spat blood and braced up and gamely started for Keith once more, maneuvering to hug and clutch. He was slower this time and the element of surprise gone, for his attack was the same. He swung the looping first punch, but Keith ducked under it and hit him twice in the belly; and when Wiley dropped his guard, Keith rammed him in the chest with his shoulder and threw all he had into Wiley's face.

Wiley reeled backward and fell. But he was still not out, however. He sat up quickly, his eyes blinking in an unfocused stare. He searched for Keith, his punished face showing no rancor or pain, only the vague surprise. He faced Keith; his blinking slowly ceased.

Keith picked up his hat, and when he turned he saw Wiley rising. His face was puffing, yet he found his feet without swaying. Wiley reached for his chimney-pot and pulled it low over his forehead and rubbed his jaw.

"I've busted ribs on better men than you," he said. "I figured you'd quit." He appeared to think that over, extremely puzzled.

"I'll be back here," Keith said, letting him know.

"Reckon you will." Wiley nodded, an inward nod, to himself. "Well, I'm not afraid of you, I'm not afraid of any man — remember that." It was important for him to speak thus, for he wanted Keith to know and to bear in mind. Keith saw all that.

They stood chest to chest for a fleeting moment until Wiley, with a wrenching motion, stretched down for his ax. He set it on his shoulder and walked off.

Coralie Dockum saw Wiley long-striding around the hill. He was out of place here on the plains, she thought, in buffalo country. He was a farmer and woodsman; from up north somewhere. A wheat man, too. She had gathered those skimpy details of his past the few times he had loosened up to talk about himself. He owned nothing but the fine ax and the clothes on his back, a neat bundle of belongings and a few blankets. He had walked all the way from Barr's Town with never a complaint, seeming to enjoy walking more than most men did riding on a wagon seat. He was the hardest working man of her knowledge, and therefore why, she knew, her father had made the partnership deal.

Wiley reached the pegging ground and roved his eyes about, apparently searching for something to do. She saw him shift the ax in his hands and stride on to camp, without a look for her father, puttering with the sprinkling bucket. He led the mules to water and back and hobbled them for the night.

Coralie, busy putting supper on the table, glanced up briefly as Wiley came in and washed at the bench. He dried his face, patting his cheeks gingerly. He hung the towel on a nail, which Dockum, in lieu of making a rack, had driven into the second sideboard of the wagon. At the moment he turned she was moving back from the table, empty handed, and she noticed his swollen jaw and puffed lips and the knot on his left cheekbone. She understood instantly and pretended not to have seen, going on to the fire. Wiley, silent, stood at the end of the wagon until she called supper.

Her father did not notice until he sat at the table, but he said no word and reached for the bread plate. After the first appeasing of his violent hunger, young Lenny, staring across the table at Wiley, blurted, "What's the matter with Wiley's face, sis?"

"Eat your supper," Coralie ordered him firmly.

Lenny said nothing more, but he kept sneaking a look at Wiley now and then.

Wiley ate faster than usual. Finished, he got up and strode off to see about the mules. Lenny had one leg up to follow him when his sister said sharply, "Young man, you finish your supper." A glance over his shoulder and he turned back to his plate.

Coralie was clearing the table when she missed Lenny. She looked up and saw him already halfway to where Wiley aimlessly fooled with a mule's hobble.

"Let 'im go," Dockum said. "How could a-body not see Wiley's face? Must 'a' been some tussle from the looks of things. Was it over you?" She continued with her work, in silence, and Dockum, in a slyer tone, went on: "You like this Hayden?"

She rested her hands on her hips, feeling an old discouragement. "Papa, I've only seen him three times." And then, remembering the first time, at the wallow, she turned her face away, knowing her father was watching her.

"So you're keeping track, eh?" Dockum teased her. He settled himself comfortably on the stump and filled his pipe. "He talks good. Reads books. I can tell that. He's neighborly. More'n you can say for most folks. All that's fine. But you keep in mind, Coralie, we don't know a thing about him or his family."

"*We don't?*" She all but laughed. "Papa, he wouldn't have me. We're nothing much. We're just trash — white trash — the way we are, goin' from one place to another. No roots. No nothing."

He swung his shoulders. "Don't you say that. Your grandpa Dockum, he fought in the Revolution. Had land once back in Ohio. You forgot that?"

"I haven't forgotten anything about us. I remember the Adair boy, too. You knew all about him. He came from a good family, but you same as ran him off."

"Why, Coralie, how can you say that, child?" Her father's round face grew downcast; in a moment she would recognize the look of mortal injury, the self-pity, and she would see the one expression she knew was real, his fear that she would leave him to fend for himself — and she would feel herself struggling and, as always, giving in to him because he was her father and she pitied him.

"I do," she said, "because you were afraid I'd

marry him. Afraid you'd be left to look out for yourself. If Mama hadn't just died and if not for Lenny . . . well, I'd have left you and married Tom Adair. He asked me more than once."

"Why didn't you?" Dockum asked, keeping his voice humble, his expression of deep hurt persisting. "You know I wouldn't 'a' stopped you, child."

"Because I didn't love him. That was the main reason."

"Aw, Coralie, you don't mean all that."

"I do, Papa. I'm twenty-three years old. Most girls my age are married and have families. In a few years, no man will look at me."

"Wiley looks at you. He'd marry you in a minute. He's a hard worker."

"Is that all that counts?"

"It's mighty important."

She poured hot water from the tea kettle into the dishpan. Dockum slapped his thigh and she saw the dreaming drift into his face. He always looked younger then. She guessed that was another reason why she hadn't taken Lenny and left him, it would be too much like hurting someone who would never face up to responsibilities, who would never grow up. He said, "We'll make us a good stake, Coralie. I know we will!" He had predicted that before, like an old tune hummed over and over, worn out, made meaningless by repetition.

"We hardly take enough hides to make our work pay," she said. "Why don't you go out early in the morning to hunt?"

"Man can sweat just so hard, no more."

"Papa," she demanded, suddenly provoked, "why can't we settle somewhere? You're a good wheelwright."

"That's what your mother used to say." He looked annoyed now.

"She was right. And now Lenny needs to go to school."

Dockum shrugged. "You can learn him enough."

"I can teach him some things. But not enough. I never went to school much, you know that."

With a heavy grunt of irritation, he idled to his feet and scanned the westward country. This time next year you'll see. Things will be better. You'll see."

Ever since she was a little girl she had heard her father speak in that vein, in dim, far-back places that stretched eastward across the Missouri and the Mississippi, his indolent face transformed, her mother standing as she stood now, listening, wearying. For a long time Coralie had believed him; now she knew nothing would come of his talk. Next year they would be camped in another harsh place, and the next year after, and after. Her father, she thought again, was more child than Lenny in some ways, hoping for better while doing little about the future. Nonetheless, in fairness to him, she knew there were many others like him, for she had seen them, all figuring prospects would be better across another state or big river, all followed by given-in women worn by toil and care. Always restless, the men, the moving a fever in them that seldom let them accumulate more than one or two wagons could carry, and behind them also, like guideposts, the headboards of their women who had died so young.

"You'll see, Coralie." He said that once more and left her.

Near dusk, Coralie saw Wiley leave his lean-to in the mesquites and approach the camp, not striding as usual. This time his steps were uncertain and his long, sandy hair was combed and he had trimmed his beard and put on a clean shirt. There was, she saw, a shyness about him.

Dockum after a sly glance toward Wiley and another for Coralie, called to Lenny, saying he had found a bird's nest down by the spring.

Awkwardly, Wiley sat on a box close to the wagon. He kept poking his thick, powerful hands in his pants pockets and taking them out. That unsureness, Coralie observed, did not extend to his eyes, which followed every movement she made while she finished putting away the washed cooking vessels.

"Nice evening," he said.

"Yes."

"Daylight hangs on a long spell in these parts." She added nothing and Wiley, as if finding new confidence in her silence, said, "It's not the kinda country I like. Me, I'm used to hills and valleys and woods — more water. You don't like it hereabouts either, do you, Coralie?"

She thought over her answer. "I like the open country, the clean sky. But it's no place for a family with Indians about."

He doubled his fist and made a short, striking motion. I've made up my mind. When we sell the hides, I aim to take up farming again."

"You mean leave? Where to?"

There was genuine surprise in her voice and she saw the assurance that gave him, saw the sternness in his face recede. "Best of all," he confided, "I like good bottom land. Like in Ioway. Would you like that, Coralie? A good farm? A good house? Snug in the winter, all fixed up just the way you want it?" When she did not answer, he stood and crossed to her, a rawboned figure looming over her, tall, strong, secure. "No man will ever work harder for you, Coralie. I never break my word."

She saw his intense earnestness and she knew he would keep his promise. He lifted a hand toward her. Hardly aware of moving, she leaned back and away from him. The expectancy in his eyes faltered as suddenly as it had gathered. His straight body sagged a little.

"You sleep on it, Coralie. I'll be around if you need me." He knew her better than she did herself, for she realized he was speaking for her, actually, making it easier for her and delaying the truth.

"Thank you, Wiley. I'll always remember that you asked me." She felt sad for him, because he was a good man. "I will —"

He left her before she could finish, before she could get out what she ought to make clear now, in finality; but his long strides were taking him out of earshot already, and it spun through her mind that her very words might be the identical ones she had spoken to Tom Adair, which seemed so long ago. She felt suddenly old.

Around her the early prairie darkness thickened like gossamer, bringing a sensation of loneliness. She was glad when she heard her father and Lenny coming back from the spring.

"Well —" Dockum began, looking wise.

"I'm not going to marry him, Papa."

Dockum frowned his surprise. "What? You've got too much pride, Coralie." A half-anger spurted into his speech. "You can't let a man dangle forever. You'll wait too long!"

"Papa!" Out of shaken hurt and sick anger and profound weariness, she was suddenly lashing back at him, both cruel and honest. "You want me to marry him so you can lean on him — don't you, Papa? That's why you're angry! That's what you really mean!" She saw the naked truth standing in his eyes, and then, realizing that Lenny heard, and biting her lips, her tears coming, she took Lenny's arm and hurried him to the wagon for bed.

CHAPTER 12

After pulling in early with a wagon load of green hides, they were stretching and pegging when Andy, facing east while he crouched over his work, paused and said, "Son-of-a-gun, looks like two white men afoot."

Keith saw two hatted figures on the wagon trail the outfit had made traveling upriver. He studied them curiously, yet with a detachment, and then pulled another limp bull's hide off the wagon. Dragging it, flesh side up, to an open place in a new drying row, he cut a slit in the neck part and commenced pegging, occasionally looking up. One of the white men was limping along. The pair halted and the lame man gave out a hallooing shout. Sam Massengale waved them in.

Keith dropped his mallet to watch. Seeing them, he experienced a stab of intrusion. Maybe it was their aimlessness. Something told him they weren't professional hunters put afoot by chance. No — just more of the motley debris filling up the country and spoiling it, even as the professionals were spoiling it. He thought of the word *scrabbling* as they hurried by the hide wagon, both walking sore-footed, and the moment he saw them up close he knew they were drifters. Goddamn drifters, and was astonished at the depth of his feeling, because runners were causing more changes than anybody.

"Food!" the first man called, demanding about it. "We need food! What's there to eat around here?" He moved in a slouch-shouldered trot. His brown beard struggled for growth on the bony ridges of his jaw and mouth. Hungry though he might be, he displayed a prying interest in the contents of the well-equipped camp. In short, he looked like any other drifter Keith had seen in Barr's Town. Nothing about him was distinguishable unless it was his sly-eyed covetousness.

As the second man hobbled in, Keith saw the reason for his up-and-down walk. One of his boot heels was missing. Burly and muscular, he was inches shorter than his companion. He seemed without a neck. His low, round head sat like a large ball on his squat, snowman's body. Dark whiskers formed a curly bush from ear to ear. A boldness simmered within the confines of the battered face, the nose broken crookedly, the punished ears warped.

Yet the man had some sense of conduct, because as Sam motioned them to the cook wagon, he scowled at the other and said, "Where's your manners — he's inviting us to eat?" And he explained to Sam: "Indians took our horses early yesterday. Cleaned us out. We hid in the brush. On our way to Barr's Town, wherever that is."

Sam nodded his sympathy, and the insight whipped across Keith that Sam was too generous for his own good, too prone to believe any hard-luck story.

"Barr's Town is south on the main trail," Sam said. "You're on the Middle Pease here. West of the trail."

"We took the first wagon road we come to, hopin' to find an outfit."

Sam might have been visiting with a back-home neighbor. "South Pease comes into the Middle Pease southwest of us. Place on it called Robber's Roost."

"We want to go to Barr's Town."

Shortly, the two were eating like winter wolves. Their only visible weapon was a holster revolver on the stout man, a Smith & Wesson Army, it looked to Keith. No one asked their names or where they had come from, and they supplied no information. Finished, the stout one got up wiping greasy hands on his shirt front. "What can we do to earn our meal?"

Keith could see that impressed Sam, who put them to chopping wood and piling it handy for Levi. When suppertime came, the two ate again at Sam's invitation. Later, he found a blanket for each man and they bedded down near the spring.

Andy and Keith lay awake under the big hide wagon. The stars were scattered like pieces of glittering silver. There was a faint sobbing in the cool wind off the prairie.

Andy rolled over on his side. "How do you size up our company?"

"Don't like 'em."

"I figure the short one is boss."

"That he is."

Following breakfast, the two showed no sign of going their way and again the same man offered to earn his keep. By this time Andy and Hub and Keith were making ready to pull out.

"Think you can skin a buffalo?" Sam asked the stout man.

"I can learn."

"You go with the boys. Your partner can help around camp today. Plenty to do."

Keith found the buffalo feeding between camp and the wallows, big and little bunches, hundreds of buffalo watering along the creek, which he now called Ranch Creek because it cut across the grass-rich flat, because the ridge he liked was near. Before eleven o'clock he had moved his sticks twice and killed all the crew could skin and haul in for the day. Southwest, he heard the occasional banging of Dockum's carbine and he considered riding by the camp, but decided it was too far out of the way today, when the skinners needed him.

After watching the hills for some minutes, he rode to the wagon. The newcomer watched while Andy showed him how to skin a cow. Most times Andy talked and joked while taking hides. Today he handled his knives in silence. When the drifter took part, his actions were more indifferent than awkward, more careless than unskillful.

In camp that evening after the meal, the short man placed a Jew's-harp between his teeth and twanged up a tolerable rendition of "Turkey in the Straw," after which Andy played his favorite,

"The Buffalo Skinners." Andy was in good form tonight, Keith thought. A young man's yearnings and searchings flowed through the harmonica's reedy notes. But the night didn't match the first one on the Sweet Water. Sam didn't sing or fetch the jug. The outfit sat around, smoking and listening, and Keith knew it was because of the drifters.

Together, then, Andy and the short man ran through "Little Brown Jug" and "The Old Chisholm Trail." And when Andy, alone, swung into the lively trail tune again, the burly newcomer unbuckled his gun belt and jumped up, flapping his elbows and joggling his head in time to the music, and flung himself into a shuffling, dust-raising, foot-slapping dance, which, if lacking grace, was rhythmic and clownishly performed, accompanied by roguish grimacing and rolling of the eyes.

Slowly Keith became aware that Andy, tiny glints of devilish amusement in his eyes, playing the time over and over, was also changing it and teasing with his music. When the dancer paused for breath, Andy played fast; when the dancer started in again, Andy let the music die, so the two of them were never together.

After several false starts, the drifter flicked Andy a look and went puffing to his seat. "Sonny," he said, breathing hard, a manifest distinctness in his voice, "you play right good."

Andy grinned back devilishly. "Want to do another dance? Maybe to 'Cotton-Eyed Joe'?"

"Guess not, sonny."

Andy was still sleeping when Keith awakened before daylight. He lingered on his bedroll, yawned and stretched, letting his senses take hold gradually, his sluggish mind resting on the thought that, after months of rising at this hour, one part of his being had become a dour taskmaster, refusing to permit his body another moment of ease. Hearing Levi and Sam stirring, he rose and pulled on his damp trousers and shirt, and stamped into his boots.

As he straightened up by the hide wagon, a subtle sound rustled the stillness, as much sensed as heard. A vague impression of distant movement. He turned, unsure of the source, and swung back again. There he caught it once more, a stirring from somewhere across the prairie southwest of camp, a feeling coming to him of vast heavy motion, of living things.

Light was spreading across the eastern sky, the streaky grayness fading, a pinkish hue coming through.

Now a faint bawling. A muffled bellowing. He stepped to the edge of camp. Hub and Sam were up watching. It was still too dark to see far.

The darkness retreated and dazzling streamers of light struck across the camp, peeling off the gray patches, and Keith glimpsed a dark blur on the prairie, passing sluggishly less than a mile from camp.

"By God — they've drifted back," Hub murmured.

Not merely a big bunch, Keith saw as the strengthening sun stripped away the murk, but all the eye could take in. To him the buffalo seemed to be flowing out of the southwest as a dark, broad river, the hundreds in front forced by the pressure of the thousands behind them.

There was a rush for rifles, and Sam cautioning, "Go down a ways, boys. There's enough stink in camp as it is."

Keith and Sam, taking turns, killed until noon, the shaggies indifferent, bent on their blind, stolid march, their nearsighted eyes fixed north

When Keith quit shooting to help the skinners, it was with a sense of excess, of too much. He felt more than a physical tedium as he took a straight-bladed knife from his belt.

Before supper, while the drifters were at the spring, Sam drew the crew together. "Looks like this will go on for days. Never saw the like of buffalo, even in Kansas. We need more skinners. What you boys think about those two?"

"I'd as soon make out as we are," Hub said.

"They're not interested in work," Keith seconded. Andy didn't give his opinion, but his expression said he sided with Hub and Keith

"I don't mean bring 'em into the outfit," Sam said. "I mean pay 'em two-bits a hide. Just wages — wages and furnish grub. That's all."

Sam's sturdy shoulders hung in a pronounced stoop. His blue eyes looked tired, in them the unmasked desire to wind up the hunting and return to Missouri, the sooner the better.

"Guess we could try 'em a day or two," Hub gave in.

"That short one worked harder today than yesterday," Andy said. "But that tall one — all he does is grumble."

Sam waited for Keith, who was thinking the issue wasn't worth an argument in a tired outfit, that the drifters would soon wear out their welcome, if they hadn't already.

"They'll hang around as long as we feed 'em," Keith said. "But it's your outfit, Sam."

Sam's eyes bared his hurry, his impatience. "If they don't pan out, nothing is lost." He was forcing the matter; that also showed.

He brought up the proposition when the two came in to eat. The short one, somewhat surprised, shook his head in agreement and a coldness curved up one side of his mouth. "Might give 'er a try. What's the pay?"

"Two-bits a hide and all you can eat."

"All right."

"We'll tally up each evening. How'll I put you down in my memorandum book?"

"Ah" — he hesitated but a moment — "I'm Parker. He's Goss."

On the second afternoon after the hiring, Keith rode back to the light wagon and tied his horse, the killing over for the day. The herd had shifted course a couple of miles to the west, still a dark-brown mass, grazing, drifting, wallowing, plodding, still in the blind, northward movement, earthen lumps which fell stolidly at the boom of his Sharps. The June day was no hotter than usual, and yet it seemed so, the sun a polished ball lodged in the west, never going down, the heat haze like fine glass over the prairie.

Keith noticed Parker skinning a bull. He would pull on the hide and cut a while, then look up and off, here and there, his attention constantly shifting. Keith took a robe off a cow, thinking how poorly the mud-crusted hide and its shedded patches compared with the rich, dark smoothness of robes taken in late fall and winter. He pulled the hide to the wagon and threw it aboard; glancing across, he saw Parker working on the same bull.

Parker moved his hands a little faster when he saw Keith watching. He was whistling, a tuneless, between-the-teeth whistle, less harmony than hiss, that galled a tired man, and when Keith started out again, Parker stood up. He came forward, in the peculiar pumping walk caused by the missing heel, something in his ambling reminding Keith of Cal Dockum — in a different way, to be fair to Dockum. Because an undercurrent of violence ran through Parker — if that was his real name, Keith thought — a constant shifting and turning in the man, a sifting and assessing of what went on around him.

"Don't see how you boys keep at it," Parker remarked trying to sound friendly.

"It's work."

"I'm findin' that out. Here I figured huntin' was easy."

"Nothing easy about it."

"You boys got it pretty easy, though."

"How's that?" Keith asked, feeling a keen irritation.

"You're comfortable. You eat good. You sleep good."

"We earn it every day — everybody works," Keith reminded him and went over to the next carcass.

Not long before dark, as Keith and Andy were starting a new pegging row, Keith heard a creaking and the loose chattering and running rumble empty wagons make. And soon he spotted a train of wagons drawing for camp, traveling upriver — six mules pulling each lead wagon and its smaller trail wagon, and a rack fixed on each vehicle for hauling hides.

Mike Cassidy waved from the passenger side of a light cook wagon, a long-barreled rifle across his lap. Looking stiff and hard-used, he stepped down to shake Sam's hand. His heavy brogue carried clearly:

"Better load up all your flints. We won't be back till the Indian scare blows over."

"Indians again?" Sam said and told him about the war party back in May. "Been quiet ever since."

"Well, the heathens are on the warpath again. Soldier boys out from Elliott an' Griffin, paradin' around, mostly findin' where the red devils been, not where they are. We'll go by a few more camps, then cross upriver some place."

Keith, remembering the Dockums and the hides they couldn't haul to market, got up and stepped across to shake hands with Cassidy. "There's a family upriver," Keith said, and added more specific directions. "The Dockums — Cal Dockum. He'll have a few hundred hides. Maybe he'll move in when he hears about the Indians."

"Dockum — Dockum," Cassidy repeated, marking the name in his mind. "I'll remember." And to Sam: "Might as well load till dark. Save time tomorrow."

"You bet."

Cassidy directed the first wagon to the nearest long stack of hides, and the loading began, while the Irishman and Sam tallied the count.

To Keith's surprise, Parker, after eyeing the scene, climbed up and took his cue from one of Cassidy's men, began helping stack the stiff robes which Keith and Andy were pitching upon the wagon frame. The floor of the wagon was crowded and Parker wasn't needed; evident as that was, he crowded in, easily tossing the fifty-pound bull hides on the stack, meanwhile hiss-whistling between his teeth or mouthing jocular remarks. Did Indians make Indian whisky? How long would it take a man to hoof into Barr's Town for Saturday night?

"Why'n't you ask Cassidy to put you on?" a freighter suggested. "We're a little short."

"Got me a job here," Parker said and grabbed another hide.

Andy, hearing, winked at Keith and grinned.

But Keith saw Parker, gawking and turning, intercept the by-play. He paused with the hide in his hands, the comical expression on his brawler's face altering, gone his role of jocular helper.

"What's wrong, sonny? Don't you like the way I peel off these stinkin' hides?"

Keith saw what Andy, still grinning, did not realize: Parker was actually angry, in a moment's flash swung toward violence.

"You couldn't peel an apple," Andy laughed back.

The easy-natured grin lingered on Andy's face when Parker charged toward him. Both Keith and Andy were standing on the long embankment of hides, the stacks butting end on end. Parker jumped on the nearest pile, worked down below the level of the wide wagon bed, and Keith, closer to Parker than Andy was, instinctively shot out a delaying arm.

Parker pawed it off. Keith grabbed his shoulder and saw the skinner whirl on him, his body low. They clinched, taking quick, tromping steps on the shifting footing, each straining to use the other as a prop to keep from falling. Keith felt his churning left boot find no bottom; then he and Parker, grappling, tumbled over the edge.

Keith struck on his left side in the short grass, and felt Parker scramble free. Keith rolled to his feet to find Parker charging in, his eyes glittering. Before Keith could gain his balance he felt himself hammered and bulled against the side of the hide stack. He struck out, two blows caught Parker's face. Parker just shook his head. His battered mouth crooked into a relishing grin. He sprang into a squatting stance and cocked his scarred fists, sliding inside, skillfully, again maneuvering to pin Keith against the stack. Keith's head rang. He sank his fists into Parker's belly. It was like hitting a sack of tamped sand. Parker kept wading in, punching as he came. Keith kept meeting him, landing blows and taking some in return.

A figure, arms prying powerfully, sprang between them and Keith heard Sam Massengale's dumfounded voice shouting, "What the hell's goin' on?"

Keith, dragging in wind, said nothing. He was too busy glaring at Parker, watching the wildness burn out in Parker's eyes, left furious by the man's unpredictable nature.

The skinner dusted off his pants. He looked around for his hat, found it, and slapped it against his leg, the makings of a grin working into his bruised face. "Guess I flew off the handle," he said, breathing fast. "My fault." Which was the very last reply Keith had expected to hear.

"Go help with the pegging," Sam ordered.

Parker left at once, looking neither at Keith nor Andy as he turned. It filled Keith's mind that he had never seen a man cool off quite so fast.

In the morning, when all the flints had been loaded and boomed down with ropes, Sam and Cassidy walked to one side and figured in their memorandum books, their voices a just-audible murmur. Cassidy drew greenbacks from a wide moneybelt and counted out a stack to Sam. They shook hands; afterward, Sam, the greenbacks bunched in his left hand, tramped to the gear wagon and disappeared inside. When he came back, he said, "Mike, can you boys spare some primers?"

"Will a hundred or so help?"

"Now," Sam replied, as though thinking possibly he had imposed, "that might short you if you run into Indians. We can make it for a while, you bet. Be going into Barr's Town in a few days, anyway."

"You're welcome, now."

"I know. But we're all right."

Nodding his head, the Irishman climbed heavily to his place on the wooden seat and the long string of wagons swung upriver.

The outfit worked through a little bunch of shaggies west of camp, and by ten o'clock Keith was left with nothing to shoot. He rode farther out, in anticipation of locating game within a few miles. But as quietly and strangely as they had appeared by the thousands migrating past camp, the buffalo had vanished once again.

He traveled past Ranch Creek and the wallows and across the wide flat where he had surfeited himself with killing. The air still smelled heavy through here, and the mossy black hair still clung to the grotesque heads lying out there, looking incongruously large on the sun-blackened, varmint-torn carcasses.

He rode beyond the flat and there he found the buffalo again, great masses of solemn, doomed creatures, filing northward through a passageway in the string of green hills. Far away to the southwest the big-caliber rifles of other outfits reached him like battle sounds on the wind.

Watching the shaggies drifting by, following their leaders, hearing the booming reports, he was conscious of the gnaw and unease of something, and knew it was the camp. Rather, the drifters. Camp wasn't the same with those two around; they were tolerated because the crew was too busy. Past time, he decided, to send them on to leech off another outfit.

That resolve stayed with him as he started back. He recrossed the littered flat and rode by the first wallows, and where the old tracks of Andy's light wagon curved on downriver, Keith turned off, holding the gelding southwest, his mind drawing on Coralie Dockum. Coming to the wide traces of Cassidy's heavy hide wagons, he followed them toward the Dockum camp.

He could see buffalo scattered in here, probably fresh from watering in the river. Cows and calves, and a few bulls growing fat and restless, for the rutting season was close.

Keith turned at the sound of voices. Along the foot of the hill, through the brush, came Coralie and the boy. She wore no sunbonnet. She carried the shotgun and Lenny swung a tin pail. She stopped as Keith angled across to them.

"Mr. Cassidy took all the hides," she said. "All but the split ones. Even so, I think he took some not so good, too. I want to thank you."

"Your camp was on his way. Perhaps now you will go to the settlements?"

"Papa won't. He's made some money. He and Wiley went out right after Mr. Cassidy left." He saw the feeling go across her face, the enduring that was so akin to resignation, and which he wished to change.

"Money's the only reason for a man to take hides," he said; saying that, he found a truth within himself: he wanted to be done with hunting.

Her glance went over him, back and forth. "Yet you stay in it," she reminded him. "Is it the music you're after?"

He smiled at her. "I like my crew." He got down to walk with her. "If Wiley's out that means he's staying."

"I don't know. Why would he stay?"

"You."

Her head tilted up in her habitual indication of defense. "Wiley's a good man," she said soberly. "If he leaves, we all go. He does most of the hard work."

"Wiley won't leave unless you do."

"No — I guess not."

He was thoughtful. "Where would you go?"

"I guess we'd just drift, like always."

He dropped the matter. Lenny ran ahead with the pail, and Coralie said, "He's excited about finding red sand plums. I've promised to make

222

some plum butter."

Walking beside her, he was aware once more of her same gray dress and same heavy shoes. She was taller than he had realized; she came to his shoulder. She moved with the even steps of one accustomed to walking a great deal. He had the impression that she liked to walk for the freedom it gave her. The hot wind off the prairie brought him the warmly pleasant scent of her body, and of soap and scrubbed clothing dried in sunlight, and the very faint scent of her long, swept-back hair — a faintness of wind and sun and sweet grass and a clean woman, lovely in her plainness, unknowing she was.

They reached the wagon in the mesquite grove and Coralie, after carefully putting the shotgun inside, offered Keith a drink of water. Seeing the bucket was low, he walked to the spring and filled it. Returning, he noticed more buffalo grazing up from the river, some close to the mesquites on the other side of camp. He had his drink and mounted, thinking to drift the buffalo away from camp.

Just then he heard Coralie call Lenny. The boy didn't answer and Coralie, looking and calling, followed to Keith's left. Through the light greenery of the foliage Keith saw movement. It was Lenny, staring at something in the mesquites.

"There he is," Keith said.

"Lenny," Coralie called in an even voice. "Come back."

The boy stood as if hypnotized, drawn in fascination.

Keith felt no alarm until he saw the stir of a small, tow-colored shape. A late spring calf, no hump yet, body fuzzy and scrawny, and Lenny was going to play with it. Now the frisky calf darted off on sturdy legs. Lenny pursued and disappeared, deeper in the mesquites. Walking his horse faster, Keith saw the calf bounding into an open place and Lenny close behind.

At the same time Keith heard Coralie's gasp and he saw the humped wedge of the buffalo mother, head down, coming to protect her baby.

Keith drew and cocked the Sharps. The calf retreated to its mother's side. Lenny froze.

"Stand still," Keith called softly, knowing that if the boy ran the cow would charge, yet hoping she would lead her calf out to the prairie.

Keith slid from the saddle, ever watching the cow. She was still advancing. He slanted the Sharps. She stiffened her stumpy tail and uttered a throaty bellow and lowered her head, ready to charge.

He aimed behind her shoulderblade and fired. The report was thunderous. The cow threw up her shaggy head with a lurching shock; by the time Keith had thumbed in another shell she was on the ground kicking.

Running up, Coralie grabbed Lenny and pulled him back, the fear in her face diminishing when she saw the calf nuzzling its thrashing mother.

"Take Lenny back to the wagon," Keith said.

She didn't understand his urgency until she saw his fixed grimness on the calf; then she whisked Lenny away, her face in strain.

Keith caught his lower lip between his teeth, listening to Coralie's fading steps, putting off what he felt he had to do. Quickly, he shot the calf and rode to the wagon for a rope.

"Did you have to do that, too?" she demanded.

"Better than letting wolves or coyotes drag him down, killing him a little at a time."

He dragged the cow behind a rise, far enough out where the carcass wouldn't smell up the camp, and then the calf. He skinned the cow and cut out the tongue and the hump and the hams, and bagged them in the hide.

Riding back, he saw Coralie leave Lenny at the wagon and come out to meet him. She searched for something to say and made an apologetic motion with her right hand, her eyes slowly meeting his. "You had to do it — I know. It's just so cruel and wasteful — all this." She gestured about her.

"It is," he agreed and ran a wondering eye over her, moved by a realization of onrushing time. "In a day or two I'll be going into Barr's Town. I will take you and Lenny, if you want to go. I will help you find a place to live. I'll see that you have means of support as long as you need it."

Her lips opened in astonishment. She was speechless.

"Be a good town there in a few years," he said. "The wild crowd will fade out with the buffalo.

Families will move in. That means a school, some decent stores. Be a church or two."

"I'd have to find work," she said, frowning over it. She looked up suddenly. "What if I couldn't? What then? How could I repay you?" She paused. Her eyes, her sudden coloring betrayed her.

"You'd owe me nothing."

She shook her head. "I can't go — I couldn't do that," she said, confused, her momentary confidence broken. She was, he saw, falling back into old ways, the damnable putting up with.

"You can't stay here much longer," he said. "It's not safe. It never has been."

He could see her hardening against his words. "I won't leave Papa."

"Even though Cassidy told him about the Indians?"

She turned away, which was answer enough. Her face was rigid as she walked to the wagon. He rode after her and unloaded the meat. Crossing back to his horse on impulse, he unsheathed the .44 Henry rifle, took a belt of cartridges from a saddlebag, and laid them on the rough table, just now realizing how few times he had fired the rifle in buffalo country.

"I'll have to show you how to load and fire it," he said. When she stood beside him he continued: "It will shoot fifteen times without reloading — sixteen with one shot in the chamber." Next he unloaded the rifle and demonstrated how to work the lever action, and how to fill the tubular magazine under the barrel, poking the cartridges in at the muzzle end, and how to adjust the sights. Finished, he made her go through the loading steps, and was encouraged to see that she wasn't afraid of the rifle.

"It's yours," he said as she finished.

She was startled. He saw the will of her refusal pulling at her lips; but he saw as well that she realized he meant it and she was touched. She laid the rifle across the table. She stood there uncertainly, only half looking at him.

There was an appealing quality about her which he had never quite noticed in another woman — a difference, an elusiveness, which he saw fully in her rather high-boned face and deep hazel eyes, and which smoothed her cheeks and left her lips full and softly turned, almost maternal, and then he saw it no longer.

He led his horse out a way. She followed him

"Coralie," he said, giving her a long look, "a man has to fight for happiness. So does a woman." He was looking directly down into her eyes. She did not move away from him. Drawing toward her, he saw her begin to lift her lips to him and he saw her eyes closing. But before he could touch her, she opened her eyes and turned her head from him. He kept on, bending closer. This time she stepped clear.

"You didn't mean it anyway," she said.

"How would you know until I'd kissed you?"

"You're used to women who live in town. I just happen to be the only woman on the Middle

Pease." That wasn't all. He was seeing again her rooted weariness and submission to her surroundings.

He swung up. He was reining to go when the unexpectedness of her voice came to him. "Will you be back?"

"Soon as I can."

Keith's mind was on the drifters when he rode into camp. Seeing them lounging around the cook wagon, talking to Levi while he fixed supper, Parker always the louder of the pair, Keith remembered what his father had said once: It was wiser to let a man go in the bright of morning. That way he left in daylight and had time to look for another job. If he worked on a farm, particularly, he wasn't around that night to indulge his temper on the owner.

Keith unsaddled and picketed, and when he told Sam where he had found buffalo, the hunter narrowed his eyes and pulled on the lobe of an ear, pondering. "That's a long way to take a wagon every day. Maybe it's time to move camp again."

The matter of the drifters rushed to Keith's tongue, but at that moment he heard Levi's hoarse summons to supper. Sam moved away. Keith saw Parker and Goss, nearest the fire, start loading their tin plates. Like wolves, Keith thought, hunkered around a fresh buffalo carcass. It wasn't that he resented the food they ate; it was their damned pushing-in manner, as if they owned the outfit. He was going to iron everything out with Sam after supper. He would offer to tell the drifters to pack, and likely then he and Parker would fight again, and that would be all right, too.

"We're down on primers more than I thought," Sam said, when the crew was settled around eating. He chewed reflectively. "And Levi's down to a week's supply of flour. Keith, how would you and Andy like to hit for town tomorrow?"

"Maybe Hub wants to go?"

"I been to Barr's Town," Hub spoke up sourly. "Once is enough. I'd rather smell buffalo stink. It's cleaner."

"All right," Keith said, though not wishing to, and he caught Andy's eagerness.

Parker laid down his plate. He swabbed half a biscuit around in buffalo gravy and plopped it in his mouth, chomped and swallowed, afterward making sucking sounds between his yellow teeth, rolling his tongue around and pushing out his furred cheeks.

"Goss and me — we're pullin' out, too," he said. "Figured we'd look over that Robber's Roost place before we went on to Barr's Town."

"You'll find anything you're lookin' for there," Hub predicted, openly glad they were leaving.

Parker laughed. "We're better at cards than skinnin' stinkers. How do you get there?"

"Just follow upriver to where the South Pease comes in," Sam said.

Parker was donning his friendly air. "Reckon

we could talk or trade you out of something to ride?"

Keith could read Sam's natural disposition to help, and just as he feared Sam would let them have a mule or a horse, the hunter, though nodding sympathetically, said, "We can't spare any stock, boys. Wish we could. I'll figure up tonight what you have coming."

"Won't be much, will it?" Parker's chuckle was self-ridiculing. "We ain't cut out for skinners. Just the same, we're much obliged to you."

When the pair left for bed, Parker going off whistling, Keith could not help but feel a certain contradiction. For Parker wasn't an agreeable man. He was a crowder and trampler, one who bulled his way in. Yet everytime Keith had expected him to cause trouble, Parker had backed off. It didn't fit the man.

CHAPTER 13

Riding downriver after daybreak to pick up the main trail south, Keith thought of the drifters, who would be hoofing to Robber's Roost by now. He didn't like leaving after what Cassidy had said about a general Indian scare, and his mind wavered between concern for the camp and the Dockums, remote from all help. Yet the trip to Barr's Town had to be made. A man could live on buffalo meat, but the primers, or caps as some older men called them, were as life itself. Gradually, as the sun shone through and the green country fanned out before him, motionless and peaceful, and with Andy's cheerful chatter in his ears when he rode by the light trail wagon, he began to enjoy the day.

At the river crossing he found the unshod tracks of Indian ponies — old tracks, not many.

Andy kept the mules fast-stepping. By evening Keith estimated they had covered twice the distance compared with when they had hauled hides back in April. They camped off the trail, backs to a creek, hobbled and close-picketed the stock. Lying on his bedroll, Keith considered the empty country through which they had passed. He was beginning to suspect this part of the buffalo range was already gunned out, which left him a sense of loss and violation he might not have felt six months ago. He would never forget riding through here last spring with Andy and Hub, and the banter that passed back and forth on the way to town, and everywhere he looked the earth seeming to move with dark-brown columns of buffalo. Once again his mind turned drowsily to the camp and the Dockums. For a mere instant, no longer, he realized, he had thought she was coming with him, she and Lenny. She had too much loyalty. She was also afraid.

They rattled into Barr's Town around one o'clock the next afternoon. To Keith's eyes, the street looked more crowded than last spring. More wagons, more cowboys, more families, more hunters and skinners and more drunks. Two new stores showed painted fronts. The Buffalo Bull was going full blast. A knot of cavalry troopers loafed outside the Texas House. Looking up and down the street, Keith knew he wouldn't feel right killing the rest of the afternoon when he and Andy could be well started up the trail by dark.

Keith halted. "Let's load up now. I think we'd better start back right after we grain and rest the team." He saw Andy's surprise, his letdown and disappointment, and Keith understanding, said, "Be plenty of time to look around. We needn't start for a few hours yet."

"Why can't we stay over?"

"We can make good time before we camp tonight."

Andy set his jaw. "What's a few more hours?"

"Plenty — if we're needed back at camp."

"Keith, I'm stayin' longer!" There was the ring of will in Andy's voice, not merely the whim of a boy hungry for a good time.

Keith eyed him. A question crossed his mind: Was it the Barr woman? He said nothing more for the moment and rode on to the general store. Andy, his face shaped in discontent, drove in front and backed the wagon in so it could be loaded from the rear.

Keith tied up and watched Andy. Like Sam said, Andy was headstrong, but no more certainly than most boys his age, no more than Keith had been. Keith felt a wave of understanding. Andy was greatly likable. He had become like a younger brother. Like Sam, Andy knew nothing but toil. Now, come to town, he longed to soak up some fun, and Keith was more inclined to oblige him than he let on. But when Keith remembered the camp, shorthanded to three men, and Levi so broken down he could hardly handle a weapon, he knew they must make tracks.

Now Andy sat on the wagon seat, glumly watching the mill of traffic on the wide street, the muscles in one corner of his mouth jerking.

"Come on, Andy," Keith said, walking out.

Andy did not move and Keith said no word. Then, taking his time, Andy looped the reins around the brake handle and stepped down over the front wheel; but when Keith saw his face he knew that Andy hadn't changed his mind. Inside, Keith ordered supplies while Andy looked around. When the wagon was loaded, Keith rode across the street to the hide yard, Andy driving the team behind him.

The man in charge recognized Keith. "Cassidy been up your way?"

"He loaded on our hides three days ago," Keith told him. "Said he was going on up the Middle Pease."

Andy went quietly about taking care of the mules. When the stock was watered and fed, Keith said, "Let's eat."

The fare proved neither better nor worse than Keith remembered, and the same faceless men in their earth-colored clothes seemed to wolf their greasy food and wait in line. Outside, Andy said, "Think I'll look around."

"I'll be at the wagon."

Keith found a barbershop. After sitting in line on a bench for the better part of an hour, he got a shave and a short haircut. Coming out, he felt a coolness about his face, neck and ears; then, his back against the flimsy board front, he watched for Andy and did not see him in the milling crowd. In that restlessness out there, Keith could detect changes. Although the buffalo trade was at its peak, he recognized the signs of a coming cowtown growing stronger, discernible in the rows of saddled horses and the dominant drawl of riders' voices.

He strolled on and was passing one of the new stores when he happened to notice the shoes in the window. He held up, his interest caught on a black, low-heeled pair with straps that buttoned across the instep.

He turned in immediately, warmed by an impulse. A man and woman ran the place. She left him bent over a ledger, a reluctance stiffening her pointed features as she stirred herself to wait on Keith. A dissatisfied woman by the looks of her peevish eyes and fussy mouth, a woman possibly given to nursing notions of faded elegance. When Keith inquired about the shoes, a question of propriety took shape in her long face.

"Do you know the size?" she asked in a lofty tone.

Keith shook his head negatively.

"Then how can you purchase the proper size?"

"I'll have to guess at it," he said. To the best of his knowledge, Coralie Dockum had a slender foot; that was all he could surmise from the bulky shoes she wore.

"If this is for one of those girls up the street," the woman informed him, disapproval and superiority like vinegar in her crisp voice, "she should know the size."

"It isn't."

And so, after examining several pairs, he made a guess and left with the box under his arms. Going to the general store, he bought hard candy for Lenny and began looking for other small gifts for the crew.

Andy entered the Buffalo Bull, working his way against the outward push of men, and reached the bar after some moments. He caught the bartender's attention. "When's Miss Thompson on?"

"She was just on. Can't you tell with the crowd leavin'?"

Andy's boots sounded on the wooden walk before he realized he had no place to go, and he regretted then leaving Keith in such rashness. The town held less attraction for him now. Disappointed, he strolled to the hide yard and visited with the man in the office; tiring of that he went to the wagon, planning to stretch out for a catnap. He climbed up and glanced back, hoping to see Keith striding after him, and when he did he saw, instead, a woman coming across the street, a man on each side of her.

A knowing froze Andy. Just seeing her again flung a feeling of lightness through him. She walked gracefully. Like a lady, he thought.

He watched them cross the street and disappear among the trees in front of the house, which lay southeast of the hide yard. All he could see of the house was the slanting roof, its new-lumber yellow beginning to turn gray. Behind the house the trees thinned, and he saw a pole corral which enclosed a low shed.

For want of something to do, he sat on the wagon seat, idly dividing his interest between the noisy street and the house. Soon a man left the trees, going back toward the Buffalo Bull. Andy, recalling that night, could imagine the other bodyguard on the porch.

He tensed, alert, when a figure left the rear of

the house — a woman. She was walking toward the pole corral. She lifted a bar and went inside to the shed; there he lost sight of her. In a couple of minutes she led a saddled horse from the corral. She mounted and rode east, easing the horse away. No one followed her.

Her careful movements brought upon him that time on the Sweet Water, when A. B. Barr had watched her like a hawk. Andy knew little or nothing about women, but he told himself that he recognized fear when he saw it.

Excitement piled through him. His mind was spinning. Before many moments he was down out of the wagon and swiftly saddling Keith's gelding and riding out of the hide yard and along the street to the yard's end, and turning east, thereby placing the house to his right.

Instinct warned him not to run the horse past the house. He heeled the gelding to a running walk, riding on east, past the low, pole fence of the yard, where dark humps of stacked hides covered an acre or more.

At last, when he turned south for the river, the house was out of sight behind the lip of a rounded hill rising above the river valley. He rode to the stream and halted, gazing up and down. He did not see her. He took off upriver in a lope. In his hurry, he tore through brush that clutched at his stirrups and pants legs; yet, as he broke free of it, he found a well-used trail angling down to the river and following it.

He rode faster, weaving the horse as the trail

weaved. At the moment he followed a bend which led to the low, sandy bank.

Rods ahead a rider was letting a handsome bay drink. A woman rider. She saw Andy simultaneously, for she jerked the bay's head up and flung about in the side saddle. At the same time Andy saw the gleam of her revolver.

He checked his horse, feeling intrusive and awkward and lost for any words. He touched his hat brim, an unfinished gesture. Her eyes, cool and direct, were as dark pools. There was a self-reliance about her. He realized, furthermore, that she didn't recognize him, and that took him down another notch. But he remembered his manners and he removed his hat and said, with some apprehension, "Miss Tess — it's Andy Kinkade."

She regarded him for what seemed an interminable pause to Andy, without hint that she remembered; meanwhile, she pointed the handgun unhesitatingly upon him.

At once she gave a toss of her head, drawing Andy's eyes to the small hat she wore and the green feather slanting from it like a plume; and she seemed to cast off her inscrutable mask as Andy saw the partial smile like a light on her pale face. "You —" she said and tucked the revolver in a holster on the saddle. "You again. We seem bound to meet."

"I didn't mean to scare you," he said, all apology.

"You didn't — but you gave me a start. I

thought you were one of the bunch that hangs around the Buffalo Bull." She was not amused. "I've been followed before. Usually someone rides with me."

He sensed a meaning, transparent in her face: today she had slipped away.

She rode back to the trail. The light found the dark coils of her hair, and he thought of sun catching the gloss on a crow's wing, for he'd never seen hair so sheeny black.

"You didn't just happen along this way, did you?" She wasn't reprimanding him; rather, she was curious.

He gave her a sudden smile. "I was in the hide yard when you crossed the street. I saw you ride off. I followed you."

"You shouldn't have. I hope you know that?"

She baffled him. Her voice said one thing and her smoky eyes another. Still, he didn't think she was angry.

"And you shouldn't ride alone," he said. "Don't you know about the Indian scare?"

"Scare?" Her lips were wry. "Indians are the last people to look out for around town."

"Indians could slip up the river," he countered, and in another breath he was telling her about the war party attacking the camp on the Middle Pease.

She listened gravely, with a manner that made him feel what he said was important.

"Since you're so concerned about Indians," she said, "you may escort me a way."

She turned the bay, but Andy saw her scout her eyes around before she let her mount spring ahead. Andy followed, feeling the wish to please her. For a while he rode behind her. When the trail widened, he moved up beside her. Whenever the trail ran through an open stretch, he saw her take the scouting look. He guessed they had covered a mile when, sharply, she reined off the trail and rode west between the trackless hills, then north behind another hill and into a mesquite draw. At the head of the draw a spring seeped into an oval pool which sparkled with gravel and red clay.

She dismounted before Andy could hand her down. She tied up and went avidly to the pool, feasting her eyes over it and onward to the glistening smear of the tiny spring; and when she looked up, gazing all around, Andy saw the kindling pleasure on her face. He tied up and stood still, his nerves tingling at the sight of her.

"I ride out here whenever I can," she told him, taking another turn-around look. "It's quiet, so restful. Barr's Town is noisy day and night."

He saw a change come over her. Unlike on the river trail, she seemed nervous and high-strung. And young as he was, he saw through to her loneliness. Only a lonely person would take long rides and come here, away from everybody. From the way she kept watching the hills, he knew again that she lived in some kind of fear or dread, and within himself he felt the determination to drive away that fear, to protect her.

"Don't you be afraid," he said, going over to her, talking as he might to any defenseless person.

"Aren't all people afraid of something?" she said, her head turned away as she spoke.

"Maybe so," he replied vaguely.

She faced him, her expression softening in interest. "What are you afraid of, Andy?"

It was his name, her saying it, that opened him up. Suddenly he was ready to tell her anything. "Nothin' bothers me much. Maybe I'm afraid of things and just don't know it. Main thing . . . I just want to grow up. Be a man — be treated like a man."

"I think you're already a man."

She was studying him through tolerant, perceptive eyes. Just talking to her and being close to her gave him a strange and wonderful sensation.

"Nobody else seems to think so," he said.

"I know you're a man, Andy."

His whole being flamed up. Deep down he was trembling. He had to drag the words up from his throat, though they seemed to spill out of him without thought. "Miss Tess — if you think I'm a man — then I'm man enough to help you. I can use a gun — I —" It crashed upon him that he was blurting and stumbling like a schoolboy. He choked on the rest, in a torment of shamed confusion. Worst of all, the self-reproof flashed through him, she, being older and wiser and a woman to boot, would laugh at him for the young fool he knew he was.

241

Overcome, he couldn't look at her. He couldn't see her clearly, anyway, because of the mist across his eyes. He wasn't expecting her touch on his arm. When he raised his head, the mist was gone and she was saying, "Andy, I don't know when anybody's said anything that honest and kind to me."

She seemed to be staring through him and beyond him. Very suddenly, as his sister might, she put her face against his and he felt her light kiss on his cheek; and when she drew back he held her instinctively, his hands touching her arms, yet feeling her lightness, dragging in the marvelous fragrance of her. For a single stroke of time he thought he felt her body give to his; in another she was straining to pull free, her face contorted. Everything seemed unreal to Andy, and the feel of her was like velvet. He kissed her on the mouth, a rough kiss, not knowing whether she met his lips or not. Before he could again, she wrenched free, and he knew, ashamed, that he had ruined himself in her eyes.

"Andy," she said firmly, her face growing hard, "I shouldn't have done that. You forget that it ever happened, understand? I was just thanking you . . . for being honest That's all it was."

She threw a searching look around; by the time she reached her horse, she had regained her control. Andy helped her mount, then stepped back.

"Miss Tess, I ought to feel sorry but I don't. I know how that sounds, but I'm not sorry."

He swung to ride beside her, but her upraised

hand stopped him. "I will go back alone," she said. "You wait a while. Circle around and ride into town from the north."

He reined the gelding in front of hers. "I'll be comin' back to Barr's Town — back to help you."

Her even features settled within their careful boundary, forming the enigmatic look he now knew so well. Her voice, flat and toneless, was empty of all feeling:

"Don't come back. Don't try to see me. Don't follow me again." Still, he thought, her face denied what she was saying.

She let the bay have its proud head. It sprang away, the muscles rippling under the blood-red hide, out of sight around the hill in a dozen lunging strides.

Andy heard the drumfire of the shod hoofs rise and hold, a running roll toward the river; suddenly the beat lessened and faded altogether.

He had never felt more alone. This was the most painful moment of his life, and the most unsure. He almost questioned his senses: the little spring unusually bright, the trees unusually green, the nook in the hills more imagined than real and as still as a cave. About. him, close, faint, he could smell the fragrance of her, but she was gone.

Miserable and shaken, he rode down between the hills and to the river and began a circling ride to the north, paying cursory attention to objects ahead of him. Otherwise, he realized suddenly, he could have avoided the rider he saw come to the point of a rise and halt to observe him.

Andy had no choice but hold to his course. The way he was traveling he would pass within fifty yards of the watcher.

He was startled to see the horseman spurring toward him. Andy snaked the Sharps free and cocked the hammer; when the rider held up a staying hand, Andy lowered the rifle.

The rider came on fast. He was only yards away when he choked in his horse. Andy saw the eyes in the watcher's deeply pitted face rake over him with a memorizing look and then he galloped south. The pitted face lodged in Andy's mind as he rode on, but he couldn't place it.

He was turning into the street north of the hide yard when he remembered. He'd seen the man that night in town after he was slugged and robbed and left on the street; in the flare of the match. One of Tess Thompson's bodyguards. She had called him Quinn.

It was after four o'clock when Keith, his packages in a sack, left the general store. A cavalryman stood on the porch of the hide-yard office. Keith saw Cassidy's man speak to him and nod toward Keith crossing the street. A sun-blistered young officer, stiffly courteous, his blond mustache a mere trace, the once bright stripes down the seams of his light blue breeches faded to a pale yellow, was waiting for Keith.

"I'm Lieutenant Nolan," he said, "4th Cavalry, Fort Elliott. He offered his hand and Keith gave his name. "I understand your outfit is hunting up north of here?" the lieutenant asked.

"On the Middle Pease."

"Possibly you can help. Besides Black Horse's Comanches, we're looking for two deserters named Cook and Fisher."

Keith's mind swung back like a sharp point, tapping out his premonition. He scowled. He started to speak, but his thought hung, unsaid, at Andy's surprising appearance on Keith's gelding, which looked hard-used.

"Andy," Keith said irritably, his annoyance spinning out, "better get down and listen to this."

Andy dismounted, an oddly guilty quietness upon him. He seemed lost in thought.

"I have detailed descriptions of the deserters," Nolan was saying. He took a paper from his blouse and began reading, and Keith was certain before he had finished. Keith's body was drawing together in apprehension. Andy, who had thrown off his preoccupation, was nervously rubbing his chin.

"Two men like those stayed at our camp a while," Keith said, deciding that Cook's description fit Parker exactly. "Gave their names as Parker and Goss."

"Where did they go?"

"Said they were going to Robber's Roost — on the South Pease, though that's not saying they did."

"Likely not. And when did they pull out?"

"The morning we did," Keith said, his voice picking up a new dread. "That was yesterday."

Nolan's young eyes showed an older patience seasoned with frustration. "A detachment came in from there only this morning. We can't send even a small detail back out there for three or four days, depending on the Indian outbreak around here. I have a company with Indian scouts northeast of here now. The idea is to intercept any raiding parties dashing out of the Territory. Meanwhile, every tough in this section of Texas comes to Barr's Town sooner or later. Probably that's our best bet." He folded the paper and put it away. "I suggest that you men take precautions for other than Indians. Cook and Fisher broke out of the guardhouse at Fort Elliott and killed a noncom. On the Prairie Dog Fork they murdered two hunters and took their rifles. Good luck."

Nolan left them, going stiff-legged across the street for the Texas House.

Keith's annoyance with Andy was long since forgotten. He looked at Andy and saw the image of his own mounting concern. Suddenly, of the same mind, they rushed to hitch up the mules.

CHAPTER 14

In the glow of the high moon the ruts of the broad trail were as sallow bands of light leading them northward. After these hours of unbroken traveling, Keith could tell the tough mules were tiring. He rode off the trail and he and Andy dipped water from the barrel for the team, fed the hungry animals corn and stationed them on picket ropes to graze, and cooked a quick meal and lay down by the wagon to rest.

Keith didn't know what to think. Parker and Goss or Cook and Fisher were to have left camp right after Keith and Andy had, early that morning. But if they were the deserters, where were their rifles, the ones they had taken from the murdered hunters? Like the lieutenant said, Indians were the main worry. More than likely the drifters were in Robber's Roost at this moment, snoring by another man's campfire, their bellies full of another man's meat and biscuits.

In less than an hour they were in motion again. Breaking daylight revealed the rolling country south of the Middle Pease. Still no buffalo — none anywhere. And that emptiness nagged at Keith and darkened his worry.

In the forenoon, coming up against the grade toward the camp, the mules stepping faster as they neared home, Keith saw in the distance everything where it should be — first the big

Shuttler hide wagon, next the gear wagon, then Levi's cook wagon — and he felt an unfurling relief.

As he rode faster and objects became truer, he seemed to be observing the camp through the eye of an ongoing telescope. The wagons were all right, not burned, which meant no Indians about — but part of the familiar scene was missing.

Another instant and Keith understood what was wrong: the stock was gone, neither picketed beyond camp nor nearby. And suddenly his mind hunted for an excuse. He thought: Sam and Hub have taken them to the spring. But at this late hour? A more logical part of himself said no.

Keith loped the gelding faster. Andy was whipping the mules. standing up in the wagon to lash them faster.

They tore into camp and thudded and rattled to a dusty stop, the sounds of their coming tapering off, until Keith was conscious of the mules shaking their harness and stamping nervously. As if fighting his will and dreading what he would find, he forced himself to look, and the first object he saw on the ground was a man lying between the Shuttler and the gear wagon.

Keith did not remember dismounting. But he was on the ground, swearing softly and gazing down, breathing jerkily through his mouth.

Sam Massengale lay as if sleeping, head thrown back. One arm across his body. His right knee drawn up. Blood blackened his curly beard. His blue eyes were wide open and he was dead.

Keith's throat filled. He shut his jaw. He turned his head tortuously. His eyes found a second shape. It was Levi beside the still-smoldering campfire. *This morning,* Keith thought, *this morning.* With trancelike steps, Keith crossed over and looked, hoping to find Levi alive. He wasn't. Someone, Keith saw, had started a fire under the wagon as though to burn it; the fire had gone out.

Where was Hub?

Behind him, Keith heard a convulsive choking and broken crying. He whipped around and saw Andy sagged down, slamming his fist repeatedly into the hard-packed earth.

Powerless, Keith had a terribleness of loss that pressed harder and harder, blurring his eyes and freezing his brain and choking his lungs. A small voice inside him tried to whisper that nothing he saw could be real, that these friends great and good weren't past bringing back; but outside him all was stark and absolute.

A massively infuriating wrath shook him that Sam and Levi had lain so long uncovered. He lunged toward the gear wagon for blankets. His boot struck a tinny object, hurled it skittering. He picked up a black tin box, pried open and empty. Although he had never seen it before, he knew it was Sam's money box, kept in the gear wagon. He ran across and climbed inside and saw the exposed false bottom in the wagon bed. Snatching blankets, he hurried back and covered the bodies.

Andy was standing slumped over, his slim face ashen with shock, his eyes sightlessly on the ground. His eyes had a wildness when he turned, and Keith saw his first savage craving for revenge.

"Indians!" Andy burst out. " . damned stinkin' Indians!" He balled his fists and shuddered with rage.

"Somebody tried to burn the cook wagon," Keith said, straining to reconstruct what had happened. "Maybe that was the idea — make it look like Indians. But Indians would burn everything to the hubs — they'd take scalps." He showed Andy the tin box. "Indians wouldn't know where to find this."

Andy's eyes clawed over the box. "Parker and Goss — hell, yes! They knew. They saw Cassidy pay Sam — saw Sam take the money to the wagon."

"Parker's tracks — those funny heel marks — are all around the gear wagon. But we've got to find Hub first."

Andy rushed afoot to the south, his Sharps cocked. Keith rode north to begin his searching half circle. One conclusion tightened as he did so: Sam, trusting as he was, and Hub, especially bitter Hub, weren't men easy to catch off guard. But if Hub had been there where was he now?

He was swinging west when he heard Andy yell down by the spring. Keith got there as fast as the gelding could run.

Andy was holding Hub's head in his lap. Keith saw Hub move. By God, he *was* alive.

But when Keith knelt over Hub, he looked,

then looked away and back again and clamped his lips tighter. Hub's eyes shed a faint but stubborn recognition. His dark skin was gray. The hole in his chest opened and closed as he fought for breath.

Keith pressed his hand. "Sure, Hub. It's Keith."

"He says it happened early this morning." Andy's voice broke. "Parker and Goss — they hung around camp till yesterday. Pretended to leave. They had buffalo rifles hid out somewhere."

"The hunters' rifles," Keith nodded.

Andy bit his quivering lips and patted Hub's shoulder, while tears coursed down his cheeks. "Happened right after breakfast," he went on. "They shot Uncle Sam first — then Hub. He played dead. He heard 'em shoot Levi — saw 'em take the money. After they left, he crawled to the spring. That was the way it was, he said."

Yet, in Hub Stratton's dark, hollow stare, Keith saw something additional, a struggle going on. He leaned in. "What is it, Hubs?"

Hub coughed blood and Keith wiped it away with his bandanna. "Dan Massengale was my friend," Hub said and coughed again.

"Sure," Keith said, wiping gently. "We know."

Hub fought harder to speak. "Time Dan was killed —"

"Don't talk. Rest. We're gonna take you to the wagon."

Hub's eyes had a fixed stare. "If I'd been on the lookout — I could 'a' shot th' Indians when

251

they came outa th' draw —"

"Take it easy," Andy said and his eyes on Keith said Hub was out of his head.

"He's trying to tell us something, Andy. Let's lift him up a little."

Hub clutched his throat. "I said Dan was far away — but he wasn't too far —" He coughed and his speech fell tumbling as he hastened to beat another coughing fit: "Not too far for me to help him — if I'd been watchin'. I was off gatherin' sand plums when I heard shots — ran to th' wagon — but I was too late." His eyes blazed up with an old and inward suffering that made Keith suffer with him. "Always been late —"

He sank back, coughing, and his coughing sogged on and on, while Keith and Andy held him, murmuring futile words which Hub couldn't comprehend now. And as Keith felt Hub thrashing out his life, it was as though Keith himself relived Hub's past, understanding Hub's moodiness, his abrupt turns from gruffness to wry humor, his willingness to lose himself in back-breaking toil from sunup until it was too dark to see the skinning knives. Keith understood everything: Hub's family, lost in the blizzard — Hub believed — because he was too late reaching them. Hub's insistence that no man, unless it was Sam, could match Dan Massengale. And his holding Keith to silence about the long shots that had killed the bull and saved Keith's life — when long shots, in time, might have saved Dan

Massengale. And might have not, Keith thought. Surely Hub had carried burdens not of his own making, burdens that could happen to any man and ought happen to no man.

When Hub was still, Keith rode to the wagon and drove to the spring and they laid Hub inside and returned to camp, suddenly faced with a rending decision.

"North on that little rise," Keith said.

It was slow digging under the ruthless sun. The tight soil resisted tenaciously the thrusts of the spades. At last, they stood hatless by the three mounds of raw earth, Keith feeling the hot wind curling out of the buffalo country to the southwest, hearing the sweet, liquid voices of meadowlarks on the prairie below.

Keith couldn't bring himself to speak. Neither could Andy. They stood like cast images until Keith realized they weren't finished.

With Andy trailing in the wagon, they scouted for outcrops and found a grayish stone about the right size, mostly upright, wide and sturdy at the base, and loaded it on. Rolling and tugging together, they worked it within a few feet of the mound, where they took turns using knives and chisel and hammer from the gear-wagon toolbox, carving crudely yet carefully on the face of the stone.

"I want *Buffalo Runners* on there," Andy spoke up abruptly in a cracked voice. "I want whoever rides by here to know."

When they had finished, it read:

Sam Massengale
Hub Stratton
Levi Oatman

BUFFALO RUNNERS

Killed by white men
June 18, 1877

As they inched the stone into place and Keith stood up, he could feel the pounding in his brain, the hurrying. Already the sun was dipping into afternoon.

A tide out of the past drenched him when he went downgrade and saw the empty camp. A hard camp but a good camp for a time. Yet nowise as good as the old ones, before the hastening tempo of killing and skinning had invaded them all like an undermining illness which a man was aware of but couldn't shake. He turned and saw Andy's despair.

"Let's put what gear we need in the trail wagon," Keith said, with effort. "Cache everything else; drive on to the Dockums." Andy well knew as he did, Keith saw, where they were going and what they had to do. They would have to hurry.

On second thought, after loading up, they unhitched and pulled the Shuttler and the cook and gear wagons into a wooded draw northeast of the campsite, hoping Indians wouldn't discover them. It was then also that Keith missed Sam's old Sharps and Hub's Spencer — both taken, of course.

So many tracks cluttered the upriver wagon trail that Keith couldn't make out any fresh mule and horse prints. Farther on, he saw scatterings of buffalo covering the trail and the valley. The shaggies soon took alarm and spooked to the northwest, rumbling off, drawing together under a brownish haze of dust, thereby telling Keith they had been shot into earlier in the day. A sudden conclusion dug into his mind while he watched them fleeing in their nodding gait: he was through hunting hides. It was over. His life had changed greatly in these six months; it was still changing. Gone were his ramblings, his gropings and vagabondage. As though he looked through unstained glass, he saw his new purpose, a violent one; likewise his responsibility for young Andy, the two dangerously crossed.

Short of sundown, they reached the Dockum camp. Suppertime was past, but Dockum invited them down to eat. Keith declined, saying they had to go on; tersely he told what bad happened.

There was a suspended silence as shock passed over their faces, Dockum's and Coralie's. Wiley dropped an armload of wood and stood motionless, his stern features thoughtful.

"We saw two men go by this morning," Dockum recalled. "South of camp. I thought it was funny then they didn't stop. They had a string of mules."

Keith felt his blood pound. "We'd like to leave the wagon and one mule. Help yourself to the supplies."

"We'll look after everything."

Andy drove around and unhitched and began saddling a mule. Keith stuffed shells into belts for the two Sharps rifles and his revolver, and sacked up a supply of food. He turned at the approach of light steps. Coralie handed him a floursack bundle.

"Your suppers," she said. "The light bread is still warm."

He could smell it as he thanked her, and realized suddenly that — he and Andy hadn't eaten since dawn. He slipped the bundle into a saddlebag, stepped to the trail wagon and found two empty canteens.

"I'll get some fresh water," she said. In a moment he saw her on the path to the spring with a bucket. He followed her, drawn by a compelling sense of incompletion. When he caught up with her, beyond the mesquites, she was ascending a path which dropped to a gravelly wash and the spring. She filled the bucket and rose. When she turned, he placed his hand partly over hers to take the handle.

"I wonder if you know what you're up against?" She did not relinquish her hold.

"We know what we have to do. That's enough."

"These men are deserters. Why can't the Army arrest them?"

"Army's looking for Indians, too."

"You can wait till the Army has time to catch them."

"That might never be."

"Whatever happens won't bring back your friends."

"I'm quite aware of that."

She sighed, as though resigned, and let the handle go. He took it and was surprised when she swung toward him, almost touching him but not. A deliberate movement and unlike her, bringing closer her disturbing warmth and the appeal of her face. She was panting a little from her rapid walk, her even lips just parted. A strand of loose hair fell across her forehead. She brushed it in place and, contrarily, it strayed back again, giving her an open, natural look. Her eyes were luminous.

That moment persisted while he saw her face, upturned to him, deliberate and yet transformed. He put down the bucket and pulled her to him and felt her unhesitating response. She met his kiss fully, warmly, with a blinding sweetness. She pressed her slimness against him. It was she who broke the embrace.

"You don't have to go," she said lingering over the words looking up at him.

He dropped his arms, feeling himself in the sway of indecision. For a bit he wanted to give to it; then he said, "We have to go — and we want to go."

"You don't know what you and Andy are getting into." There was no gentleness in her now. "I know where you're going. It's that terrible place on the South Pease, isn't it? That hangout. I know — a hunter told us. It's a den. Men wanted from other states."

He picked up the bucket to start up the path. She stepped across in front of him. "You'll find more men just like the ones that murdered your friends. They'll all be against you."

"Is that what this was all about — to stop us? Was that all it was?"

He had spoken out of impatience. He saw the hurt tear into her face; before he could say anything more she turned up the path, walking fast.

He followed slowly, regretting his words but at loss how to withdraw them; and now there wasn't time.

At the trail wagon he filled the canteens and mounted. Andy swung up on the mule, which humped its back and bucked a few times, awkwardly, and settled down, though cantankerous about the bit.

Keith glanced around for Coralie. She stood not by the Dockum wagon, where he expected, standing back, hurt, but at the geldings flank and she was holding up the Henry rifle. He had never seen her so still and tense, her attention on him so concentrated.

"Keith," she said, "take this — and I want you to know I didn't do that just to stop you from going."

She didn't have to say that. Now Wiley knew. Keith saw that as Wiley, with a start, turned to her. Keith shook his head, that for her also. Then he and Andy rode through the mesquites.

Keith was in the lead, coming in on an old, deep buffalo trail that ran gouging down to the river, when he remembered the new shoes and the gift for Lenny, still in the trail wagon.

He traveled without much caution, figuring that darkness would overtake them in an hour or so, feeling the long day's pressures ganging up on him at last. Every step of the gelding and the mule sounded as loud as a shot, for the evening was quiet and humid. It was curious how a windless day in buffalo country made you jumpy. To him the rolling country below the Cap Rock had a voice of its own and the wind was that voice.

Emotion swelled in Keith when he glanced back at Andy, who hadn't said more than ten words since leaving the old camp. Andy rode slumped, in a state of benumbed grief. Today, Keith thought, in one great crushing shock, Andy had passed through the ordeal of manhood.

The South Pease was not yet in sight when Keith halted for the night. Andy watered and hobbled the mule, then sat with his back against a chinaberry tree, staring out over the darkening valley, his eyes brooding. Keith took one look at him and decided to risk a fire for coffee, taking care to hide the blaze in a wash.

Andy took a tentative sip of the black brew and put down the tin cup. He nibbled on Coralie's generous supper; finally he laid that aside also and sat back again, the torrent of his grief pouring into his face.

"You've got to eat," Keith told him.

"All I can think of is them two."

"You'll need your strength and steady hands. Better eat."

Once more Andy tried. After a minute, he rose and went striding down to the river. Keith let him be, knowing Andy needed to be alone. A long time later Keith heard him stumbling into camp; in moments he was snoring.

Keith awakened before daylight. Andy lay in an exhausted but restless sleep, moaning softly. Keith slipped off to see about their mounts. He built a low fire in the wash and put the coffeepot on. When it was boiling, he climbed the short slant and knelt to wake up Andy. Seeing the slim face, boyish in the pallid light, in these moments free from yesterday, he hesitated before touching him.

Andy sat up and opened his eyes. For a moment he was his old self, yawning, stretching. And then Keith saw him sink back, moaning and remembering, and press his right hand to his head.

Keith forced roughness into his voice. "Come on. You won't be worth a damn if you don't eat and drink something."

The day began as it had ended, gray clouds hanging in woolen pockets over the shallow river and the air sticky. A stifling heat rose off the short grass as the sun bit through.

Before midmorning Keith saw the glitter of a small stream, down to summer-low pools and shallow necks, bending in from the south to join the Middle Pease. Keith put his horse down the bank to drink, but the gelding, after a bit-shaking taste or two, refused. Keith scooped up some water in his hat and tasted, and like the line in "The Buffalo Skinners," it was true: *Pease River's as salty as hellfire — the water I could never go.* Only a buffalo could drink it. That meant, Keith reasoned, that Robber's Roost was back off the South Pease, near a supply of sweet water.

Not long afterward, Keith started hearing the deep tones of buffalo rifles, west and southwest, and the stink from the hunted-over country became near gagging. For the next hour no minute passed without the big-caliber rumbling. The gloomy clouds were burning off; the wind was rising. Keith felt better. By this time he and Andy rode side by side. There was a fresh alertness in Andy, an eagerness to ride ahead.

When a low-banked creek trickled in from the west, they rode into its mouth and the gelding and mule drank their fill That was enough to send Keith up the bank and riding upcreek.

In a short while he spotted the first hide tents on the flat, and a few dugouts against the slope, and near the creek, a long oblong hide structure that had to be a store. Behind it dark stacks of hides and a corral enclosing two horses.

"There it is," Keith said.

"What're we waitin' on!" Andy demanded, keyed up, and he clapped boot heels to the mule's flanks.

Keith sprang the gelding ahead of the slower mule. He swung his arm. "Hold up! Rush in there — you'll get your head shot off. We'll start at the store."

They rode in behind the hide-and-pole place and got down. Keith, scrutinizing the horses in the corral, felt his hopes fade a little. He didn't know these hard-used saddle animals nor the poor mules in another corral, hitherto hidden by the tall hide stacks. Holding their rifles, he and Andy entered through a hide-flap door at the rear. Here was a sort of storeroom, jammed with barrels and boxes.

Keith heard voices beyond. He listened a bit. None sounded like Parker or Goss, and he would know Parker's cocksure voice anywhere and Goss's grumbling.

With Andy at his shoulder, Keith pushed aside another smelly flap and found himself inside a catch-all store and saloon. He halted when he saw a hunter and long-haired Tobe Jett hunched over the counter at the other end. Ol' Tobe, as Sam had called him, looking as dirty as ever, if not dirtier, wearing what appeared to be the same greasy red shirt Keith remembered on the Sweet Water.

Jett glanced around, his cranky face forming in complaint. "Why'n't you runners come in the front way? You raised in a barn?"

Keith saw Jett's foxy eyes focus on him, and lift after a long moment. Jett didn't recognize him. The hunter paid for a bottle of whisky and left.

Keith and Andy moved along the counter, mounted on whisky barrels like the one on the Sweet Water. Jett was frowning. He sized up Keith again.

"Well, Tobe," said Keith, "how's the sugar sand?"

"Who th' hell are you bustin' in here?" Jett's tobacco-chomping jaws suddenly paused.

"Still got your little tin cup?" Keith inquired.

"You —" Acrid recognition flared in Jett's murky stare, a bitterness. "Can't you let a man alone? You boys wouldn't let me make an honest livin' on the Sweet Water."

"All we want is some information. Any new faces ride in here yesterday or today from the north?"

"How th' hell would I know?"

"You'd know if anybody would. Did they, Tobe? Two men? Leading a string of damned-good Missouri mules? One beanpole fellow? Other one built like one of your whisky kegs?" Keith's eyes, meanwhile, were busy. Behind the counter, below the shelf of whisky bottles, Jett kept an assortment of odds and ends, apparently stuff he had traded for: a bent-up brass pot, some cheap watches, belt buckles, spurs, bridle bits, and three old buffalo rifles leaning against a box. One a big side-hammered Sharps.

"Naw," Jett grunted, "been nobody new here. Same old bunch."

Keith shifted his looking and immediately

sensed a tugging within himself, and he pivoted back to meet Jett's eyes cutting at him. Keith fixed his eyes again on the rifles, on the Sharps. And fast, he stepped around the counter, laid his rifle on a box and picked up the Sharps. An old Sharps — he saw, the strangest of feelings came over him — the stock once mended with green buffalo hide, dried now to a flinty hardness, as any runner might wrap a busted stock. His mind was whirling as he turned the rifle and saw the walnut forearm and the whittled initials *S.M.*

"Gimme that!" Jett snarled, his whining compliance vanishing. He grabbed for the rifle. Keith rammed the butt into Jett's stomach. Jett let out a cry and caved in like a straw man, doubling up on the floor.

"Uncle Sam's old rifle," Andy choked, his eyes blazing up. "They sold it here."

Handing it to Andy, Keith seized Jett and slung him to his feet. "Where are they?"

Jett's Adam's apple bobbed like a cork. "They — they — pulled out this morning."

"Where to — damnit?"

"Barr's Town."

"You're lying." Keith knew Jett was lying and he shook Jett until the man's head rolled, until Keith grew tired of shaking him and asking him over and over. He threw Jett against the counter and seized him and demanded again, "Where are they?"

"I told you — Barr's Town."

Keith shook him again. Jett's body was soft and

pulpy, and he wouldn't fight back; therein lay his strength. Keith released him and saw Jett slither down.

They left Tobe Jett writhing on the dirty floor. They mounted and swung around in front. A wagon road running west from the store toward the hunting grounds provided the semblance of a rough street, which crooked past scattered hide tents and on over the low ridge and the dugouts there like swollen eyes peering down on the windy part.

"Maybe they did go on to Barr's Town," Andy puzzled.

"Except they know that's the most obvious place the Army would watch."

At the first tent, Keith looked inside and saw an undersized man, naked to the waist, morosely loading bottlenecked cartridges. A mere glance and he bent over his work again. Riding ahead, Keith found the next two tents unoccupied. In the next, four men played cards under hides laid over chinaberry poles. The day was hot and as Keith rode along he saw that the sides were up on the shakers.

Approaching the last tent where a horse stood saddled, Keith heard a woman's flat voice. He drew up. At that moment a man came out, mounted and rode toward the store. Keith stiffened, then relaxed, seeing the bearded features of a stranger.

The dugouts on the ridge presented more problems. At the first one, Keith dismounted and talked briefly with the two tight-lipped occupants, while Andy sat guard on the mule. Thereafter they rode to each gouged-out habitation, seven in all; having learned nothing, they returned to the road and paused where it climbed over the ridge.

"Parker and Goss are too lazy to dig a dugout or put up a tent," Keith brooded. "They're around here somewhere."

Keith became silent, watching, thinking. The light swimming over the flat fell yellow and harsh, and the southwest wind, bringing the stink from the rottenness on the hunting grounds, was a fetid breath that wrinkled the nostrils. He turned in that direction, hearing the strident booms like the bronzed strokes of a smithy's hammer.

A minute later he and Andy disappeared over the ridge, perhaps to seek out the runners busy at their killing; instead, they circled back to the south. Thirty minutes passed; from a patch of stubby cedars on the broken face of the ridge, they observed Tobe Jett's village while they ate the last of the supper Coralie Dockum had prepared.

Afternoon crept in with a cruelty of blazing sunlight, raising heat waves which turned the flat into a lake of shimmering fire.

On the red earth below, a man left his hide tent and jogged his horse across to the store; when he emerged, Keith saw sun-glitter on the bottle in his hand. The rider jogged to the tent where the woman was. He paused without dismounting. After some moments he rode back to his tent.

A team of bay horses pulled a light wagon, loaded high with hides, down the ridge road and on to the store and behind it; later Keith saw the team drawing the empty wagon to a tent.

He spoke on a jarring thought. "Andy, if a man slipped up from the creek behind the store and went in, we couldn't see him from here. Not the way ol' Tobe's got hides stacked around down there."

"Mean if they hid out along the creek?"

"Guess that's what I'm thinking."

Andy, who had been dozing a little, sat up suddenly and leaned forward in concentration. "Keith — along the creek is the *only* place we didn't look sharp. Remember? We had our minds on the tents."

"When it gets dark, we'll go see."

Keith watched the sun wane. The flat seemed to writhe feverishly under a batting of unworldly glare. Now Keith dozed while Andy watched.

Mauve light was thickening against the slope when, at last, they led down through the cedars to the scrub timber which lined the creek. Across it, the flat was shaking off the drowse of afternoon and stirring visibly. Lanterns burned here and there; horsemen gravitated toward the store-saloon.

In late-evening gloom, Keith and Andy stopped opposite the store, which squatted in a dull glow of light about fifty yards north across the creek. Keith thought how wrong they had guessed. There wasn't one dugout on the creek or near it.

They tied the gelding and the mule to a mesquite, back from the creek, and returned to hunker down and watch the store. Before long a man staggered out, whooping like an Indian. He clambered aboard his horse and went charging up the road, whooping again.

Full darkness wasn't far away when Keith noticed a motion of white on the road. A walking figure which presently, instead of continuing to the store, left the road to move parallel to the creek.

For a short pass of time Keith lost sight of the walker. But now he heard light steps scuffing the rocky bed of the creek, and quicker, distinct steps as though the person had jumped from one rock to another, and he saw suddenly a white figure coming up a cut in the creek bank.

Andy gave a start beside him just as Keith, peering through the muddy light, saw a woman.

She went on purposefully. Keith puzzled why she chose that direction, for beyond her stretched the vague continuation of the rolling flat as the land sloped toward the South Pease.

Keith and Andy rose to follow. She passed their tied mounts without notice. She turned east, walking faster. Farther on Keith saw a dim path slanting in from the creek. She followed it southward. Keith quickened step, feeling the unevenness under him, dipping, rising, as the ground grew rougher. Andy kept pace on Keith's right.

The woman's light-colored dress made her easy to follow. He saw her outlined grayly on a small knob. In moments, he expected to see her moving beyond it, but after waiting he did not catch sight of her again, as if the twilight murk had swallowed her.

He stepped faster. A voice floated back from the dimness ahead — a woman's — a tentative calling, uncertain. He reached the knobby little rise and dead ahead he saw the brokenness of an eroded gully fanning out below him, and the woman standing on the edge, peering down.

"You're late," a man's blurred voice was saying.

"I came when I could." The woman sounded peevish, somewhat afraid.

"Too slow for me — to me."

"You want me or not?"

The man said, "Come down and see," and uttered a hissing, peremptory whistle.

Meaning exploded through Keith. That overbearing voice — the shrill whistle — belonged to Parker. Keith started forward. He saw the woman descending the gully's side, and he saw Parker's thickness at the bottom. Where was Goss?

Keith froze as a harsh braying trumpeted behind him, as loud and clear as a bugle call — Andy's mule. And immediately, while Andy's mount was still honking, the drawnout, raucous voice of another mule, unseen, answered down in the gully.

Keith saw Parker jerk an upward look at the gully's rim and spot him, and at once grab the woman, who screamed as Parker, holding her in front of him, began backing down the gully. If Keith fired, he would hit the woman.

Keith dropped over the edge and stumbled to his knees in loose rock. He saw the woman breaking free. She flung herself to the gully wall. So quickly did Parker loom before him that Keith was unprepared. He struggled up, seeing, almost too late, the knife in Parker's right hand.

Keith slammed the butt of his rifle against the down-chopping forearm. Parker yelled and spun off, hurt, but Keith, trying to find footing, felt the rubble shift under him. He went down on one knee. Parker was coming for him, low and fast.

Still braced on the knee, Keith shot him. The blast of the Sharps crashed thunderously in the narrow space of the gully. The Big Fifty slug knocked Parker backward. He opened his mouth and cried "ah-ahhh" and clutched his chest. He made a reeling turn, his boots clacking on the loose rock. He flopped and sprawled heavily, he gagged a couple of times and his thick body did not move again.

Behind Parker's body Keith saw Goss rushing around a turn in the gully, pointing the muzzle of a carbine. Keith dropped the empty Sharps to reach for his handgun, knowing he didn't have time. He heard a boom, but strangely he felt nothing.

Goss dropped his weapon and staggered against the gully's side. As the noise died away, Keith heard the soft scraping of Goss's back sliding down the gully wall, and then the softer thump of his body as he hit the ground.

Keith turned. Andy stood on the gully's rim. Even as Keith looked, Andy snapped open the breech of his rifle to reload.

There was a sound nearby. The woman. Keith had forgotten her. He saw her move now, drawing her hands from her mouth. She broke to run up the path.

"You wait!" Keith ordered, knowing she would run to the store, and saw her shrink against the wall again. "Andy — the mounts — be quick," Keith called and struck a match.

Parker was as dead as a lung-shot bull. He looked dirty and evil beneath the wavering eye of light; still dangerous somehow, the boldness clinging to his broken-nosed face even in death. Keith, kneeling, searching, found a roll of greenbacks in Parker's shirt pocket. But Keith knew there should be more.

Hurrying, he found another roll on Goss and beside him Hub Stratton's old Spencer carbine, which he took also. Inside a shallow dugout he struck another match. His eyes swept over whisky, food, two buffalo rifles — the dead hunters' rifles — blankets, and Sam Massengale's saddlebag. In it Keith discovered more greenbacks, and he realized this was all he would find.

When he came out, the woman had gone. He ran down the gully and untied the mules and Sam's saddle horse, shooed them toward the river and hastened back.

Andy came leading the mounts.

Between the creek and the store Keith could see a lantern bobbing. A bullet whined and he heard a rifle go *pumm*. More slugs began whistling over the gully. Keith opened up with the Spencer. On the third shot the lantern went out and he heard a high-driven yell. He laid two more shots in there. The rifle quit.

And then he and Andy were mounted and rushing east toward the river, following the widening jaws of the gully, hearing the racketing roll of the mules and the saddle horse fleeing before them like wild things suddenly freed, seeing their dark shapes scudding through the leaden light.

CHAPTER 15

They slept in the brush on the other side of the river, and as morning sent a tide of dawn light flowing over the shallow valley, they bunched the stock and struck north. Keith took the point. After him, on Sam's gelding, Andy hazed the mules, which drove readily in familiar hands.

A weary satisfaction continued to possess Keith. He supposed he ought to feel some prickings of conscience because he had killed a man, but he did not. A state of mind which he would have shied from not long ago, mindful of the usual proprieties and of due process of law and shunning the violence which his present New England people abhorred, yet with which his hardy forebears had doused themselves during the decades of Indian fighting to advance the frontier from the Atlantic Coast.

But always he would blame himself for not insisting that Sam Massengale send the drifters on earlier. Keith realized he would live with that the rest of his life.

Thus, in the bitter light of what had happened to his friends, he set to thinking about the Dockums in realistic terms.

To have a clear view around him, he led away from the river bottom; therefore, because he had that vantage, he saw the ruffling motion while some distance away.

A rider, another and another, bodies shining like greased metal in the smoky gloom, and light flashing on rifle barrels. Eight Indians, he counted, riding single file, passing through a wooded outlet in the hills which opened on the river.

He sucked in his breath and signaled Andy to hold up, and waited with the Sharps across his saddle. He was above and slightly behind the Indians, unseen for the moment, unless they looked back.

He saw the lead Indian's horse grow still, the Indian gazing right and left along the river, then westward, watching far across the river where the hoarse bellowings of the slaughter never seemed to cease.

For long-lasting moments the Indian sat there looking; then he clapped heels to his bay horse and rode straight ahead, and Keith felt the sharp edge of his tension drop away. Certain the entire war party was following in file, he eased back to help Andy with the mules; and when he looked again, the Indians were riding through the tall grass by the river.

Thereafter, Keith moved more discreetly. The sun was high as he came once more to the littered and stinking expanse through which they had hurried yesterday. He and Andy held their noses and batted at the swarms of green flies punishing them and their stock. The stench seemed banked in tainted layers over the sun-flooded valley. Many of the buffalo which Keith saw, lying like rotting brown logs off from the water where hunters had bombarded them as they drifted in to drink, had not been skinned; that meant only the tongues had been taken. There was constant motion in the hot sky of vultures diving, climbing, hovering, skimming. Wolves and coyotes prowled among the bloated hulks. Otherwise, Keith saw no living things, and as he rode through the kills an unforgiveness of waste stifled him and stuck with him, oppressively, even after they had passed the worst of it.

At noon Keith reached the Dockum camp. Riding in to get lead ropes for the mules, he saw Dockum and Wiley working around the hide stack; its size indicated a steady rate of kills. Coralie, who stood by the trail wagon, swept a look of relief over him. Wiley and Dockum, with Lenny tagging after his father, hurried over to hear the news.

"We caught up with them," Keith explained. "We got back everything." He got down to go to the wagon for rope and paused at Dockum's inquisitive voice, "Where'd it happen?"

"That big hide camp — on the South Pease."

"Some shootin', eh?"

"Some," Keith said and climbed up and rummaged until he found a long coil of rope, and realized that he didn't care to talk about it now. But Dockum was waiting when Keith came out. "Later, Cal," Keith said. He noticed that Coralie was setting the table.

He and Andy tied the mules in the mesquites,

came in and washed and ate in ravenous silence, broken only by Dockum's questions and Keith's brief replies. After dinner, Dockum lighted his pipe and turned to Keith with a further expectancy.

"Not much time for talk, Cal," Keith said, getting up from the table. "You've all got to get out of here today. We just missed a war party this morning."

"War party?" Dockum looked impressed, yet he said, "No Indians around here. We been on the lookout, too. Huntin's sure been good. We're stackin' 'em up. Look over yonder. Before long, me and Wiley will have us a nice stake."

"Cal," Keith said, "that's straight talk You've got to get out of here. You owe it to your family."

Dockum swelled up at Keith's bluntness. Wiley's lean humorless face bore a stamp of indifferent neutrality, uncaring whether he stayed or not. His tawny eyes reached for Coralie, who considered her father with an even-lipped gravity.

"Leave?" Dockum said indignantly. "Just when prospects are good?" He made a scoffing gesture.

With a suddenness that startled her father, Coralie stood between him and Keith. She turned to the others. "I want to talk to Papa alone. Lenny, you go play. But don't go far."

Wiley overcame his surprise, his grim mouth slowly reshaping its stern line. As he walked off he seemed to hunt for something to fill his powerful hands. Lenny trailed him. Keith and Andy went to the hide stack. Glancing back, Keith saw Coralie turning to Dockum, who was standing now.

Already her father was wearing his face of humility and self-pity. It was suddenly too much for her. "Papa," she said, "this is no time to pretend. We've got to do something — like Keith said."

"So it's *Keith,* is it?"

She ignored that. "I've been thinking about this a long time. I'm going to take Lenny to Barr's Town."

"What'll you do there?"

"I'll find something. I'm a good cook. I can make dresses. I can even start a subscription school in the fall."

"If none of that pans out?"

"I'll go to another town."

"How — how you aim to get by, meantime?" Satisfaction, rather than concern, rubbed through his tone.

"On part of the money Mr. Cassidy paid you for the hides. I've worked, too, Papa. Worked hard. Part of that money is rightfully mine."

A ruddy pink gushed into his cheek points, and after it, like a doleful mask being drawn on, she saw his face convey the all too familiar expression of injury. "Never figured you'd run out on me," he said, shaking his head. "Me gettin' on in years, too."

"It's not safe here," she said to him, finally at the last pinch of her patience. "That's the main reason, Papa." She gazed at him with pity because he couldn't see for himself, or what he refused to see. "I'm going to pack now, Papa."

"Now — Coralie!" He stepped toward her and the cloak of his pretension fell from him. As in an old book, read many times over, she knew what was coming last, because he had exhausted all other means: his predictable fear of her leaving him. That much about him was sincere. And in spite of her knowing, she could feel her will weakening, and seeing him that way, his face turned just so, chastened, perhaps, she could not yet bring herself to go.

But to her surprise, her silence seemed to anger him. Desperation and resentment gleamed in his eyes, and a little terror also. "You're just like your mother," he accused, his mouth curling. "You two always figured you's better than us Dockums."

Coralie stood aghast, sick at heart. She and her father had seldom reached open argument. Never this. Her astonishment and deep hurt retreated. As if through a harsh but honest light, terrible in its clarity, she saw her father for the first time. Tears clouded her eyes. Her voice choked.

"Mama *was* better than you," she got out, the gall of bitterness on her tongue. "She always was. You're lazy — you're shiftless. Because of you, she died young. I know that now." Head down, she wheeled blindly toward the wagon.

"Coralie!" Dockum shouted. "— you listen to me! You come back here!"

278

She did not stop. She lifted her skirts and stepped on the hub and pulled herself over the front wheel. Once she was inside, the blinding tears came. She sank to her knees, her shoulders shaking uncontrollably.

After a while, she sensed the stir of a hidden strength which slowly but surely began to sustain her. She began packing, sniffing as she worked, determined as she had not been before in her life.

Keith saw Coralie go to the wagon and Dockum follow her a few steps and stop, his plump shoulders sagging. He stared dejectedly at the ground. Keith couldn't help feel a little sorry for Dockum, he looked so damned shaken and left. And as he watched, Dockum dug out his tobacco plug, bit and wiped his mouth, and quickened his step across to Keith.

"You started all this," Dockum shouted, wagging a pudgy forefinger. "I'm gonna hold you responsible for her and Lenny. ⸺ I will!"

"Cal — your head's like rock — why don't you come along? You can come back after the threat is over."

"When'll that be — ten years from now?" He flaunted his raw contempt, prodded by his boastful nature. "You can't buffalo an old soldier. I'll stick it out — I'll make my stake." He was shaking with rage. His blustering voice skied higher when he saw Wiley striding over. "Coralie's leavin' us, Wiley. You aim to stay or hightail it with the rest?"

Wiley raked his dislike across Keith. "Indians

don't scare me — white men, neither."

"Your choice," Keith said and left them.

At Coralie's instructions, he and Andy started loading into the trail wagon her belongings and Lenny's, and the Henry rifle and shell belt, a small box of cooking utensils and tableware. It pained Keith to see how little clothing the two of them had, and he wondered again how she kept herself and the coltish boy so clean. Growing up in a well-fed, well-clothed family, Keith had associated poverty with grime; it wasn't so with her.

Dockum observed the preparations with an attitude of great unconcern. Wiley watched impassively; seldom did his stern gaze leave Coralie.

When everything was aboard and the mules stood hitched, Coralie looked around once more, her high forehead gathered in a final thoughtfulness. "We have to go now," she told Lenny. "Tell Papa goodbye." She was, Keith saw, in strict control of her emotions.

Lenny kissed and hugged his father, who tickled the boy and lifted him wiggling to the wagon seat beside Andy. "You be a good boy," Dockum said and turned abruptly away.

Coralie waited by the wagon for her father's embrace, her face smooth, pensive yet firm. He seemed not to notice her. He stepped back and appeared to inspect the wagon's running gear.

"Papa," she said evenly, "— my share of the hide money."

"Ah —" Dockum hunched up his shoulders as if the matter had slipped his mind. "By grab —"

he said and took out a farmer's flat pocketbook, dark and limp from being carried and sweated on in his overalls. He opened the metal catch, his stubby fingers fumbling and grudging over the greenbacks. He unwadded them and gave her some.

She accepted them with hardly a look. "Thank you, Papa. You will come to town soon, won't you?"

"Don't know when," he answered, certain she saw his self-pity and need.

Her calm expression did not falter. "You will be careful, won't you, Papa — you and Wiley?" And she looked at Wiley and, seeing her concern for himself as well, his eyes were like fanned coals.

Dockum shrugged carelessly.

She could hold back no longer. She kissed her father on his bearded cheek and turned to the wagon. Keith helped her up, next to Lenny, who was waving at his father. Andy shook the lines over the mules' rumps and the team hit the traces with a jangling eagerness.

Coralie looked straight ahead, a new and nameless ache upon her. Suddenly the mesquites passing before her eyes blurred to a green webbing, and soon, likewise, the wooded hill swam mistily, shimmering and vague in the glassy light. She sniffed.

Gradually the cup-shaped buffalo wallows came into view, now the beckoning line of the creek across the flat. It was not until then did she remember the money in the patch pocket of her dress.

Leaning over the seat, she found her mother's old cloth purse and opened it. Starting to place the greenbacks therein, she noticed the size of the roll for the first time. Counting, she shuffled through the bills and grew still with shame. She could hardly breathe.

In her hands lay more than two hundred dollars, more money than she had ever seen. Half her father's share of the hides. Half his stake.

Toward evening Keith chose a camping place and formed the wagons — all of them and the cache found intact in the draw near the outfit's old camp — into a corral. Around him, open and still, flowed the rolling country south of the Middle Pease, the twilight wind scented with the sweet odors of short grass.

Swiftly Coralie had biscuits baking in a Dutch oven, hot coals on the lid for browning, bacon frying, dried apples stewing, coffee going. There was a cheerful competence under her gravity, and as she moved about in her heavy shoes he was reminded of the overdue gifts; hence, after supper, he gave Lenny his sack of hard candy, which seemed insignificant indeed, and saw the boy's exalted delight. Not wishing to make a ceremony of the shoes, Keith hesitated.

"Here's something for you," he said, handing her the box. She caught her breath. Before she could speak, he stepped on to go outside the corral.

Returning later, he expected to find her gone to bed. But she had added wood to the fire and was standing in that renewed glow, admiring her glossy black shoes. He pulled back into the shadows with a sense of invasion, yet did not go. He saw her sit on a box and pull her skirt above her ankles and arch one slim, graceful leg out and turn her foot, this way and that, held fast by her admiration.

Then her eyes moved and she saw him and came across. "They're the most beautiful shoes in the world, Keith."

"You look nice."

She became perfectly still. Facing him, her back to the firelight, her face was shadowed and he couldn't see her eyes. Lenny's sleepy voice sounded thinly in the light trail wagon. She turned away then.

Standing the first watch, Keith stationed himself where he could see past the grazing stock. Andy was sleeping under the hide wagon. A few coyotes yowled from the moon-bathed ridges; otherwise, the night seemed quieter than usual.

In a while he heard someone coming from the wagons. It was Coralie, slim in the dim light.

"I couldn't sleep," she said.

He slid an arm around her waist, the smooth feel of her charging through his senses; to his surprise she did not pull back, yet neither did she come fully against him. He touched his lips to her hair, to her temple, and she did not deny him; but when he bent to kiss her, she turned her head away as his mouth brushed hers.

"What is it, Coralie?"

"I don't know how to say it," she began, in a searching way. "Maybe I don't know what I mean." He waited and she went on. "Keith, is she still on your mind? Is she still part of you?"

Taken back, he was a moment answering. "What made you ask that?"

"I've heard it said that men come to buffalo country for three reasons. They're running from the law. They want to make a stake — or —"

"It's a woman," he finished with a low laugh.

"Well, I don't think you're in trouble, and I don't think you need the money like Papa." His arm tightened around her, but she kept a space between them. "Keith," she said, going on painfully, "don't make love to me because I'm the only woman around. I don't want that, even though I want it."

He was amused, but he asked quietly, "What do you want, Coralie?"

"I don't want you to unless you mean it. And I don't want you to feel pity for me — never."

"Pity?" His hands on her became rough. A strange feeling, gentle but mixed of protest and anger, took hold of him. "It's not that. I love you. I want you to be my wife."

She swayed toward him, her face upturned. Her sweetness burned his mouth. He could feel her trembling. His body was rigid. When she drew back a little to catch her breath, his lips brushed her eyes and cheeks, and he found that she was crying. And holding her, he seemed to catch the doubting restlessness in her again. Her voice reached him, small and far away:

"Keith, I'm afraid."

"It's because of what happened today."

"No — though Papa needs me."

"What, then?" He was puzzled.

"You come from a different world. I know. I can tell. Way you talk; the things you do. I'm no lady, Keith. My people never had anything. I've slept more times in wagons than I have in houses."

A growl rose in his throat. "Get that nonsense out of your head. We'll be married in Barr's Town. If we can't find a preacher there, we'll go to Fort Griffin."

She stepped back to look at him, her eyes immense, warm pools. She gave him a long kiss, and the pressure of her body and arms enveloped him in a smothering sweet haze. She looked at him again. "I haven't yet said I love you. I do — no matter what happens."

She touched his face with her fingertips. She regarded him intently, with a strange and consuming tenderness, and walked away.

Following her with his eyes, Keith realized that he was scowling fiercely, that he was vaguely troubled. Was the past — the endless wanderings of the Dockums, the grinding hard times, the young sorrows, the everlasting disappointments — combining to make her doubt her own happiness?

Keith sighted the cluttered ugliness of Barr's Town under a sinking sun next day. After the silence of the hollow vastness to the north, for Keith had seen no buffalo, the buzzing drone was an alien intrusion. They drove down the street and parked the four wagons between town and the river; by the time Keith and Andy had tended to the stock, Coralie had supper started.

Having a woman and child in camp made a great difference. Both Keith and Andy were constantly trying to please her, to make things easier for her, bringing wood and water, fetching things.

She was composed and cheerful as she worked, her lips lightly pursed. She must have felt Keith's eyes on her, for she turned and caught him looking, and the light of a feeling stood forth in her face and her plainness vanished, absorbed by the radiance there.

After the meal, Andy took a towel, soap, and clean clothing and went to the river. When he returned, his wet blond hair, which he still wore long, like a hunter's, was carefully combed. He looked young and strong and trustworthy, handsome and clean, and older also after what had happened. The wake of these recent days was a somber print on his smooth, tanned face. He had filled out since that December on the Sweet Water; gone was much of his awkwardness. He had seen the elephant, like Sam had said. Andy was a man now. A damned good one to have at your elbow, Keith knew, and was proud of him.

"You could be going calling," Coralie teased, giving Andy her approval.

"Going up town a while," Andy said, flustered at the compliment.

"Andy," Keith said reflectively, "I've been thinking. We need to let Sam's family know. And did Levi and Hub have any relatives?"

"If they did, they never said so. What about their shares?"

"We can put the money in trust somewhere. I'll see if Cassidy can arrange for Sam's money to reach his family. Cassidy has banking connections through Lobenstein." Andy nodded and Keith continued. "Sam owned the wagons, all the stock. I think we can sell everything to Cassidy. I know he'll want those big Missouri mules and the Shuttler."

A frown of disagreement creased Andy's forehead. "I hate to see the mules go. I've handled 'em from colts up."

A single thought was forming in Keith's mind, warming his whole self with anticipation. "Possibly they don't have to be sold to Cassidy."

"What do you mean?"

"Andy — I want to go into ranching — up on the Middle Pease. I can get backing in the East." His words were tumbling, yet too slow for his racing vision. "I want you to come in as a full partner — with Coralie and me. We can freight till it's safe enough to run cattle up there. We can buy the wagons and stock from Sam's family.

How's that strike you?"

Andy's face lighted up. He whooped and did a quick little dance and gripped Keith's extended hand, saying over and over, "Son-of-a-gun . . . son-of-a-gun."

When Andy rode out, Keith walked beside him. "When I said we're full partners, I mean it in every way. I'm here if you need me — if you want to talk about anything."

Andy checked up. "Much obliged. See you later." He went off at a fast trot.

He had sounded sort of overeager. Keith recognized the signs. It was a woman — the Thompson woman. He walked back to camp, dissatisfied with what he had said or tried to say, thinking that the best advice in the world fell short when a young man was in love.

Out of the settling dusk a nighthawk swooped low over the camp, zigzagging after insects, crying shrill *peenks,* so close that Keith caught the whispering rush of the bird's erratic flight.

Lenny, who was playing around the cook wagon, glanced up in fear and ran to Coralie. "Sis, I want Papa."

"He'll come to see you before long," she assured him, drawing him to her.

"We have to stay here?"

"For a little while."

"I don't like it here."

"You'll like it better tomorrow."

Lenny shook his head and held on to her, drawn up in a child's taut and baffled loneliness.

Keith was moved. It occurred to him, and with some guilt, that the boy had been overlooked. "Lenny," he said, "in the morning we'll see what we can find for you in town. I promise."

"I don't want anything. I want Papa." He buried his head against his sister, and Keith said no more.

When darkness came, Coralie saw Lenny to bed. After a time the boy's sleepy voice dropped off and Coralie came back. "It's the first time he's ever been away from Papa," she said.

"We'll get him some things in the morning."

He saw her gravity lessen at his words, saw it disappear as her mouth softened. He saw the paleness of her throat as she turned her face to the lilac sky.

"It's a lovely night," he said.

"Yes," she said, sighing, "and tomorrow I'm going to buy my wedding dress. Oh, Keith, it is true, isn't it?"

She was, he felt, still unsure. She was still trying to make certain.

CHAPTER 16

Reaching the top of the grade at the edge of town, Andy looked off where Tess Thompson's house crouched behind the dark shield of trees. A lone eye of light gleamed there. He rode on, in him the keenness of a newly found recklessness and confidence. He passed the lighted Texas House and tied up next to the rowdy Buffalo Bull and pushed inside.

His nostrils wrinkled at the close stink. Funny, but he hadn't minded the smell before. It was exciting then. He maneuvered to the bar and, remembering what had happened to him the last time he drank whisky, bought a mug of beer instead. Leaning there, he thought of Tess Thompson. His common sense told him he should avoid her, that trying to see her would be dangerous; but when he viewed the alternative of never seeing her again, he felt a kind of sick desperation.

Minutes later, out of the dark mass of milling and shoving men, he saw a dimly familiar face.

"Hello, kid. No see for long time. How about a drink?"

It was the same sporty little man, narrow of face, in bowler, fancy coat and vest. Andy, aware of a pointed annoyance as he recalled the man's prodding questions, returned him a cold nod.

"Hello, kid, you remember me. I'm Nate Ives, the newspaper correspondent."

"I remember you," Andy said, leaving it there.

"How about a drink?" When Andy shook his head in refusal, Ives ordered whisky for himself and swung around with anticipation. "How long you gonna be in town?"

Andy shrugged and kept to his beer. The insight jabbed through his mind that he had passed out a heap of free information that time when he was half drunk on Ives' whisky. "You're too damned nosy," Andy told him.

"That's my business, asking questions."

"Well, you rub me wrong," Andy replied and stepped away from Ives, who did not follow.

Andy stood near the end of the bar closest to the stage. On his left two drunken hunters argued the merits of the Sharps as opposed to the Remington, and whether bottle-necked cartridges were superior to straight ones. The place was growing louder by the minute as the time approached for Tess Thompson to sing.

Andy finished his beer, ordered another and left it untouched, only to hear the bartender growl, "Listen, sonny. If you're gonna drink like a hummin' bird, make room for somebody that's thirsty. I work on a commission."

"I paid for it. All stand here and drink it as I please." He saw the hardness behind the pale eyes dull and sink down. Grumpily, the bartender turned to another customer.

Andy heard a man say it was ten o'clock. Soon, the Professor and Little Ned drifted wearily to the bar for refreshments. Around Andy the expectant crowd shoved and gabbled. Business at the bar picked up as the dance-hall girls urged their partners to buy drinks. Andy saw a door open between the bar and the stage. A man posted himself there, his bulldog stare watching for trouble. It was Tess Thompson's pock-marked bodyguard — Quinn.

Soon the musicians returned to their places. On that signal, the nimble master of ceremonies appeared. After his showy introduction, the red curtain sailed upward, the Professor and Little Ned lit into the racehorse fanfare, and Tess Thompson glided on stage as graceful as smoke.

While the crowd whooped and stomped, Andy stared at the glittering green figure. She sang "When Johnny Comes Marching Home," and the appreciative crowd whooped and cheered for another number. She bowed, she gestured graciously to the Professor at the piano, his head turkey-cock high, and to Little Ned, who deftly twanged his banjo at her attention. She smiled, her features as pale as marble, while her dark eyes, meantime, seemed to caress the crowd in that special way she had of reaching each lonesome patron.

Somebody shouted for "Lorena." After a provocative pause, she inclined her glistening dark head left, center and right, and the Professor light fingered the keys, a tinkling evocative to Andy of water rippling over mossy rocks, and so "Lorena" it was.

She looked tired when she finished. Although

the crowd clapped and whooped and stomped and called for another number, she bowed and left them with the consolation of her half-smile.

Just as the hubbub slackened, Andy heard the two hunters' quarrelsome voices resume:

"Any jackass'd know that!"

"You callin' me a jackass?"

A meaty whap muffled the reply. Andy whipped around to see the two hammering each other. A house man pawed a path toward them from the other side of the room. Another figure rushed past Andy, pulling and shouldering men aside to get at the hunters. Andy recognized the pock-marked Quinn. Now the two hunters wheeled to meet their attackers, and other hunters joined them. Girls screamed. Glasses shattered as crashing bodies bowled over tables and chairs.

An awareness of his position filtered through Andy. He stood alone at the end of the bar, free of the milling fight. The musicians were standing up to watch. There was no one near the door where Quinn had stood.

Andy was almost in motion with the thought, tasting a wild excitement as he drifted toward the door. One backward glance and he opened the door and passed into a hallway. To his right a flight of stairs led to the stage and on past to a landing, where steps doglegged back to the second story.

He froze. Down the hall Tess Thompson was unlocking a door.

She turned in alarm at his sudden step. He saw recognition change her expression. "What are you doing here?" Concern and not a little exasperation struggled for order in her mouth and eyes. "You've got to get out of here at once."

Coming steps struck through the thin wall of the saloon. Without hesitation, she flung open the door and motioned him inside. A lamp was burning. The violet fragrance Andy associated with her scented the room like spring. She locked the door behind her and rested her back against it, the smokiness of her eyes mirroring relief and vexation with him.

"Andy — you fool," she said guardedly, coming forward.

"I had to see you."

She flung up an aimless hand. She dropped the key on the table by the lamp. He heard her drawn-out sigh and he saw some of the tension leave her body.

"You're so innocent," she said, shaking her dark head. "So damned innocent and honest."

Andy heard a door slam and bootsteps rapping down the hall. She touched a finger to her lips. The boots halted outside her door. A heavy voice panted, "You hear anybody come this way?"

She placed her graceful white hands on green-spangled hips, and when she replied her voice had a sibilance, a discipline, which Andy had not heard. "How could I with that war going on?"

"A blond kid slipped through the door. The

Professor saw him."

"Maybe he went upstairs to see the girls."

"I'll look."

"You do that, Quinn. And my name is Miss Thompson — not *you*."

"Yes, Miss Thompson," the voice answered, thinly mocking. That, and Andy heard Quinn pounding down the hall and up the stairs.

Tess Thompson turned, her eyes angry. "I detest that man," she said. And then she seemed to sweep that feeling from her face as she regarded Andy. "You're a stubborn one," she said, and he saw that she was no longer provoked with him, just puzzled. "I told you not to come back, ever. Why did you do it?"

"To take you away."

"Away?" Her even lips formed an incredible *O*. "Oh, Andy, you *are* innocent. I should have told you." She averted her face, but not before he saw her biting her lips.

Brushing at her eyes, she stepped behind a dressing screen. He heard her step out of her high-heeled shoes, and he heard the rustling of the spangles on her dress as her white hands and arms, pulling, appeared wandlike above the screen. She was undressing. Not till now did that understanding crash over him. He felt an engulfing embarrassment, a headlong excitement. He kept turning the brim of his hat in his hands as he stared at the screen, then the floor. She was hurrying back and forth. He could see her small, stockinged feet. A chair squeaked. There was the stamp of heels. Again, the round, white arms rose languidly above the screen.

She came out in a dress of conservative gray. She held a cloth purse. He stared his open-mouthed admiration. She paused. He saw feeling touch her face. Now, it came to him, she was herself — not posing, not afraid of Quinn, not hard to figure. As if seeing a part detached from himself, he saw his big right hand lift to rest on the rounded point of her shoulder. She did not shrug it off, nor did she come closer. She could be a waxen figure, a sad smile drawn on the pale shell of her face.

There was a twisting inside him to his roots, a strange suffocation in his chest. With effort, he brought his hand to his side. She had not moved. Her smile was frozen. But because he had to, because he couldn't help it, he took hold of her with both rough hands and he kissed her tenderly on the mouth.

Her body felt wooden to his touch, her lips lifeless. He was raising his head when all at once, to his wonderment, she returned his kiss. His breath caught. His whole life seemed to burst forth. A magnificent strength became his. There was a mighty roaring in his ears.

As he felt all this he also sensed her restlessness. Each let the embrace fall apart.

He saw that her eyes were glistening wet. She touched an absurdly tiny white handkerchief to her nose. He moved toward her again. Her gesture checked him. Already, he saw, she was willing herself to composure. When she spoke, in the flat, toneless way he hated, because he knew it really wasn't like her, it was as if nothing had happened:

"Quinn will be back in a few minutes to escort me home. There's another bodyguard outside. I will lock the door. After we leave, you wait a while. You can get out by going upstairs and down the long hall to the outside staircase."

She gave him the key on the table, took another from her purse and waited for Quinn.

"Miss Tess," Andy said protectively, his earnest voice just above a whisper. "I said I came to take you away. I will now — tonight. We're camped down by the river."

He watched, spellbound. It was terrible for Andy to observe her transformation: the dark eyes growing cold, the even mouth hardening, the wrinkles at the corners of her eyes revealing themselves. She seemed to be growing old before his eyes.

"You moon-struck young fool," she lashed out, her mouth a harsh line. "Can't you see?"

"I don't understand."

"Then I'll tell you. I'm A. B. Barr's woman."

"I don't believe you."

"A. B. Barr's *kept* woman — if that makes it plainer. I have been for years."

He shook his head dazedly. "You're just sayin' that," he said in a crushed voice, still expecting her to soften as she had before.

But her relentless voice stayed the same. "It's

true. If you come back, you'll be killed. They already know who you are."

Boots beat the stairs. She gestured to the closet. Andy squeezed in, though he didn't much care whether he hid or not, and got behind a rack of dresses. He heard Quinn's voice at the door. He heard Tess Thompson walk out and a key's rattle in the lock. Her light steps blended with Quinn's heavy tread to the hall's end. Another key rattled. Voices rose outside. The door closed, was locked again. It stuck in Andy's mind that A. B. Barr ran a tight establishment.

Within a short time, he was climbing the stairs to the second floor, the noise from the saloon below reaching him as a subdued roar. He opened a door and looked down a narrow hallway, dimly lighted by wall lanterns, and saw the open door at the other end. Men's and women's voices droned in rooms along the hall.

Andy, moving quietly, was nearing the hall's length when he saw the parlor to his right. Two women and a man sat inside. As Andy started by the doorway, the man leaped up and yelled, "There's that blond kid!"

Andy had the notion to run. But seeing he couldn't make it, he swung about to meet the man dragging out a revolver as he lunged through the parlor doorway. Andy grabbed the gun arm, twisted backward. The man grunted his pain. The handgun slapped the wooden floor. A woman in the parlor screamed like a panther.

Andy took a solid punch in the chest. He hit the man in the belly and got a swiping sidearm across his neck. It was a painful blow that drowned the last of his caution. He charged in swinging and felt the house man's soft body give with each punch. Andy was faster, his body harder. He threw blow after blow into the generous belly and at the wedge of the bearded face. A step or two beyond, Andy could see the open door to the outside landing. The house man was racking for air. He tried to wrestle, to bring his weight to bear. Andy's fist caught him high in the neck. He went reeling backward through the door.

There was the shriek of splintering wood, and the house man's scream as he was smashed through the railing, clutching at the darkness as he fell.

Andy tasted blood, hot, salty. He glared at the broken railing while he gulped for air. Behind him the woman was screaming again, and he legged it down the stairs to the walk, knowing that he had taken out part of his frustrated, shaken hurt tonight on the unlucky house man.

Tess Thompson knew A. B. Barr was in the house before she had walked all the way through the trees, flanked by Quinn and the new bodyguard. The lights told her. The entire house was alight. She had always thought it amusing for a strong-handed man like A. B. Barr to be afraid of the dark.

She went up the porch stairs and opened the door, but paused when Quinn started to follow her inside. "I don't recall that I asked you in," she said sharply, blocking his path.

"I want to talk to Mr. Barr."

"Your manners haven't improved in the year you've been with us. When you speak to me, you will address me as Miss Thompson or ma'am."

"I forgot. But I take my orders from him."

"— and from me." In the past, she had overlooked much of his arrogance, which was a mistake. Now, when she stood him in his place, he feigned forgetfulness or resorted to roundabout talk. Holding the partly opened door, she said, "Get it straight for the last time. You're not bullying one of those poor, half-frightened girls at the Buffalo Bull. You are addressing Miss Tess Thompson. Got it?"

His hostility toward her, never well concealed, burned in him like a bed of banked coals, and she was quite aware of the main reason. Quinn had never had his way with her; he never would. So he liked to annoy her by various practices: coming for her before she was dressed; dropping innuendoes, his conversation brushing insult.

She held her ground. Finally, he said, "All right, Miss Thompson."

For still another moment she exhibited her loathing for him to see. At that, she went in and he followed. The door to her bedroom stood wide open. She smelled the familiar cigar stink.

A. B. Barr sat where he could watch who entered. A large, roly-shouldered man in rumpled brown suit, an oversize gold watch chain arching across his broad vest, each big link, she had mused many times, symbolic of the sturdy string of enterprises he had planted like cedar posts westward from Kansas City. He always wore dull brown suits. His beard was a curly brown. His pomaded brown hair was plastered down and parted in the middle. He was smoking a cigar and had been figuring on the back of an envelope, as usual. He raised his eyes from the envelope and she saw the deceptively mild brown eyes project a question. He took the cigar from his mouth. His thick lips stirred:

"I can tell there was trouble tonight."

Tess shrugged. "Quinn seems to think so."

"Plenty," Quinn declared, stepping deeper into the room, eager to tell his story. "That blond kid — the hunter — he slipped in below when there was a fight goin' on. He got away."

"How?"

"Don't know. We looked everywhere."

Barr's eyes, on Quinn, acquired a keener directness. "You go back — you find out everything. See me in the morning. Early." Barr's curt inclination of his head dismissed Quinn, who turned to go, but he flashed her his look of triumph before he went out.

Tess closed the door and sat down, her uneasiness deepening. Barr made a tsssking sound, shaking his head as he did so. She had learned to dread these habitual signs of pious disapproval for what they presaged.

"Greasy hunters who call themselves buffalo runners," he scoffed. "Louse-infested skinners who work for twenty-five cents an animal. Dumb cowboys who think twenty dollars a month is richness."

"You never refuse their money."

"If I didn't take it, other people would. They are fools who throw their money away. And you — you're acting foolish, too, Tess. You seem to forget where I found you."

She felt a flaring resentment. "How would I?"

"Isn't this better?" — he spread his heavy hands, then locked them across the broad slope of his vest — "than the upper parlors of the Teller House in Central City, Colorado?"

"I've paid you back, A.B. Many times." Her people had died long ago, on the trail from Missouri; when she was a mere girl. She had survived on the frontier, in a man's demanding world, and paid for it over and over. So she faced him without apology or humility. The fear she felt was not for herself.

His nature was not to admit. He did not now. "You've pretty much done as you pleased, Tess. I let you perform before the ogling saloon crowd. You seem to enjoy that."

"Would you close me off completely from the world?"

"I should, maybe, to keep you out of trouble — and to protect my own name. A man's good name is important above all, associated as I am with captains of commerce. The Eastern newspapers say I'm a trail blazer, a pathfinder, opening the buffalo frontier to the advance of civilization." She expressed a dim smile at his fondness for overweening statements, for self-rhetoric, and he saw her smile, just as she intended for him to see it. "Now," he said, visibly annoyed, "you have allowed this damned fool of a boy to fall in love with you. You have no doubt encouraged him."

"I have not."

It was as if he had not heard her. "The boy is losing his judgment. It was bad enough when he rode after you, and the two of you were gone from sight for sometime. Now this. Brazenly breaking into private quarters at the Buffalo Bull. I can't have that."

She rose and stood by the window. "That's Quinn's story — not mine. Quinn hates me. He would say anything to hurt me. You should get rid of that man, A.B."

"Why?"

"Some day he will ruin your good name."

"He does what I tell him to do."

"In his own way. Yes, I am followed and watched and peered at. I am something valuable. Like a fine-blooded horse. A good wagon. A stack of hides. I am property."

"If you dislike security," he said, keeping to his calm monotone, "why have you stayed?"

That drew her back, near him. "You know

why. Because I'm afraid. Afraid — if I did leave — it would be like before. And I'm not young anymore. That's your hold over me, A.B."

The conversation, she realized, was boring him. He had never liked discussions of human feelings. He got up and towered over her, a dogged, phlegmatic, immovable figure. "You won't see the boy again, understand?"

"I've never tried to see him."

"I think you're lying."

"I am not!"

His great paw of a hand enveloped her wrist. He pulled her to him. It was like the tug of a horse. "What happened on the river that day?"

"Nothing happened — nothing." In her intensity, she was driving her denial at him.

His grip tightened. "If so, why are you so flushed? Tell me."

"I told you. Nothing happened. You're hurting me." Somehow, suddenly, she wrenched free.

He picked up his hat. "The boy has gone too far. Now breaking and entering. There are laws of society, no matter where men are."

Her impulse was to sneer at him. Yet she dared not now. "Let him be," she said. "Don't hurt him. Nothing happened, A.B. That's God's truth."

Barr was at the door.

"A.B. — what are you going to do?"

He opened the door. He had to duck his head as he went out.

She heard his heavy, measured steps go down

the hall and across the porch. And as those sounds faded, the old fear clawed up through her and she realized she was utterly alone, as she had been, always.

CHAPTER 17

Leaving Andy to tend camp, Keith drove the gear wagon to town and tied the team in front of the general store. A detachment of cavalry trotted in from the north, dusty figures who laid longing appraisals on the roistering Buffalo Bull.

Keith handed Coralie down. Turning, he noticed the watching man. A bowler-hatted individual, jaunty, in sporty clothes, who held a searching scrutiny on him, who turned away as Keith stared back, feeling an elusive recognition pass.

Lenny's first gift, a jackknife, took a matter of moments; but the clerk rummaged and chin-tugged at length before he found a tapering wooden top, as red as a farmer's barn, and the right size string to spin it, and a bag of varicolored marbles. New brass-toed shoes, overalls, and a blue shirt followed.

For once, Lenny was without words. His soft hazel eyes were enormous over the stack of things in his arms as he trailed Keith and Coralie out of the store. At the Ladies' Ready-to-Wear where he had purchased Coralie's shoes, Keith left the boy with Coralie, who was going to pick out her wedding dress. The problem of a ring was already solved: Coralie would wear her mother's.

Troopers passed on the board walk. As Keith started across the street, blue-clad arms encircled him from behind, hugging him, and a deep-chested voice, expelling a fog of whisky fumes, spoke in his ear, "Friend — heap friend."

The powerful arms released him and Keith, turning, found the broad heavy-lipped, smile-cunning face of High Medicine, the Cheyenne of the Sweet Water, who now pumped Keith's hand and said again, "Friend — heap friend."

"Friend," Keith said, smiling in turn.

"Come on, High," a trooper said. "Let's go water the horses."

The Cheyenne grinned amiably at the trooper and turned his attention back to Keith. "Friend — where you hunt?"

Keith pointed north and northwest and shook his head, indicating no more. "White men killed three of my friends."

High Medicine scowled his sympathy. He blinked, his black eyes growing worried. "Hunt buffalo — bad — heap bad. Heap Comanch'." He made scalping motions. "Keep gun one hand all time. Get wood one hand, gun other hand. Make little fire," he cautioned, holding one hand low. "Cook meat one hand, gun other hand. Take gun ever'where — never see Comanch'. Leave gun — see plenty heap mean Comanch' damn quick."

Keith thanked him. High Medicine pumped his hand ceremoniously; then the coppery features split in a fawning smile. "Friend buy whisky?"

"No whisky," Keith smiled back. "Heap friend just the same."

High Medicine's smile flickered out. At the trooper's call he turned reluctantly away.

Heap Comanch', Keith was thinking. For one who had witnessed the buffalo slaughter, he wondered what had kept them so long.

He found Mike Cassidy puzzling over ledgers in the hide-yard office, and through him made arrangements to send a wire from Fort Griffin to the Massengale family, Sam's money to follow; the offer for the wagons and stock, yet to be worked out with Andy, would come later.

"It's these hardcases that be the ruination of the buffalo trade," the Irishman said, saddened and outraged at the news. He nodded his favor of Keith's plans. "You can freight goods out from the railroad at Fort Worth. Take back hides or bones. The boys are gettin' a penny a pound a mile on freight. Bones will be the business in a year or two . . . Mules are faster and grain is high. Bull teams are slower and cheaper to feed. Take your choice . . . You'll have the one big Shuttler. Fine. A Shuttler is low, easy to load . . . You could start makin' a profit for yourselves tomorrow. Haul hides for me to Fort Worth."

"Not yet," Keith smiled. "I'm getting married. Is there a preacher in town?"

"A preacher? Now that's the only thing you won't find in A. B. Barr's fair city. Possibly there's one in Fort Griffin."

Keith accompanied Cassidy to the entrance of

the Texas House, declined a drink, and turned along the walk up the street, his mind on Coralie and the boy.

Several doors from the Ladies' Ready-to-Wear, in front of a new saddle shop, in the brief shade of the square overhang there, he saw a little man in a bowler hat standing beside a slender, well-dressed woman. The man moved off a short way and swung around, watching, his deliberate actions drawing Keith's eyes. As that happened, a stronger recognition reached Keith and he remembered at last: the cocky, brash-mannered man at the Texas House the time he and poor Hub and Andy had hauled in the hides.

Keith's interest switched back to the woman. Something strange was plucking at his senses. He paused. Something about her. Her face was hidden behind a dark veil. She wore a blue traveling suit of obvious elegance and fitting, and gloves and a flowered hat of high quality, and she held herself in a certain manner, head tilted slightly, a suggestion of superiority — in a manner that hurled a stiffening shock through him.

She stepped toward him. She said, "Keith, dearest . . . I don't believe you know me," and she lifted the veil and kissed him on the mouth, a lingering kiss. He felt a stir, an awakening. He breathed an eddy of verbena.

"Yes — Charlotte, I know you." *My God,* he thought, *she's as beautiful and perfect as ever, unchanged by time.* And he asked himself, why, damn it, the physical feel of her should yet affect him? Why, after all these years?

"Keith, we can't talk here."

He was finally collecting his senses. "There's nothing to talk about."

"There are many things. Your father —"

"What about him?"

"He isn't well, Keith. He . . ." Charlotte Van Tine let the rest lie unsaid, on the brink of her perfect lips, within the green mystery of her veiled eyes. "Please let me talk to you at the hotel. Everyone is staring."

So they were, Keith saw, and no wonder, for she was indeed beautiful. Shaggy runners, sun-browned cowboys, burly teamsters, and two envious, overpainted girls from the Buffalo Bull.

Nothing seemed quite real to Keith as he walked stiffly beside her to the Texas House, where the pasty-faced clerk bowed not once, but again and again, staring openly at her as she swept past.

Charlotte Van Tine unlocked a door at the end of the hall, to a room farthest removed from the noisy street, and Keith entered behind her, leaving the door ajar.

Her intimate laugh floated back to him. "Are you accustomed to leaving hotel doors open out west?"

He frowned and closed it. "Now what's this about my father?"

"He isn't well, Keith."

"How bad is he?"

"Not bedfast," she said, uncertainly, and by

that he suspected the story was a pretext to get him here. "But he can't carry on as he used to, Keith. He wants you to come back and take over the business."

That, Keith knew also, was old news.

She removed her hat and veil and laid them on the dresser, and touched her exquisite hands to her gold-colored hair, standing just so, the room's dimness as another veil softly over her perfect face. As lovely, he realized, as the evening he had found her in the carriage house with the older man she later married.

"Would you like something to drink?" she asked. "I believe you used to prefer a certain whisky made in Fairfax County, Virginia. I brought some for you."

"Nothing, thank you. Did my father tell you where I was?"

"Of course not." Her voice was gay. "I had to find out for myself."

"Remarkable."

"It's an easy matter to hire Pinkerton detectives if you pay them enough. To have them watch every incoming wagon and learn the identities of the people. To check with the drivers on Cassidy's hide wagons. When I found out you were in the vicinity of Barr's Town, I came to Dodge City. When I was doubly certain — after learning you were with an outfit on the Pease Rivers — I took a stage to Fort Elliott and now here."

Listening, he saw where the bowler-hatted

man fitted in, and he was not surprised at her determination to get what she wanted. Yet, for all that had happened to Charlotte and himself, and it seemed long ago, he saw her as a stranger might for the first time, seeing only her undeniable surface beauty. He had saved himself from her by forcing simplicity and order into his life, by following a dim destination, which he had found by the grace of faith and circumstances — though never quite able to forget her.

"You look better than I've ever seen you, Keith, dear. You look big and strong. You look happy. I hardly recognized you at first, when I saw you bring that — that girl — to the dress shop. Ives pointed you out from the saddle shop."

He said nothing, for he realized he had nothing to say to her, for inside himself she was dead to him. Still, he felt he must hear her out after she had come so far.

Her fingers played with a button on her dress, her first sign of uneasiness. "I just missed you in New York when you returned from Europe. I expected you to come home, but you didn't. You went west." By dress, carriage, and gesture, she had always sought to draw attention to herself, not that a man minded that in a beautiful woman; if failing, she exaggerated and affected the dramatic. He heard her voice grow unnatural. He saw her fling out an arm to him.

"Keith, I've been hunting you for three years, I've never remarried. Doesn't that mean something to you? Isn't it in you to forgive?"

"I never hated you for what happened that night."

"So you do understand?" She started toward him, then, watching his face, she checked herself. "Oh, I was wrong, I was foolish — I admit. And money isn't so important as I once thought it was, although I'm a wealthy woman now, Keith. My husband died soon after we married. He left me a great deal."

"Fortunate. I remember he was much older."

"Keith, you sound so distant, so formal. That foolish part of our lives is over. Can't we begin again?"

She waited for him to touch her, and when he stayed motionless, he saw the appeal deepen in her face, and also her desperation and humility. One lovely hand rose to her breasts, a motion which drew his attention to the brooch pinned at the neck of her stylish suit, and to the ring she wore, long-ago gifts of his which seemed coldly impersonal now — displayed today to sway him.

"Keith," she said, a catch in her voice, "why did you run away so soon? Perhaps, if you'd stayed . . ."

"I was trying to find out who I am. I know now. I'm not going back."

She came closer, and the nearness spoiled a trifle of her perfection, letting in the just perceptible pouting of the full lips. He saw an awful concentration in her eyes; in another moment she would be begging. To spare her that, he turned away.

She bridged the space between them with her body, pressing herself to him, her arms around him, a frantic clinging in them. She strained upward to kiss him, her lips warm and seeking and desperate. It seemed cruel for him not to kiss her, not to embrace one so lovely. His hands touched her and dropped.

She sensed all that. She looked at him through misty eyes, and he saw the terrible truth inscribed in her face, as naked as raw pain. "It's gone, isn't it, Keith?"

"It is."

"I remember how it used to be. How real it was. Surely there's something of that left in you for me?"

"I loved you once, Charlotte. It took me a long time to get over it — but I did." He would not tell her how much she had taken from him; how far the loss of her had driven him.

"I wanted too much," she said. "I wanted everything. Today, when I saw you with that plain looking girl . . . Why, she's no more than a servant girl!" She stopped, seeing his keen anger; but before he could speak, she said as impulsively, "Keith — forgive me that. A woman's last thrust at her victorious rival."

"It's still the same, Charlotte. There's nothing to forgive." He looked at her for the last time. "You are still beautiful. All your life you will be."

He wanted to leave her that. He went out and closed the door.

Ives, the detective, was waiting in the cramped

lobby. He slid his bowler back and met Keith's eyes with satisfaction.

"Don't let Mrs. Van Tine go back by way of Fort Elliott," Keith said to him. "It's too dangerous."

"That's considerate of you — *Mr. Keith Madison Hayden.*"

Keith seized him by his coat front and grabbed him under the crotch and dumped him in a corner. He landed heavily, the breath jarred out of him. His bowler bounced to the floor. Picking it up, Keith yanked it down over Ives' ears and walked outside, conscious of a freedom that was light and swift. He hurried.

He came to the ladies' shop and looked in. Coralie and Lenny were gone, which wasn't surprising as late as he was. A look at the sun told him a good deal of time had passed. He glanced up the street for the gear wagon; it wasn't there. He rubbed his jaw. So tired of waiting, they had gone back to camp. Possibly Lenny was sick.

He rushed into the street, striding for the river. At the top of the slope he began trotting.

The moment he swung off the road he saw the light trail wagon was missing, but there was the gear wagon. He started running, calling Coralie's name and Andy's. There was no answer. He ran to the camp circle, looking, looking. It was strange. Everything seemed undisturbed. He looked inside the gear wagon and ran to the cook wagon.

On the seat, arranged side by side, rubbed

clean of dust, were Coralie's new shoes. Underneath them was a sheet of paper. He lifted the shoes and took the paper. It was written on. Swiftly, he scanned the penciled words:

Keith
    It was wrong for us to come. I know that now. We're going back. Papa will return the light wagon and team. Thank you for helping us.
                                        Coralie

He folded the note with meticulous care, creased it between thumb and forefinger, folded and creased it again, and stuck it in his shirt pocket, staring without seeing, and slumped down on the wagon tongue, too shaken to think straight just yet. He was glad she had let Lenny keep his small boy's gifts; that was different. And presently, brooding, he decided there was yet time to catch up with her. Time to head her off from going back into Indian country.

Now another thought struck him. Andy? Where was he? Andy's gelding was out there on picket. Keith circled camp, calling Andy again, and he ran to the river and called up and down it, and ran back and called again. He heard no answer. It wasn't like Andy to leave camp untended.

A horse was running on the river road, coming from town. Keith heard it slow up as the rider took the camp trail, and then he saw a woman in

316

riding habit on a blood-red bay. A woman of striking paleness and delicate features.

"I'm Tess Thompson," she told him. "You must be Andy's partner." Keith nodded. Her manner was matter-of-fact, but her trembling voice betrayed her. "They arrested Andy. Took him just before the woman and little boy came back."

"They?"

"A. B. Barr's marshals. Least, that's what he calls them. Andy's in jail. Behind the Buffalo Bull."

"I'll pay his fine and get him out."

She cast him her worldly knowledge. "I'm afraid it's not that simple. They'll make it look like he tried to escape. Then kill him. It's an old game."

He found all that too much to swallow, and he didn't trust her. "If they want to kill him, why don't they take him out and shoot him?"

"It's the hunters — the saloon trade," she explained. "Hunters stick together. They don't like Barr's business methods. It's got to look right. Even here."

"What's the charge?" He asked it with an angry contempt.

"Breaking and entering. Barr has a so-called judge, too."

Keith gave her a contemptuous laugh. "Has to be more than that behind it. My guess it's you."

She leaned toward him, earnest and without apology. "Andy came to my dressing room last night. Barr thinks something has been going on between us. It hasn't — not that much. I don't want Andy hurt. That's all that matters now."

He believed her. He slapped his empty belt. He went to the gear wagon, buckled on his gunbelt. A second thought caused him to take the loaded Big Fifty and a belt of shells.

"You can't just barge in there."

"Hell I can't."

"You have a little time. They need to set him up first."

"I can't wait long," Keith said, thinking of Coralie. "Neither can Andy."

"You can't help him dead." The high-strung bay made a nervous turn. She reined the horse back, her pale features settling into a willed calm. "I'm going to help you."

"Can I trust you?"

An unqualified scorn for him leaped into her eyes. "You'll have to. I know a way you can ride in close and not be seen."

On that, he saddled his gelding and Andy's, tied on Andy's Sharps, crammed the saddlebags with sacks of the big cartridges, and threw a light pack on the fastest mule. As he took the lead ropes and mounted, he asked her, "When this is over, mind getting word to Cassidy to look after our wagons and stock?"

She replied with a curt nod and led away, traveling south along the winding river, Keith trailing her. They rode for ten minutes or more, longer than necessary, in his mind. He was closing up to question her when she turned north. They climbed out of the low valley, wound through scattered, cedar-clad hills, going hard. Again, just when Keith began to wonder at her purpose, she veered eastward, riding fast, skillfully weaving in and around knots of stubby timber.

She reined up and Keith, coming alongside, saw Barr's Town sloping away from below them, and the back side of the Buffalo Bull, behind it a rectangular picket stockade higher than a man on horseback, no larger than a tight horse corral.

"There's the jail," she said. "The gate faces the saloon. Andy is in a picket shed."

"How many on guard?"

"I don't know." Her hard, capable assurance seemed to desert her all at once. "I could ride up to the gate, maybe . . . while you . . ."

He shook off the notion, meanwhile sorting out calculations and running up against rigid facts. Neither circumstances nor time allowed elaborate plans. Only directness, only surprise and quickness could free Andy.

He came down and unsheathed the Sharps, saying, "You cover us on the way back," and seing how slim she was he had his misgivings.

"If you're wondering whether I can handle that cannon," she taunted him, "I can — just show me."

He showed her how to open the breech and load, how to steady one elbow on her knee when firing. On afterthought, he gave her Andy's lighter rifle and handed her a bag of shells.

Keith's foremost thought had been to approach on foot. Now, seeing that meant crossing an open hundred yards or more, he changed his mind and slid the Big Fifty back in the saddle scabbard and took off.

Riding north, he saw that he could keep the high-walled stockade between him and the rear of the saloon once he turned east.

The hot sun stood high, in drowsy flame, as he made the eastward turn, straight for the stockade. The town's noontime monotone gradually sharpened to distinctness, the drone of voices, the tired clop of freighter's teams, the creaking of burdened wagons. When the rough picket wall began sliding past on his right, he drew the Sharps and slacked it across the saddle. Not two rods on, the wall made a right-angle turn.

He turned with it, and dead ahead he saw the wooden gate, iron-hinged, sagged open. A guard on a box dozed in the opening. He roused up at the padding of Keith's horse, surprisingly alert for a dozing man, and came openmouthed when he saw Keith.

As the man started to his feet, Keith booted the gelding headlong at him. The guard dodged, flung up his rifle protectively, and was too late. Keith, two-handed, laid the long barrel of the Sharps across his head like a club. He heard the solidness of octagonal steel meeting bone, the grunted cry, and felt the blow through his wrists.

Even as the figure crumpled, Keith was plunging the horse through — and sighting the shed and cutting for it, and suddenly, improbably, Andy ran out. Keith got a glimpse of his taut face as he wheeled the horse for Andy to swing on behind, and then they were rushing toward the gate. It was still open. The man was still on the ground. And as no one ran up to block the opening, the rescue seemed almost anticlimactic to Keith, for this was too easy.

His horse shied at the prone figure. Keith forced the gelding ahead; it jumped over the man and in doing so struck the box and shied on that splintering sound, scraping Keith against the gate as they broke clear, throwing Keith half around in the saddle.

A hatless man was running out the back door of the Buffalo Bull. A chunky man with a rifle. His pitted face had a savage look. He snapped a shot as he ran. Keith's horse screamed, jerked. By now Keith had the Sharps up. Its roar swelled in his ears. He saw the rifleman throw up his hands.

As they whipped around the corner of the stockade, Keith booted the gelding harder. It seemed to falter, then lurched ahead running. They ran humping down that side, shielded from behind for the moment.

Keith felt the faltering again when they turned across the open stretch to rim for the trees, though the horse went on, doggedly, in ragged stride.

It happened fast. The sickening give of the straining muscles, the thrusting hoofs falling slower and slower, the fine head jerking, the fore-quarters suddenly breaking down. Keith, kicking free of the stirrups, went sailing over the horse's head. He struck sprawling, still gripping the Sharps. Dazed for a whirling instant, he flung around and saw his horse floundering and Andy on hands and knees.

Keith ducked at a bullet's whine and heard the *splat* of a rifle, and another, and saw smokepuffs behind the saloon. As if in answering rage, a Sharps bellowed from the trees on the slope; in seconds, again. Two figures behind the saloon scurried toward the stockade.

Keith raised up. Mouth creased, he shot his horse with the six-gun. A backward glance, and he and Andy ran for the trees. There, slowing up, Andy turned. "Keith — you saved my life." Keith gave him an onward push.

Black powdersmoke smudged Tess Thompson's pale cheeks. Andy could only stare at her, thunderstruck. Keith, taking the rifle and handing it to Andy, tipped his head to her, admiring her.

"Chain on the shed door was loose," Andy panted. "Guard dozing. Gate open. It looked fishy."

"It was," Keith said. "One step through that gate you'd been dead. That man was waiting."

"Quinn," nodded Andy. "It was Quinn. Miss Tess, he won't bother you again."

Keith spun the two of them a perceptive look. "Andy," he said, "Coralie went back to camp.

Hurry." He walked away to watch below, already imagining the distance to be traveled, and his horse dead and a mule to ride. A curious crowd was collecting behind the saloon. Before long Barr would be sending somebody up here.

She looked younger, Andy was thinking. Her dark eyes lively with excitement. She was still breathing fast, her breasts rising full and round against her jacket. She held her lithe body straight and poised, like a lady. He had a sudden rush of feeling for her.

"You better come with us," he said.

She raised her head higher. Her eyes glowed, yet he saw more than excitement there. "Andy, I'm leaving Barr's Town for good. I'm going alone."

"You don't have to. You can come with me."

"It's better this way, Andy. Believe me I know." He was hearing the strangest softness in her singer's pleasant voice, as if he listened to bitter-sweet fiddle music way off on a warm summer night. "I'll go to Fort Griffin first," she said. "I have money. I may travel in the East."

Utter despair smashed him. A lump of sickness was balling up within him, rising to smother his chest and stifle his throat. He said shakily, "Barr will try to stop you."

"Not with Quinn gone. I know."

"Miss Tess, I'm asking you for the last time. Come with me." He realized this was the moment for him to tell her how he felt about her.

"It can't be, Andy," she said, and he realized

she had read his thoughts.

"Why not?"

"Time helps us see many things, Andy."

She untied the reins. He lifted her easily to the saddle, the lightness of her, the wonderful feel of her, leaving a shivering ache in his body. When she looked down at him, he saw an understanding there beyond his years. A dreadful sense told him he would not see her again.

"Thank you, Andy," she said simply, yet with a baffling, too, of other, deeper things.

He couldn't breath, he couldn't speak. He was too choked up, grasping for elusive meanings, knowing, yet not knowing. He loved her. He knew he loved her, except he couldn't find the unadorned words.

At the final moment her face changed, pushing out of its inscrutable mask, softening. He saw her lips stir to speak, and he had his hope. It passed, as quickly, as he saw her half-smile return.

He watched her ride off. A trim, bobbing shape, little by little dropping from sight as the land sloped toward the river, till only her plumed hat was visible. Then it, too, vanished. He stood fast another moment, resisting what his eyes told him. She was gone out of his life.

A dim sound pierced Andy's consciousness. It was Keith coming back. He felt Keith's touch on his shoulder. Andy nodded, knowing they had to go at once. He groped toward his horse, feeling a thousand years old, part of him understanding; maybe, in time, the rest of him would.

CHAPTER 18

North of Barr's Town, Keith slid off the long-legged mule and shifted part of the pack to the gelding; after that, they took turns riding the mule. Keith was discouraged, though he said no word to Andy. At best they were three hours behind Coralie and Lenny.

Later still, through the quivering heat of early afternoon, Keith sighted a low mass spread out on the trail ahead. Biting back his dread as they approached, he saw the remains of a burned wagon and the shapes of two men prickly with arrows. The discovery was enough to make him question even more whether she had slipped through, for this was only a few hours old.

Hurrying, they crossed a vast flat dappled with old buffalo droppings, and toiled through the jaws of a row of reddish hills. The massive emptiness of the country peeled away before Keith's eyes, the horizon swimming in hellish glare, the vaporous waves creating an imaginary effect, the land seeming more liquid than solid.

Far off, scattered, on guard, he saw the broken battlements of solitary buttes. At each open expanse he searched the wavering lines of the wagon road for movement or another crumpled mass.

In one suspended interval, while they traversed a mesquite plain which sloped eastward —

eroded, gashed, breaking off into wicked little draws and brushy canyons — the country sprang to tremulous life. Bright flashes on a butte. Flickering mirror signals answering from a butte to the north.

Andy swallowed. "Never saw that before. Pretty slick."

Watching, Keith thought of what Sam Massengale had said: if a man with a Sharps kept to open country, away from the breaks, he could stand off quite a pack of Indians.

The fluttering flashes died, not repeated. An ominous calm seemed to settle down.

"Let's pull off west," Keith said. "But keep the trail in sight."

Before many minutes, Keith, eyeing the northeast, saw a spur of dust roiling up from the mesquite brokenness. He watched it bear rapidly to the west, a long coil of brown feathering eastward on the hot wind, its unseen riders on a slant to cut across the wagon road ahead of the white men.

That single streak of dust grew to a fuming whirlwind, much larger, much nearer. When Keith saw riders bulging on the trail near a hill, he yelled:

"Andy! Throw your horse!"

He was swinging down off the mule, pulling free a piece of rope. But the mule, like all mules, took a sudden perverse notion of its own, and went to jumping sideways. Taking the bridle by the bit, Keith yanked the long head toward him.

Then bending, reaching, he jerked up the offside fetlock and drove with the point of his shoulder. The tripped mule landed sidebelly with an explosive grunt. Keith spun a loop around one hind shank, then the other, tied fast, and looped across to the front cannons and hogtied.

Andy was doing the same.

On the hill the dust was settling and the Indian riders swarmed as if around a hive, restlessly. Keith laid the Sharps across the mule and waited, watching the Indians riding in tight circles and making insulting gestures. Some fired rifles. Keith heard a few whistling shots.

"They're just outa range," Andy swore.

"Wait'll they come closer."

Hardly had Keith spoken when four riders came dashing toward the flat, quirting their horses, yipping like coyotes. A short run and they veered off, circling for the hill, their hooting cries hanging over the flat. Keith saw all the Indians come together, and get down for a parley. They seemed unhurried.

The yellow sun drew a slanting bead on the heat-soaked flat. A stirring now on the hill. The powwow was breaking up.

Keith's pulse jumped as the Indians began mounting and streaming downhill. Hot as the sun was, his skin felt cold as he saw them reach the bottom, flowing there, massing there, some wearing feathered war bonnets which danced in the wind. Dust boiled up under cavorting war ponies.

He tensed as the war party bunched and moved forward in a brisk trot. After a hundred yards the trot became a steady lope. The dust was blooming into a brownish fog. The tough war mounts flattening out, in a drumming run, flashing their solid, earthy colors — bays, blacks, duns, roans, paints. Just when approaching accurate rifle range, the Indians swept off in a dusty circle.

All but a knot of riders rushed straight on from the tail end of the circle. The leading warrior rode a big chestnut.

Keith rose to one knee to fire. At his sudden move- ment the rider threw himself low on the withers of his horse, and at that instant Keith fired.

The chestnut went down with a gush of dust. The rider tumbled. Two Indians swooped forward, one catching the unhorsed rider by his hand, another his foot. They were cutting back for the hill when Andy's Sharps boomed. The brave holding the foot rolled limply off his horse, which raced ahead, and the rescued Indian became a ball of spinning dust, then sprang up running.

Andy whooped and thumbed in another shell. Keith saw him start to say something, and cease, for the Indians were bunching once more, faster this time. Keith threw a slug into them. But they kept swarming. Flailing their war ponies. Still bunched. Charging like buffalo. Howling like wolves.

After these first shots, Keith's coldness left him. He heard Andy blasting. An Indian slipped from his yellow mustang, but the charge never wavered. With his next shot, Keith saw a pony spill and its rider flipping, ridden under, lost in the dust. For the first time, Keith wondered if they were going to be overrun. He worked the Sharps faster. He heard Andy come in with the carbine.

But as that fear caught at Keith, he saw the wedge of riders open like a precise fan and split, sheering off to make running passes. As the first Indian on Keith's side drew abreast, the rider slid to the opposite flank of his pony and hung a naked leg over his pony's backbone and clung there, suspended by a rope looped around the pony's neck. Keith glimpsed a painted face. The Indian fired underneath the pony's neck. Keith shot and missed.

Now, above the yammering yells, he heard feathered whisperings mixed with gunshots. The mule was struggling to get up, kicking, head-rocking, wall-eyed, squealing. Two arrows protruded from the brown rump.

Keith put the muzzle of the Sharps on a fleet dun war pony which seemed to skim over the flat. He followed it, leading a trifle. When the face blurred under the surging neck, Keith fired. A brown shape twisted away, rolling like a log on the swift millrace of the short grass. Two Indians veered out of the line. Hanging low, they scooped up the limp body without even slowing their ponies.

Keith reloaded and looked across through the

film of drifting dust, stared hard, and slowly exhaled. As though a bunch of stampeding buffalo, the Indians had passed. He could see them circling back through the yellow-brown haze toward the hillside. Loosely, they collected there, but not to parley. At once, Keith and Andy bombarded them. The distance was too great to tell if they hit anything, but presently the Indians began moving off.

A pony was down on Andy's side, its dead rider pinned underneath. Keith pulled the arrows out of the mule's rump, and ran a cleaning patch through the bore of the Sharps. He passed the canteen to Andy, who gulped a swallow and handed it back. Keith drank, and his mind sank on a thought. The fight here had killed his last chance of reaching Coralie and the boy in time. And if he and Andy left here in daylight, they'd be dead, too.

Watching the loitering afternoon sun, watching the light weaken and die, measuring the change by the east face of the hill from where the Indians had charged, there where the first purple gloom of twilight stood banked, feeling the light wind rising — abruptly, Keith could wait no longer. He got up and untied the mule and roused it, suffering and staggering, to its feet, swaying with stiffness.

With Andy leading his horse ahead, Keith trailed behind, listening, probing the changing light. He heard not a brush of sound behind them.

They mounted and rode west a way, then turned north to ride parallel to the trail. When a deeper darkness fell, they swung in on the rutted trace, for they had to follow it, dreading what they might find. A gray-ghost moon was rising.

Coralie watched the summer-brown prairie. Under the humid glaze of the straight-down sun, objects lost their reality and assumed fantastic shapes, twisting, bending, sinking, rising, shivering, beckoning. There wasn't a fluff of cloud in the blue vault of the sky. Heat waves flowed like quicksilver, fooling the eye, deceiving the judgment, lulling the senses. One fold of land, she thought, could hide a whole tribe of Indians.

But, living close to prairie life, she recognized the distant creatures out there to the west. A little sentinel band of antelope grazing into the wind. They looked like white dots scattered on the dun-colored slope. She understood why. Antelope had pillow-white rumps and snowy stomachs. When they ran in fear, their rump patches glittered like signals.

She turned back to the wagon and built a fire. A smaller one than usual, a caution upon her, thinking of her father and Wiley, who were coming in for the noon meal. Much needed to be done after her absence. Washing. Baking. Cleaning up. She and Lenny had driven into camp early that morning, before the day's hunting started.

"I knew you'd come home," Cal Dockum said.

"You got better sense than gallivantin' off when you're needed."

He didn't ask her why she had come back, and she didn't explain. It was enough for him, she could see, to have her back under any terms. He looked slyly at Wiley and went to funning with Lenny.

"Mighty glad to see you, Coralie," Wiley said, and she saw the undisguised pleasure in his tawny eyes. He stood a further moment. An awkwardness stiffened him, turned him. "I'll get water. Hustle up some wood." He strode to the spring and back. Soon she heard the quick, strong strokes of his ax. He brought in an armload of exactly cut lengths of wood and dumped them.

Pressing on her mind was the talk she had heard in town of the Indian scare. "Wiley," she worried, "have you and Papa seen any Indians about?"

He stacked the wood slowly, piece by piece. He was an uncomplicated man and he wished not to alarm her. She could see him struggling over his reply.

"You've seen some, haven't you?"

"Just a little bunch," he discounted. "West of here. Yesterday. Cal threw a couple of shots at 'em. They hightailed it fast."

Before they left to hunt northwest of camp, she insisted they take the Henry rifle. Dockum patted his old carbine; with a show of pleasing her, Wiley laid the shotgun and some shells in the hide cart.

She kept watching while she worked. Lenny was playing in the lacy shade of a mesquite, completely happy again, engrossed with his gifts. She hadn't had the heart to make Lenny give them up. Now, just seeing them brought back the tearing hurt. But by watching and keeping her hands busy, by concentrating on everything she had to do, she managed to shunt the thoughts aside, yet never far away in the background of her mind.

She took her things and Lenny's out of the light trail wagon, for it was impelling that she separate herself from reminders of what had happened in Barr's Town. Every few moments she watched the antelope.

Having used the water Wiley had brought her, she called to Lenny and they walked to the spring to fill the bucket and walked back. She lifted the bucket to the bench and let her eyes search the encircling open prairie. She thought of the burned-out wagon on the trail north of Barr's Town, and the bodies of the two men lying in the blackened ruins, their shapes pin-cushioned with arrows.

Hence, she had punished the mules severely for the next several miles, until the undisturbed country on both sides of the trail and in front reassured her. Later, seeing flashes on an eastward butte, she turned off the trail and waited a long time, hidden among some mesquites; still later, she saw more signal flashes, mirror flashes, she supposed, from two buttes, and presently she heard firing to the south, downtrail, behind her, booms which sounded like buffalo rifles. It seemed a wise time to leave. Since she could see the wagon road by moonlight, she had driven the tough mules most of the night, halting only to rest them, while Lenny slept on a quilt behind her on the bed of the wagon.

She was getting sleepy again, but her wide-awake caution wouldn't let her rest. Not until she saw the men coming in would she relax.

Coralie spread the oil cloth on the rough table and set the tin plates around and tin coffee cups for the men; turning, she glanced again toward the antelope, started on and glanced again, keenly, stiffening, and stood still, her heart hammering.

The white dots were darting away, the white rump patches in glittering motion from left to right across the brown face of the hill.

She did not hesitate. She whirled, calling high-pitched to Lenny, and hastened to the wagon for the Henry and the shell belt and a water jug. Lenny came fast. His eyes looked huge, his small, round face solemn; so she knew that he understood.

Without a word, she took his hand and they ran for the wooded hill.

Keith heard rifles popping before he and Andy crossed Ranch Creek. One rifle's sound stood out. There would be the slap of a shot and a charged silence, and several shots jammed together and long-running silence, then the shoot-

334

ing would start again.

He saw the smoke when they turned south-west, a sullen cloud overhanging the Dockum camp, and the leaping scarlet of a burning wagon.

The rifle slammed again, and he saw the swish of an Indian pony among the mesquites. The shot had sounded from the wooded hill to Keith's left. As he recognized the light crack of the Henry, a mighty relief wrung him when the Henry opened up furiously. A wildness in the fir-ing, a frenzy, a helplessness, apparently directed at something in the distance.

He hauled about, seeing the hide cart bumping in from the west. Two figures hurrying alongside it. The shorter one turned and Keith heard a carbine bang. That was Dockum. Wiley was handling the mules while Dockum covered the rear. Behind them Keith saw weaving riders. Dockum stopped to fire again. The riders hung back.

Keith hit the ground and sighted along his rifle, only to damn his frustration as he lowered it. Dockum and Wiley moved between him and the Indians. He laid a futile shot over the heads of the white men. He heard Andy go.

Keith, reloading, saw that Dockum was falling behind, unable to keep up. Wiley slowed for him. Keith fired again, but saw the Indians rushing forward unchecked and Dockum clawing vainly at his carbine. Dockum ran toward the wagon. And suddenly, as if hearing the Indians upon him, he spun and swung the carbine by the barrel. A swarm of riders enveloped him. Keith, trying to fire into them, thought he saw Dockum's carbine swing once more.

Wiley was running back to help Dockum. With his motion came the deep tones of a double-barreled shotgun. Now Keith saw him throw the shotgun down and run to the cart. The Indians left Dockum to rush Wiley, who faced them with his ax. He struck all about, a berserk wild man. He knocked a rider off his pony. But even while that shape was still tumbling in the grass, the Indians coiled around Wiley.

Instantly: a savage snarl of ponies, of half-naked bodies and slashing arms. Wiley seemed to rise above the dusty swarm, swinging his ax. Keith saw him briefly. Another moment and the ponies blotted him out.

As Keith and Andy began firing fast, the riders broke away, scattering back. Wiley was down.

Keith could think of Coralie and the boy now. The Henry was still. He was loping the mule along the base of the hill, looking upslope, Andy close behind him, when an ocher-streaked Indian rose like smoke behind a clump of brush, rifle lifted.

Keith tried to swerve and get his Sharps up, but the black mouth of the muzzle followed him. He saw the spout of flame as he felt blinding, terrible pain in his head and tasted blood in his mouth. He kept saying to himself he must stay conscious, else he would fall and die. But already he was falling into a pit of blackness and, last, he thought he heard the roar of Andy's buffalo rifle . . .

In this strange place where he drifted aimlessly, there was no sky, no earth. His mind was clear, but he could not speak. He could see, but he saw nothing distinct. He could feel, but he had no feelings. He could hear, but only muffled murmurs reached him. All sense of time was lost, yet time did not matter. He was nobody.

It was the green dome that puzzled him most. It arched up where the sky should be. It was generally there when he opened his eyes, though sometimes not; then everything was pit black. It seemed near enough to touch. But when he strained upward, he went tumbling off into utter blackness; thereafter, when he saw the greenness again, he let it alone. To him it represented all remaining life and hope. It was the best he had.

And then, haunting and torturing him, he began seeing dim, bygone faces whose identities eluded him. But as they drifted toward him, he recognized each one and a wrenching emotion passed through him. Sam and Levi and Hub. Nearly formless figures standing forsaken at the edge of camp, sheered in mist.

He cried out, but as he ran forward to throw his arms about them, they began fading before his eyes, even though he was shouting, "Come in, boys! Supper's ready! Andy's here! There's a bottle in the wagon! Come on!" He came to a stumbling stop where they had stood, sorrowing, seeing them glide backward, receding in the roiling gray haze, their unforgettable faces forever calm.

He saw Charlotte, too. Oh, he saw her. Everywhere he turned he saw her, clad in the luminous dress, posed so he could not miss the soft light glowing on her perfect face. And so he ran away, ran until exhaustion drove him into the pit again.

He saw Coralie. She was firing the Henry. He saw her on the shaggy hillside. He shouted. But when he climbed the hill, she wasn't there. A searching moment and he sighted her a second time, higher up. He scrambled there, ragged of breath, full of expectation, and looked all around, bewildered. She wasn't there. He called her name. Neither did she answer. He was alone.

He saw Andy come out of the Buffalo Bull between two men. He saw the appeal on young Andy's face, and he started after them. In his haste, he stumbled and fell, though the street was perfectly level. By the time he got up, they were out of sight. He could hear Andy calling him, but he was powerless to move his wooden arms and legs.

There came a vague interval when he could see real sky and red hills and short, curly grass and he could hear and feel the wind like the warm voice of an old friend. He stood on a high hill and the river valley below was teeming with buffalo. He hurried down there and set up his rest sticks. An enormous guardian bull took his eye. A long shot, but everything Keith did today was flawless. He killed the bull with a single bullet. But when he bent down to skin the bull, a dreadful remorse overtook him, sharpened with shame; and when he looked up all the buffalo had vanished. He was alone again. He was nobody. He was nothing.

In the timeless void that followed he commenced to grasp that the faces no longer haunted him, that although still alone he could sense reality somewhere near him. A low voice, a cool touch told him; always he was struggling to find his lost identity and his friends, but never quite.

He had no warning. He became aware that the drifting had ended and he was rising through vaporous space, rushing toward the green dome and the core of light shining beyond it.

He opened his eyes and all his senses sprang exalted and wondering, and the greenness, he realized, was a lacework of mesquite branches and the light breaking through was the open sky. Rolling his eyes, he saw enough to recognize the Dockum camp. He heard a faint stir and looked into a face, lost until this moment. He heard a voice croak hoarsely from his throat:

"Andy — you . . ."

"We thought you'd never come to." And Andy shouted, "Coralie!"

She was suddenly close and Keith tried to speak. "Be still," she said. "You must rest."

He sank back into sleep. He awoke to find her gone. He was alone; in panic, he feared he was drifting again. He cried out. He heard the rush of boots, then Andy's voice:

"It's all right."

"Where's Coralie?"

"She's here."

". . . Lenny?"

"He's fine. They're down at the spring."

Like a thrown rock the past struck Keith awake. "Cal? Wiley?"

"Both dead. Indians."

Keith groaned. "God, I remember now." It seemed that he had been gone a long, long time. "When was that?"

"Two days ago. An Indian shot you. I got 'im. Your head looks like a grasshopper plow ran over it."

Keith touched his head. It felt as large as a watermelon. "Tell me —"

"You're gabbin' too much. Rest some more."

He slipped into a wonderfully soothing sleep that took him over calm waters. Next time Andy was there to feed him. He slept again and felt much stronger on awakening. He lay on a crude cot made soft by several buffalo hides; he could smell the spongy hides.

Now, on this second day after his awakening, lying in the dappled shade, he was content to watch between naps. Lenny came visiting, shy, curious, displaying his gifts. He touched Keith's hand. He stayed until Coralie called him away.

Keith followed her with his eyes. Each step she took back and forth, in the intolerable workshoes he so hated. Now and then she waited on him and spoke to him, but she never lingered or said or touched him more than was necessary, and her voice, though concerned, could have been for any man, for any stranger. She was, he realized, as apart from him as in his thrashing nightmare.

That afternoon he had Andy help him to the edge of the mesquites and back. That evening he ate at the table. By the third day he could walk unaided to the spring. All this time, other than a few words and to pass food, Coralie Dockum did not go near him.

Depression bore him down. He saddled up and rode to the wallows and beyond to the big flat. Today an exhausted stillness seemed to hover over the country, and he thought of the quiet after a storm. Far out, he was surprised to see a few buffalo. By God, it felt good just seeing them again. He watched them, thinking how he had seen the great southern herd in all its bounty, how he had taken part in its ruthless slaughter and hastened an inevitable end. In a way he was proud; in another he wasn't. But he had memories of damned good men and good times, and he was grateful.

Riding back, he noticed for the first time the two graves at the foot of the hill. Earlier he had tried to convey his feelings to Coralie, but she had left him abruptly. He reached camp to find her alone. At once her hands became overly busy. When he dismounted, she turned to take the path to the spring.

"I want to express my sympathy," he said, and saw her instant start of bitterness. "Seems the time wasn't proper until now."

"Papa always wanted to be somebody." Her voice had an old sound, a resignation, entwined with regret. "He never was. He liked to say he was in the Battle of Gettysburg. He wasn't — he was miles away."

"Your father was a brave man. Wiley, too. Andy and I saw it happen. They came back. We all did."

"Yes," she said, tonelessly, "everybody came to help." She jerked her head, a tossing off motion. "I hate what this country's done to us — all of us. It's taken so much"

"It's given us something, too, Coralie."

"What on God's earth could that be?" she tore at him and gestured bitterly toward the foot of the hill. "Is that your music, Keith?"

"We have found ourselves here," he said, touching her arm. "Hard as it's been." She drew back from him and he saw the deep print of her hurt and uncertainty. He said, "I know. You saw the woman on the street that day, didn't you? You saw me walk with her to the Texas House?"

She looked away, but he knew she had. When she looked at him, it was with the unwillingness of one accepting dreaded loss. "She's so beautiful, Keith. How could you not love her? And she found you. She *came* to you — way out here. She must love you very much. She's so beautiful —"

"She went back. I wanted her to go."

He saw the sudden swell of her feeling, but as well her gravity and persisting doubt. "I thought I had lost you," she said. "When I saw you again, I thought you were dead, and I blamed myself. I still do."

"I'm hard to kill."

"In my lifetime I just want to love once. I wouldn't have enough of myself left over for another man."

She came to him and he saw her face smoothing, all her self-doubts gone, changing ever so softly, as light itself changes, and he knew that at last she was sure of him and herself.